676

HARLEQUIN®

$3.75 U.S.
$4.25 CAN.
April

AMERICAN ROMANCE®

Valerie Taylor

THE MOMMY SCHOOL

RISING
STAR

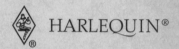
HARLEQUIN®

ISBN 0-373-16676-1

9 780373 166763

50375

Janet's To Do List

7:30 a.m. Wake the three girls.

8:00 a.m. Feed them a hot, nourishing breakfast.

8:30 a.m. Scrape breakfast off wall, get Carly and Heidi to school.

9:30 a.m. Clean house, water plants, keep eye on baby.

10:00 a.m. Call Poison Control. Are houseplants poisonous?

11:00 a.m. Work in home office, keep eye on baby.

11:30 a.m. Call Poison Control. Is ink poisonous?

12:00 p.m. Take aspirin. Work in home office.

1:30 p.m. Pick up girls at noon. Oops.

2:00 p.m. Feed girls lunch. Change baby's diaper. Treat rash with Vaseline.

2:15 p.m. Call Poison Control. Is Vaseline poisonous?

2:20 *Call Mommy School!*

Dear Reader,

This month a new RISING STAR comes out to shine, as American Romance continues to search for the best new talent...the best new stories.

Let me introduce you to Valerie Taylor. She's been an avid reader since age four. At age thirty-two, following the emergency C-section premature birth of her first child, she realized she was no longer afraid of anything and decided to become a writer, too! A lifelong midwesterner, Valerie lives in Cincinnati with her husband of seven years and her children, Jane, two, and Mick, five, and a very fat cat named Squeak. Valerie would love to hear from her readers. Contact her via E-mail at ValTaylor@poboxes.com or by writing to P.O. Box 428825, Cincinnati, OH 45242.

Now turn the page...and catch a rising star!

Happy reading!

Debra Matteucci
Senior Editor & Editorial Coordinator
Harlequin Books
300 East 42nd Street
New York, NY 10017

Valerie Taylor

THE MOMMY SCHOOL

Harlequin Books

TORONTO • NEW YORK • LONDON
AMSTERDAM • PARIS • SYDNEY • HAMBURG
STOCKHOLM • ATHENS • TOKYO • MILAN
MADRID • WARSAW • BUDAPEST • AUCKLAND

This book is dedicated to the women and men of Genie RomEx,
who provide virtual hugs, cheers, advice and support to all in
need; to my most wonderful and honest critique partner,
Jennifer Crusie, whose critiques usually begin with "You'd
better pour yourself a glass of wine"; to my parents, Mariellen
and Gordon Taylor, who raised me to believe I could succeed
at anything; and to my best-of-all-possible-husbands, John,
without whose unquestioning support this book would not
have been possible.

ISBN 0-373-16676-1

THE MOMMY SCHOOL

Copyright © 1997 by Valerie Taylor.

Prologue

Gib Coulter nibbled one perfect pink toe and was rewarded with a high-pitched laugh. He raised his head to look into Lissa's startling blue eyes. "Did I ever tell you how beautiful you are?"

A sigh was her only response.

"Oh, a woman of mystery, hmm? We have ways of making you talk." Pressing his pursed lips to her stomach, he made a razzing sound, and Lissa shrieked in delight.

"Okay, enough fun for one diaper change." He pulled the one-piece romper down over her fat little six-month-old belly and fastened the snaps. "Let's go find your mom." He slung the baby over his shoulder, provoking further delighted screams, and carried her down the stairs.

Laura Jason stood at the base of the stairs, wringing her hands. The threat of tears shone bright in her eyes.

Gib gave her a kind smile. "Don't worry, Laura, you're going to do fine." He handed Lissa to her mother. "You're ready to be on your own. More than ready."

Laura's eyes filled with tears. "Please don't go. I need you. Lissa needs you."

This always happened. No matter how clearly he told them he'd be leaving someday, no matter how readily they agreed to his terms, they always ended up begging. It wasn't that he wanted to cause them any pain. He didn't. It was just that he wasn't looking for any long-term commitments. On any front.

And besides, he really did know what Lissa needed right now—and that was a mother with her confidence back. Laura, young and pretty in a vague, undecided way, had completely lost confidence in her ability to care for her baby after the child had fallen down a half flight of stairs in her walker. The stairs were carpeted, and Lissa, though bruised, was basically unhurt, but to Laura the world had suddenly become a frightening place, full of unpredictable dangers. Gib had been here for two weeks, and he could see she really was a very good mother indeed, but she needed to see it for herself. And she couldn't, until he left. So he was going, tears or no tears.

But Gib never liked to see a woman cry. And he particularly hated it when he was the cause of the tears. Unfortunately, in this job, he was the cause all too often—every time he walked out a door, in fact.

What he wouldn't give to have a client, even one, *suggest* he leave—tell him he'd done his job perfectly and there was no more reason for him to stay. He just wanted one client to say, "I can manage on my own now. You can go. We'll be fine without you." Was it so much to ask?

It didn't really matter, though. He was going to take one more job after this one, make one more addition to his sister Sheila's college fund, and then he was through for good. Through with diapers and babies and raising other people's children for them. Through with responsibilities and duty to family. His own life had been put on hold for twelve years now. It was long enough. He had a chance at the brass ring, and he was going to take it.

So he made his voice as gentle as he could, but he was firm. "You knew I couldn't stay when we started. We talked about the fact that I wouldn't stay. I told you this day would come."

"But I didn't realize how much..." Laura's voice died away in a heaving sob. A single tear ran down her cheek as she followed him to the door, hugging Lissa to her chest.

"Do you really think I'd leave if I didn't think the two of you would be okay without me?" He leaned in close to kiss Lissa's cheek. "'Bye, sweetie." He bent to pick up his carryall. "Laura, you're a good mom. You're going to be fine."

She watched him cross the lawn to his white van. As he drove away, the name on the back of the van grew smaller and smaller, until her tears obscured the red-painted words: The Mommy School. Everything Mom Forgot to Teach You About Being a Mom.

Chapter One

Janet Resnick frowned as she tried to fasten the tape tabs on her eleven-month-old niece's diaper. They just wouldn't stick, and of course it was the last diaper in the house. She'd tried not to get the tabs wet this time. Maybe they had talcum powder on them. She leaned in for a closer look, and baby Emma grabbed a handful of Janet's curly auburn hair.

"Ouch!" Janet groped for the tiny fist and peeled open one finger and then another to release her hair. Just as she freed herself, Emma's other hand fastened on her earring. In one movement, the purple clip-on disk went from earlobe to tiny mouth. "No, Emma!" Janet grabbed the little girl by her chin and nose and pried. Emma gagged, but she opened her mouth, and there was the earring, still right in front. What a relief. Janet let go of Emma's chin to grab the earring, and Emma snapped her mouth shut tight again.

Once more Janet pried the small mouth open. This time she flipped the little girl over and jiggled her up and down. The earring dropped out, and Emma gagged and spit up—onto the bedspread.

Janet sighed in exasperation and set her niece down. She was going to have to wash the bedspread. Again.

When would she learn? The changing table was
stacked high with clean clothes, so she'd taken a
chance and changed the baby on the bed. A little talcum powder on the spread was no big deal—at least
Emma hadn't peed on it like she had last time—but
curdled formula? Yuck. As Janet mopped at the puddle
with a baby wipe, Emma pushed herself onto all fours
and started toward the head of the bed, where the cat
lay curled sleeping.

"Ah! Gah!" Emma gurgled, obviously pleased with
herself, as she reached for Clementine's tail. Clem
opened one eye and twitched her tail out of the way.
Emma shrieked with delight and reached for it again.

"Oh, no, you don't. No fun and games 'til we get
this diaper on." Janet grasped one chubby ankle and
pulled the laughing baby back to the center of the bed.
Okay, she needed something to fasten a diaper with.
Masking tape? Maybe if she got a long enough piece
and wrapped it around Emma's waist a couple of times,
the diaper would stay on. She picked up Emma and
the diaper and carried them both into the temporary
office she'd set up in the spare bedroom of her mother's
house.

She winced at the condition of her in-basket—and it
hadn't even been four whole days yet. Had she actually
thought she'd keep abreast of her employees and clients while taking care of her three nieces? But her mom
had really needed the vacation, and the girls needed
someone to stay with them. And Janet's mom was
right—after losing their parents, the poor kids really
needed a family member, not a baby-sitter. So Mom
had gone to Florida to visit Aunt Mary, and Janet got
stuck with the kids for two weeks.

Well, not exactly stuck, she thought, smiling at

Emma as the naked little girl twisted in her arms, giggling as she reached for Janet's earring again. Luckily they were really great kids. And it almost took Janet's breath away how much all three of them looked like Georgie.

Georgie'd been such a great mom. Her oldest daughter, Carly, had learned to read by the time she was four because Georgie read to her so much.

And Heidi—what a kid! She was Georgie all the way, full of fun and high spirits and always, *always,* saying exactly the wrong thing at exactly the wrong time, just when it would be the most embarrassing. Georgie had done that all her life.

Janet hugged Emma tighter, sticking her nose in close to breathe in that delicious warm-baby smell. Of the three girls, only Emma didn't remember how wonderful Georgie was, what kind of mom she'd been, how nurturing and supportive and patient. Janet couldn't even remember ever hearing Georgie raise her voice to one of the kids.

Janet, on the other hand, wasn't really much good with children. She'd always been the swoop-in-bringing-presents-and-swoop-back-out-again kind of aunt rather than the stay-overnight-giggling-and-making-popcorn kind. Janet took after her father—everyone always said so—a good mind for business, but not much else. As a single mom, even a temporary one, she was the pits. No one had any clean clothes, and it was amazing how quickly even a four-year-old would start to complain about having pizza again.

She *had* gotten herself a new client yesterday, though. On the way home from picking Heidi up from preschool, they'd stopped for ice cream. Inside, the woman behind the counter had handed Janet the cones and smiled in a friendly fashion, but she'd looked a little harried.

Janet had smiled in sympathy. "Busy day?" The little shop was empty except for them, but you could never tell.

The woman shrugged. "Busy enough, what with doing everything myself. I just opened a couple months ago. I can't afford any help yet, and I'm just about drowning in the administrative details."

Janet gave her ice-cream cone a thoughtful lick. "If you could get rid of one job, one administrative hassle, what would it be?"

"Easy. Bookkeeping. But I can't afford to hire even a part-time bookkeeper."

"How many hours a week do you spend on bookkeeping?" When the woman gave her a strange look, Janet laughed and introduced herself. "I'm sorry, I sound nosy, don't I? I have a business that provides home-based temp workers to people just like you. If you can give me a few details, I might be able to find you a way to afford that bookkeeper after all."

While Heidi finished off her cone and Emma spooned most of hers down her shirt, Janet discussed the ice-cream parlor business with Mrs. Goody, the owner. By the time the ice cream was gone, Janet had estimated that Mrs. Goody could probably hire someone for an hour or two a week and save herself around five hours a week. "Since you're not really an expert at bookkeeping, plus you keep getting interrupted to deal with customers, it probably takes you two or three times as long to do the books. An experienced bookkeeper working at home, with no interruptions, could probably do the job a lot faster. If you like, I can send you a detailed cost estimate."

Mrs. Goody, surprised and delighted, had agreed, and Janet had left the ice-cream parlor feeling rejuvenated. Another potential client. It was amazing how there was one on every corner.

But it really did go to prove how much she was like her father—he had always been turning pleasure into business.

Well, she only had ten more days to go, and then she could go back to her own apartment and peace and quiet. And back to being just an aunt, instead of a temporary single mom.

She balanced Emma on her shoulder and dug through the desk drawer for something that would fasten the diaper shut. No masking tape. Scotch tape? No, it probably wouldn't hold. Stapler? She laid Emma on the desk chair and carefully balanced one knee on the infant's chest to hold her still while she stapled the diaper shut.

When she finished, she smiled at the baby in satisfaction. "And your grandma thought we wouldn't be able to handle this for two lousy weeks. Not a problem! But remind me to get some more diapers soon." Emma, obviously delighted she was being consulted, gurgled a happy response.

Janet carried the baby to the stairway and started down. The first floor was silent as she reached the landing.

Too silent.

Where were the girls? Mrs. Murphy would be here any minute. There was no time to lose to make sure everything was in order, or there'd be trouble. There'd been enough trouble already with Mrs. Murphy.

She pulled Emma upright against her shoulder.

"Carly? Heidi?" She listened for a moment, grimacing when Emma drooled into the neck of her sweatshirt.

No answer.

"Hey, guys, where are you?"

Nothing. That was odd. She frowned and pushed open the door from the landing into the kitchen.

Janet gasped. The entire kitchen was afloat in a fine white powder. "What in the...?"

Sunlight streamed through the windows, giving the floating dust a fairy glow. It had an almost mesmerizing beauty, but just then Emma sneezed, and Janet backed out of the kitchen fast, pulling the door shut behind her.

She held the baby up and anxiously examined her face for signs of blueness. Emma, pink as ever, sneezed again. Relieved, Janet rushed into the living room and plopped Emma into her Exersaucer.

Taking a deep breath first, she opened the door into the kitchen again. The dust was starting to settle on the counters. She stuck her finger into it, and then touched it to her tongue.

It tasted like...flour?

She took a step forward into something slippery, and her legs flew out from under her. She landed flat on her bottom. From her new vantage point, she could see under the table and into the shocked faces of Emma's sisters. Carly, age eight, stared back at her, her hands over her mouth, eyes round. Heidi, age four, had her hands over her eyes.

Janet bit her tongue to keep from laughing out loud.

"We were making pancakes for breakfast, Aunt Jannie." Carly's voice was a bare whisper. "We didn't mean to make a mess. Heidi dropped the eggs, and when I stepped on them, I knocked the flour down. It went all over.''

Another firm chomp on her tongue kept Janet from smiling. ''I *see* it went all over. And then you went under the table?''

''We had to. We heard Mrs. Murphy's car.''

Right on cue, a key scraped in the back door lock, and Janet heard a gasp as Mrs. Murphy saw the state of the kitchen.

Mrs. Murphy sneezed.

Janet ducked her head in pained anticipation. This was it. This was the end of life as she knew it.

She covered her ears. Carly's hands went back to her mouth. Heidi never had uncovered her eyes.

Hear no evil, speak no evil, see no evil. Janet couldn't help herself. She laughed.

Mrs. Murphy, her flowered dress starched to stiff attention, stumped over to stand in front of her. Janet raised her eyes to look up at Mrs. Murphy's face, set into disapproving lines and topped by a tight, iron-gray bun.

''I'm glad you find this situation amusing, Janet. I'm sorry to say I don't see it the same way.''

Janet scrambled to her feet, skidding as she rose. She wiped something sticky from her palm onto her jeans. ''I'll clean it up! I'll clean up the whole thing. You just sit for a few minutes and relax, and I'll make you a cup of tea, and then I'll clean everything up.''

Mrs. Murphy rolled her eyes and shook her head in rejection of any such idea. ''If you'll remember, the last time you cleaned up, it took me two days to find everything you'd put away. No, thank you, Janet. I've had just about all I can take of your solutions. I'm not a young woman. Your mother understands that. I do my work, and she manages the children. You, on the other hand, are managing nothing.'' She turned and stumped back to the door, waving her purse to clear the flour dust from the air in her path.

Janet, heart pounding in panic, followed her to the door. ''Please don't leave. I need you. The girls need you. What will my mother say?'' She'd never cooked an actual meal in her life—what was she going to do to feed three kids for ten days? ''Wait!'' Mrs. Murphy stopped and turned around, her hand on the knob. ''At least tell me what kind of baby food to buy!''

Mrs. Murphy rolled her eyes again—the mannerism was starting to grate on Janet's nerves—as if the situation was so hopeless, no amount of last-minute coaching could save it. ''I've been cooking and cleaning for your mother for ten years. And they've been good years. But, as I told you last time, and the time before, I can't keep walking into messes like this. When your mother gets back, tell her she may call me.'' And with that, Mrs. Murphy turned and walked out.

Janet slumped onto a kitchen stool. She'd been barely scraping by for the past four days with Mrs. Murphy's help. And tomorrow was Friday and the last day of school before spring break—both older girls would be home all day, every day, for a whole week. How was she going to manage alone?

When the phone rang, Janet knew the gods were out to get her. It could only be one person—the one person whose radar was precisely attuned to Janet's stress level. The one person who could take even the minor disasters of Janet's life and somehow turn them into looming catastrophes.

Her mother.

Janet picked up the phone. ''Hello?''

"Janet? Is that you?" Her mother's voice sounded weak. But then, it always sounded as if the distance it had to travel was too much for it. But there was something more. Her mother's voice also sounded stressed, and Janet had a paranoid moment where she wondered if her mother had already talked to Mrs. Murphy. Maybe they'd been discussing her inadequacies all along.

Maybe the whole situation was all some big experiment cooked up by Mrs. Murphy and her mother to see how quickly Janet would go over the edge.

She almost laughed at herself.

Almost.

Okay, she'd gotten that out of her system. She took a breath, determined to hide the hopelessness of the situation from her mother. "Hi, Mom."

"Janet, what's wrong? You sound anxious."

Leave it to her mother. The woman had some sort of crystal ball. Janet manufactured a couple of panting breaths. "Nothing, Mom, I was just running up the stairs to get the phone."

Suspicious pause. "Has Mrs. Murphy been complaining about Clementine again?" Okay, so the crystal ball was working, but it was a little foggy.

"No, Mom, Mrs. Murphy hasn't said a word about Clem." How nice not to have to tell a lie. Janet suppressed a nervous giggle. "What's up?"

"Well, dear, I'm in the hospital."

Janet jumped to her feet. "Mom! What happened? Are you okay?"

"Oh, yes, I'm fine now. I thought I was going to die yesterday, though, I really did. I had a gallbladder attack yesterday afternoon. I really thought it was my heart, Janet, but it was my gallbladder, can you imagine? The pain! And they had to do emergency surgery.''

''Surgery! But...what happened? Are you coming home? Do you need me to pick you up at the airport?''

''Well, no, that's the problem, dear. Between the medication, and the surgery—as I understand it, abdominal surgery is really quite a problem. And my doctor is really quite adamant on the matter, he's really almost a bully. I'm not allowed to fly for six weeks. Oh, Janet, I just don't know what we'll do!'' Her voice rose to a wail as she reassessed the enormity of the problem.

The walls came closing in on Janet. Six weeks! She'd barely survived four days, and that was with Mrs. Murphy.

With one part of her brain, Janet continued to talk to her mother, reassuring her that they'd get through this latest disaster. With the other part, she held a small, private pity party for herself.

Slightly dazed, phone cradled to her shoulder, her mother's voice fretting in her ear, she went through the motions of mopping the kitchen and loading the dishwasher. She reached under the counter for the dishwasher detergent—then remembered. They were out of that, too. Mrs. Murphy had complained about it yesterday.

She reached for the bottle of dish soap on the counter, squinted at the label. Not for Use in Automatic Dishwashers. Probably wasn't as strong—she'd just use a little more. She squirted it into the dispenser in the door of the dishwasher, closed it tight, and started it up.

''And, honey, maybe you should get Mrs. Murphy to start coming every day. Sometimes she'll do that, if it's important. Keep the children away from her, though. You know how she gets about the kitchen.''

Janet decided not to tell her mother about Mrs. Murphy yet. ''Mom, you just concentrate on getting well. Don't worry about us—we'll get by.'' Somehow. They'd have to.

''All right, honey. Now, don't forget Heidi's ballet class— Miss Rita doesn't like it if the girls miss. And the recital, of course. Clementine's got an appointment at the vet's in two weeks—it's marked on the calendar. She's having her teeth cleaned, poor baby. She just hates it. And Carly's birthday, get her a Baby Talks A Lot, she's been asking for it for weeks. And I told her we'd have a party if she'd just stop checking with me about it every day, she's just so anxious since Georgie and Paul…''

Her mom's voice trailed off into the threat of tears. They'd all been so worried about Carly, who had retreated into an anxious shell after her parents had been killed in a plane crash. Carly still had a difficult time telling anyone she loved goodbye, even for short periods. The poor kid had wrung her hands, an occasional tear running down her face, for the entire two hours between the time her grandmother's airplane had taken off in Ohio and the time it landed in Florida.

Janet cleared her own throat and broke in before one of them could start to cry. ''Don't worry, Mom. I have everything under control. We're getting along fine. You just take care of yourself, and I'll take care of things here.''

But as she hung up the phone, Janet knew she was in trouble. She hadn't worried too much about neglecting her business for a week or so, but another month and a half? She had a million phone calls to make just today, and it was already past ten o'clock. If her business was going to survive, she had to get upstairs, shut herself into her office, and get some work done for her clients.

First, she made sure Carly and Heidi were absorbed in a video and Emma was still happy in her Exersaucer. "You kids stay right there on that couch. Do not, under any circumstances, go back into the kitchen. I will make lunch. Understand?" She looked from face to face, getting a solemn nod from each. "I'll be right upstairs."

Upstairs, Janet dug into her in-basket, which she hadn't seen the bottom of since she'd gotten here. Usually, her goal was to touch each piece of mail only once before dealing with it. Today, she just wanted to put out any fires.

The first two pieces of mail were junk. She threw them in the trash. The third needed a quick letter response. She dashed it off on her computer and slotted it into an envelope, ready to be mailed. The fourth piece of mail required a phone call. As she reached for the telephone, she heard a timid knock. She groaned and looked at her watch. She'd only been working for ten minutes. What could they possibly need already? She got up and opened the door. Carly stood there, her face a tight knot of worry under her silky, light-brown bangs. Heidi peered around from behind, her tiny features screwed into a conscious imitation of her sister's frown.

"What is it?"

"Aunt Jannie, there's a funny noise in the kitchen."

"A funny noise?" Janet walked to the railing to lean her head over. "Did you look?"

The girls exchanged an uncertain glance before Carly answered. "You told us not to."

Now Janet could hear the noise herself, an ominous gurgling sound. Almost a heaving, like some giant cat was bringing up a hair ball. Not a pretty sound.

She squeezed Carly's shoulder in quick reassurance, then brushed past the girls and down the stairs. Pushing open the door, she stepped down the last step into the kitchen. Her feet went out from under her, and once again she landed flat on her bottom.

Only this time, she was sitting in a pile of white suds leaking from the dishwasher and fast threatening to overtake the kitchen table.

As she watched in openmouthed disbelief, more suds poured out of the machine. She scrambled to her knees and splashed over to flick the power off. The suds slowed and lost their vigor, and soon they dripped out only intermittently.

She frowned at the dishwasher and the suds covering the floor, then looked at the girls, who had followed her down. "Has that ever happened before?"

"No." Carly looked at Heidi, who shook her head.

Janet picked up the bottle of dish soap and squinted at the back of it. "Maybe I used too much?"

Carly sighed, a huff of exasperation she must have learned from Mrs. Murphy. She stuck her hands high on her nonexistent hips. "You can't put that in. You can only put the powder stuff in. The blue stuff in the bottle is only for delicates."

"Delicates?" Janet frowned. "Delicate dishes?"

ALMOST AN HOUR later, Janet sighed as she finished mopping the kitchen floor. Straightening, she put a hand to her lower back. Without a doubt, this was the cleanest kitchen floor in all of Cincinnati. Maybe in all of southwestern Ohio. And she didn't care if a bomb went off in here, she wasn't mopping another square inch today.

She'd gone ahead and fed Emma, as long as the floor was going to be mopped again, and given Heidi and Carly a peanut-butter sandwich and half a jar each of something called capers, which looked like it had been in the pantry forever and which both girls rejected out of hand. Janet didn't blame them—whatever capers were, they didn't look or smell very good. But they were the only thing resembling a vegetable left in the house. This afternoon, she really had to go grocery shopping, three kids or not.

Finally, back to work. Then she groaned, remembering the bedspread. Who would have believed three little girls could cause so much work? After the last few days, Janet had a new respect for her mother. For all mothers. Especially single mothers.

Emma fussed as she walked past, so she took the little girl out of the playpen and set her on a blanket on the floor in the family room, where Carly and Heidi were playing with their toy kitchen. As Janet watched, Heidi stuffed everything she could find, including a doll and a toy box of crackers, into the toy dishwasher and slammed the door. "And stay in there!" the little girl scolded the machine. Janet bit her lip, torn between laughter and chagrin.

"Carly, watch your sister for a minute while I strip the beds and put a load of laundry in. If you hear anything funny, come and tell me right away."

With the master-bedroom bedspread and the sheets from all the beds in her arms, Janet carefully felt her way with her toes down the stairs into the basement. She loaded the bedspread in by itself and started the washer. Then she took a moment to sort the sheets into whites and colors and pull a load of dry clothes out of the dryer. As she was folding the last of them, she heard Carly shrieking her name.

"Aunt Jannie! Aunt Jannie!"

Janet took the stairs two at a time and skidded to a stop in the kitchen. Carly stood there in tears, holding Emma up by her armpits. Emma's face and hands were smeared with something clear and sticky.

"She ate it! She ate the whole jar!"

"Jar of what? What did she eat?" Janet grabbed the baby and swiped her fingertip through the smear. The goop came off on her finger. She sniffed it. No odor. "Carly, what is it?"

"V-V-Vaseline!" Carly hiccupped. "She ate the whole jar!" She held up an empty one-pound jar of Vaseline, which Janet knew had been at least three-quarters full that morning.

Janet grabbed the jar and turned it over to look for warnings. "Not meant for internal use. If ingested, call a physician or poison-control center immediately." Poison control! What was the number?

She skidded over to the phone, flipped open the phone book to find the number, and punched the buttons with shaking hands.

A woman's calm voice spoke in her ear. "Poison Control."

"Vaseline! I have a baby here who just ate Vaseline!"

"You mean the petroleum jelly?" The woman's voice rose in disbelief.

"Yes."

"Well, that's a new one. Let me check." The woman clicked off.

Janet clamped the phone to her ear with one shoulder and peered into Emma's face. Emma looked okay from the outside, but who knew what petroleum jelly could do to a baby? She tried to pry open the little girl's mouth to look inside, but her fingers kept slipping.

After a few seconds that seemed like hours, the woman was back on the line. "Hello, ma'am?"

"Yes?"

"How much of it did she eat?"

"About three-quarters of a pound, I think. Maybe a little less."

"Does she seem upset in any way?"

Janet's fingers slipped a little as she pulled Emma's face around to take a look. The baby grinned at her. "No, she seems fine."

"It doesn't look as if there's any problem with petroleum jelly. Call your pediatrician to see if she wants to see the baby, but our information indicates that the petroleum jelly should just pass right through. You might want to keep an extra-sharp eye on her diapers, though, and change them right on the dot. When that stuff does come through, it's going to come through with a vengeance."

Janet fought back tears of relief. "Oh, thank you."

"I just need a little information from you for our files. First, can I have your name and address?"

After Janet hung up, she sagged to the floor, shaking, cradling the slippery Emma in her lap. She held out her free arm to Carly, who was wringing her hands, silent tears streaming down her face. "Come here, Carly. Emma's going to be fine, they said the Vaseline wouldn't hurt her." She pulled the older girl in close, and the three of them sat on the kitchen floor for a moment in silence.

"I'm sorry, Aunt Jannie."

"Oh, Carly, no. I'm sorry, honey, it's my fault. I told you I'd be right back upstairs, and I should have been." And besides, what sorry excuse for an aunt would leave an eight-year-old in charge of an infant, anyway?

Before she went back to work, Janet set up the playpen against the wall in the family room. "Here you go, Emma, you can play right here by the window. Look at all Grandma's pretty plants." She brought her in-basket downstairs and sat at the kitchen table, where she could keep a closer eye on things. While Emma played happily in her pen, Janet reached for the next piece of mail.

A few minutes later, Janet looked up to see Emma gurgling happily in her playpen while Heidi stood by her, handing her things to play with.

Janet smiled. "Are you playing nice with Emma? That's nice."

Heidi giggled. "She thinks they're good."

"That's sweet." Janet looked down again at the letter in her hand before her brain pounced on Heidi's choice of words. "Good?" She jerked her head back up for a second look. "What's good?" What was that on the floor of the playpen? She walked over for a closer view and reached down to pick up what looked like a leaf. A wet leaf. A chewed-up wet leaf. She gaped at Emma, who gave her an open-mouthed grin. As Janet watched in horror, a second half-eaten leaf fell out of Emma's mouth and fluttered to the floor of the playpen.

Janet grabbed the baby and the two goopy leaves, ran to the phone, and hit the redial button.

"Poison Control." The same calm voice.

"Hello, Poison Control? This is Janet Resnick again, I just talked to you, just a little while ago, the baby who ate the petroleum jelly, Emma? She just ate a leaf from a houseplant."

"What kind of plant, and how many leaves?"

Janet looked at the chewed leaves in her hand. "I guess it's a Boston fern, and I don't know how much, exactly. I was sitting right there!"

"A Boston fern won't hurt her. But you might want to check the house for any poinsettias or philoden-drons—they're poisonous. Get those up out of her reach. Also dieffenbachia."

"Thank you...what's your name?"

"Rhoda, Ms. Resnick."

"Thank you, Rhoda. I'll be more careful from now on."

When Janet sat down again to work, she kept Emma safely in her lap. When she needed to make a phone call, she carried the baby with her upstairs to her desk, and held her, squirming, on her knee while she pulled open the desk drawer and dug out some index cards. She handed one of the cards and a pen to Emma, hop-ing to occupy the baby while she made a quick phone call. One arm around Emma's waist, the phone shrugged to her shoulder, Janet leaned over her desk and wrote notes to herself with her free hand while she talked. As she hung up, she looked away from the notes she had taken just in time to see Emma bite down on a plastic ink cartridge. The pen lay in two parts on the desk. As Janet watched in paralyzed disbelief, Emma coughed and swallowed, and a little trail of blue-black ink ran out of the corner of her mouth. She looked up into Janet's horrified face and grinned.

"POISON CONTROL." Rhoda again.

"Hello, Rhoda. This is Janet. Emma just drank ink."

"How much ink, and what kind?"

"As much as comes in one of those refills for fountain pens."

"Hold on a minute, Ms. Resnick." Rhoda was off the line for a moment. "Ms. Resnick? That much ink won't hurt her, but we'd like to send someone out for a visit this afternoon. Will you be home for the next hour or so?"

Not long after, an earnest young man with horn-rimmed glasses and a notebook showed up at the door. He introduced himself as her caseworker, Mr. Dooley, and he followed Janet around the house, taking notes and saying "Mmm-hmm" every once in a while.

At least the kitchen floor was clean.

Janet led him into the family room, where the girls were playing. As the social worker watched, Heidi planted her doll in a toy high chair and shook her finger at it. "No, no, baby. Do not eat the dish soap!"

Then Emma turned to grin at them, her mouth a wide black-smeared crater with six ink-stained teeth.

Way past the point of embarrassment, Janet just gave the social worker a sick smile.

Mr. Dooley asked Janet a few questions. "The law requires us to ask these," he explained in a dry voice. He spent some time alone with the girls, playing on the floor. "Just routine," he said.

Then he told Janet he was satisfied. "I can see you have your hands full here." He pulled a brochure from a pocket in his notebook. "These folks are good.

We've recommended them to a lot of people. Give them a call. You'll be glad you did." He looked her straight in the eye and a perfunctory smile flickered over his lips. "*We'll* be glad you did."

Janet got his drift.

After he left, Janet looked at the brochure. The Mommy School. Everything Mom Forgot to Teach You About Being a Mom. And in smaller print: Immersion Programs and Refresher Courses Available.

Sounded expensive. Well, there was Mrs. Murphy's salary—Mrs. Murphy certainly wouldn't be getting it. And there was always the girls' money. Her mother tried not to dip into that because the money was earmarked for their education, but she'd given Janet access to it before she left, in case of emergency.

Janet had been sure she wouldn't have any of those.

She needed help, no doubt about it. Maybe she could get some nice, grandmotherly type in here to help take care of the kids. And now that Mrs. Murphy wasn't going to be coming by, she could sure use some help with the cooking and housekeeping, too. She picked up the phone and dialed the number.

"The Mommy School. This is Sheila."

Janet pictured a smiling brunette to go with the warm, strong voice. "Hi, Sheila, my name is Janet Resnick." Janet's voice cracked, and she took a deep breath and started again, trying to keep the desperation out of her voice. "I'm having some trouble keeping up with my three nieces. I need some help."

"Well, ma'am, you've come to the right place."

Just listening to Sheila's voice made Janet feel calmer already. "What all is it that you offer?"

"Ma'am, it's probably best if we just send someone out for you. It's a lot easier to explain it in person."

"Are you going to be sending whoever will be working here?"

"Yes, ma'am."

"Well, fine. Just make sure she's got plenty of energy. I've got three active little girls here and a big house to take care of. This is not going to be the easiest of assignments."

"No, ma'am, it never is. Motherhood is not for wimps."

"Uh, when can you get someone here?" Janet hated to sound desperate, but she was beyond trying to keep up a front.

"How about tomorrow morning? Say, 10:00 a.m.?"

That meant Janet would have one more breakfast to deal with, and then she'd be home free. "Perfect." Janet hung up. She was exhausted.

What a day.

What was she going to tell her mom?

Chapter Two

Gib Coulter watched his sister hang up the phone with a flourish. She spun her desk chair around to report to him.

"You have a job," Sheila crowed.

Gib gave her a wry smile and sat down on the couch in their living room. "Motherhood is not for wimps? I don't think that's in the brochure."

Sheila tossed her head. "That was my own personal touch."

"You aren't supposed to touch anything, remember?" He pulled himself upright. "So, what's the deal?"

"Desperation is the deal. This poor Resnick woman sounded harried. She's taking care of three kids, including a toddler— sounds like someone ran off and left them with her."

He grinned. "Desperation is not necessarily a bad thing in a client. I only need another few thousand for your tuition for the next two years—with that and your scholarship, we'd be home free."

"We could have been home free with the last family. That Mrs. Jason really was desperate. She'd have kept you on forever."

Gib wrinkled his lip. "Laura Jason needed to be alone with that baby. If I'd stayed any longer, she'd think I didn't trust her to handle things on her own." He shook his head. "When her husband shoved us on her after that trip to the emergency room, it just about destroyed her self-confidence. She needed that back a lot more than we need the money. Still, it would be great if we could get one last client, a little more money in the bank, before I ride off into the sunset." He grinned at his sister. "I don't want to have to tell anyone where I'm going, ever again—except my editor, of course."

Sheila hesitated. "Gib, you could do that now, if only you'd listen to me."

Not this again. Irritated, but controlling it, Gib leaned back on the couch.

Sheila plunged ahead. "I found this great place. It's perfect. It was a dance studio once before, it has a great floor. All it needs is mirrors, barres, a fresh coat of paint. And the rent is really cheap...."

"After you finish school."

"But, Gib, it's—"

He dismissed her reasoning with a short sweep of his hand. "It's settled, is what it is. We've discussed this before. I've spent the last twelve years getting you kids started in life. I am not going to quit now, when I can see the light at the end of the tunnel, and neither are you." He pushed his body deeper into the cushions of the couch, forcing himself to relax. The argument was over.

"Gib, I'm twenty years old. I'm not a kid." Sheila whirled her chair around and leaped out of it. She almost seemed to fly to her bedroom at the end of the hall, where she slammmed the door to punctuate her exit.

Gib took a deep breath and let it out, controlling his irritation. Why was it always Sheila? Always Sheila, being difficult. Always Sheila, needing extra attention. Of his three younger siblings, Sheila had always given him the most trouble.

At sixteen, she'd put the car in a ditch, after Gib had told her and told her about how she should avoid that one bad curve out on Columbia Parkway.

At eighteen, she'd accepted a date with an obvious jerk—against Gib's clear advice—and ended up in a pool hall on the wrong side of town, calling Gib at 1:00 a.m. to come get her because her date was getting drunk and rowdy.

And now, at twenty, she wanted to drop out of school and open a ballet studio, of all things. She was a talented dancer, and an even more talented teacher—she'd been instructing for years—but a ballet studio? Could there possibly be a more risky idea?

It was almost as if she listened to his advice and then went out and did the exact opposite of what he said, for some perverse and incomprehensible reason of her own.

Patience. After all, she'd only been eight when their parents had died—of course she needed the extra attention. It wasn't her fault that, at eighteen, Gib hadn't been ready to be a parent to his siblings. It certainly wasn't her fault that in the past twelve years he hadn't become any more ready.

For a moment, he was back in the stark hospital corridor, seated on that hard, uncomfortable bench. Sheila, eight, sat on his lap, her head on his shoulder. From her even breathing, he assumed she was asleep.

His brother Paul, ten, was also asleep, leaning against Gib.

John, fourteen, paced. "What are the doctors doing? Why don't they come talk to us?" In the previous weeks, John's voice had started to change, and now it cracked with anxiety.

Gib tried to speak, but his throat was too tight. He swallowed to relax it. "I guess they'll come out as soon as they know anything."

He shook his head to clear it of the scene—it was still clear as day, even after all these years.

After their parents died, Gib faced the threat that his brothers and sister would be taken from him, split up by well-intentioned adults and parcelled out to various relatives. Frantic to keep that from happening, frantic to prove that he could handle the job of parenting his siblings, he started reading child-care books, at first so he could fool people into thinking he knew what he was doing, and later because most of the books were full of great information that he actually used with his brothers and sister.

By the time John was capable of taking care of Sheila and Paul overnight, the insurance had run out, and Gib had turned a baby-sitting business into The Mommy School. From child-proofing to nanny-training, he did it all. And he'd been doing it all for twelve long years.

Now, he was finally ready to move on.

He loved his sister—he'd lay down his life for her—but he was looking forward to the day when she'd be safe on her own and he'd have no more responsibility for her. He felt as if he'd been looking forward to that all his life. No one else to look after, no one but himself to consider. Parenting was a full-time job. There were no holidays, no sickdays, no overtime. Sheila had been right…it wasn't for wimps. It never let up.

Well, he was ready for it to let up now, and by God, Sheila wasn't going to screw things up. If she didn't graduate from college, who knew when she'd be on her own? Who knew when she'd stop needing him here, supporting her financially and looking after her constantly and making sure she didn't make life-wrecking mistakes every time she turned around?

He just had to keep his eyes on the prize. He was so close to the end now, he could almost taste it.

Freedom.

Freedom to travel, to write. Freedom to take care of himself for a change. Freedom to do what he wanted when he wanted to do it.

Over the past three years, since Sheila was old enough to stay on her own, he'd taken several jobs that involved travel. Argentina with one family to help train a new nanny they hired there. China and Tibet with another, and other places besides, each time combining child care with training. And each time, he kept a journal, writing about traveling with a family in a foreign country.

One of his clients had found his travel journal and, with his bemused permission, read it. She'd laughed out loud, she'd cried, she'd sent the journal to her sister who was the managing editor for a travel magazine in New York City. The sister had asked for some revisions, bought a section of the journal as a piece on traveling with small children in Greece, and asked for more.

Three articles later, she was ready to offer him a regular column on exotic travel with kids, which it seemed was a new trend. He could make a living at it.

It would be a subsistence living—no spare change for younger siblings' college tuition—but it would be plenty to support him.

Gib wanted it so badly he could taste it, and he was going to do it.

Just as soon as Sheila graduated from college, that is. Just as soon as he earned enough money to make that possible. Just as soon as he finished up with this one last client, this Resnick woman.

FRIDAY MORNING, as Janet was wiping orange juice off the wallpaper in the kitchen, the doorbell rang. Janet looked at the clock. Ten a.m.—if this was Mommy, you couldn't fault her on her punctuality. She swiped a splash of juice off the face of the clock, scooped Emma up out of her high chair, and pushed through the kitchen door.

Through the glass in the front door, she could see a tall man, back turned to her. Not Mommy, after all.

But also not a bad view. She paused for a moment, Emma on her hip, to enjoy it. From behind, this guy looked like an athlete. His shoulders almost filled the window in the door. A well-cut houndstooth jacket emphasized his lean waist and hips.

Janet suppressed a grin of enjoyment before she opened the door. Could this guy's frontside possibly live up to his backside?

He turned, and she looked up at him, and she had to close her mouth and swallow. Blue eyes, the bluest blue eyes she'd ever seen, put a lump right in the middle of her throat. Dark hair waved back from a strong forehead.

It wasn't that he was so impossibly handsome—he wasn't. In fact, his features were uneven, and when he smiled, his face became lopsided in a way that promised intelligence, humor, an easy-going nature. But when he smiled, Janet forgot what it was she'd been about to say. She wasn't sure she was still breathing, so she took a deep breath to be on the safe side.

"Ms. Resnick?"

Janet nodded.

"I'm Gib Coulter." He paused for a moment, waiting for a response Janet still felt unable to give. "From The Mommy School." Another pause. "May I come in?"

Beyond him, she spotted a white van parked in the driveway, The Mommy School painted on its side. She looked back at him and at the empty van. "Oh."

Brilliant recovery. She stepped back and held the door open for him.

He walked past her and into the entryway, and then followed her into her mother's blue-and-white living room. "I think you were expecting me?"

No, she wasn't expecting him. She wasn't expecting anything like him. "Not exactly."

He smiled that transformational smile, and it had the same effect on her this time as it had last time. "Don't worry, a lot of my clients have the same reaction the first time they meet me."

"I can imagine."

"They wonder how a man can possibly be capable of dealing with children, much less capable of training others how to do it. And I don't blame them. Most men have a hard time doing the things most women do as a matter of course." A confident smile. "But most men aren't me."

"You don't say." Now that she was breathing again, Janet tried to dredge up her conversational skills.

Surely she still had some. "And you've been working for The Mommy School for how long?"

That flash of smile again. Janet found that if she looked off to the side, it didn't have the same disastrous effect on her equilibrium.

Great. All she had to do was avoid looking at him. With an effort, she concentrated on what it was he was saying.

"I *am* The Mommy School. There really isn't anyone else."

"But on the phone..."

"Oh, Sheila. My, er, answering service." His gaze flickered, and Janet's heart dropped just a little. Of course he was married—or something—to this Sheila. She checked his left hand; no ring. Definitely "or something."

He continued. "We've found that if we tell prospective clients they're hiring a man to show them how to run their household, they're a little reluctant. But if I show up first, I can reassure them, or at least get them to let me in the door." He smiled, and Janet had no trouble at all believing that any woman he met would let him in any door he knocked on.

But not her. This was not the picture she had in her mind of a white-haired, nurturing type to take care of the kids and house so Janet could work. She set Emma down at her feet and opened her mouth to tell him that she didn't think it would work out.

Out of the corner of her eye she saw Emma pick up something from the floor and pop it into her mouth. "No, Emma!" Janet grabbed the child by her chin and nose and pried her mouth open. "Can you grab it? I think it's a penny!" Emma gagged.

He reached for Emma. "Not like that, you'll choke

her." He pulled Janet's hand from the baby's chin. Emma stopped gagging, and her mouth snapped shut. Gib levered a finger into the corner of her mouth and fished out the penny. "Lesson Number One—anything small and shiny goes right in the mouth."

He handed Janet the wet penny. "Those earrings, for instance. I'm surprised she hasn't already taught you that lesson herself."

Janet's hand went to her right ear; the earring slipped off to lie beside the penny. She frowned, but she dropped onto the blue-flecked couch and motioned him into a nearby chair. "It's not lessons I need, it's a nanny."

His gaze flickered to Emma and to the earring and penny in Janet's hand, and Janet could feel herself flush. But when he looked back at her, his eyes held no guile, and he nodded. "Okay, you don't need lessons. Instead, you need a nanny. But you might as well take advantage of me while I'm here—I can teach anyone. And it's part of the service. Here's our brochure."

Janet took the brochure from him. It was the same one the poison-control people had given her. Of course, she didn't have to tell him that.

But then, he might already know about the poison-control incident. For all she knew, he had some sort of deal going with them. She gave him a narrow look before she opened the brochure.

This time one phrase leaped off the page at her.

"Live-in?" This man was planning to move in here with her and the three girls? "I'm not sure I really want anyone living in the house with us."

His voice was reassuring. "It's really the best way to get things in order for you, at least at first. Don't worry, you'll get used to it."

"I don't want to get used to it. I just want to get through the next month and a half and get my life back on an even keel. The last thing I need is one more person living here, keeping me from getting anything done."

"Well, then, we'll work fine together. I'll keep the children safe and out of your way, and you do whatever it is you do."

How was she going to get out of this? Even if he was as good as he said he was—which had to be a stretch—there was no way she was going to be comfortable living in the same house with a man she couldn't even look at without turning into an idiot.

She had to get rid of him and find someone more...traditional.

"I don't need your kind of help. It's not that I don't know what to do, I just don't have time to do it. All I really need is someone to come in a few hours a day to deal with the kids while I work."

"Oh?" Gib gave her a calm gaze. "And where is the baby?"

Janet jerked her head to look at the floor beside the couch. "She was right there. Just five seconds ago." She jumped to her feet and scanned the room. "Emma?"

"It's okay, she's right here." He reached down behind the small end table next to his chair. "But she was reaching her hot little hand toward the cord to that table lamp. In another minute, she'd have pulled it down onto her head. Or maybe she was going to jerk the plug out of the outlet." He gave Janet an almost apologetic smile. "Which I see isn't childproofed in any way."

Janet swallowed, and looked from him to Emma,

who was once again making her way toward the lamp cord. All she needed was a couple of trips to the emergency room to round out Mr. Dooley's file on her and the girls.

He was right. She needed help. Maybe she even needed lessons. Surely through repeated exposure, Janet could get used to his smile. Familiarity breeds contempt, right?

She turned back to him. "Okay. Let's do it."

Chapter Three

Janet figured now was as good a time to start as any, so after she gave him the ten-cent tour, they settled down at the kitchen table.

Gib set the baby on his knee. "So, why are the kids with you, or why are you with them?" He reached into his pocket and pulled out a set of keys, which he shook for Emma.

Emma opened her mouth wide in delight and grabbed for the keys. She put the key chain in her mouth.

"Don't worry," he told Janet. "I put the whole key chain through the dishwasher this morning."

Janet almost laughed out loud; it hadn't occurred to her to worry about germs on a key chain. "It's that obvious they aren't mine? They're my sister's. She and her husband died—" Janet stopped for a moment, swallowing her automatic tears "—not quite a year ago, in a plane crash. Since then, the kids've been living here with my mom. I was just taking care of them while she was on vacation down in Florida, but then Mom had emergency surgery, and now she's going to be gone for another six weeks. At least."

He gave her a sympathetic look. "Sounds like you've all been up against it lately."

Janet averted her eyes and hurried past his sympathy. As frazzled as she was feeling, if anyone was nice to her, she'd end up crying. Not that she would have minded weeping on that nice, broad shoulder, but she'd done enough crying since they'd lost Georgie; they all had. "Anyway, any port in a storm, and the poor kids are stuck with me. And my problem is that I don't have time for them. I think it's important that I be here with them—that someone in the family is here, anyway. And I've always run my business from my home, so that's not a problem. But I'm going to start losing clients if I ignore the business any longer."

"What business are you in?"

Safe on the subject of work, she looked up at him. "I run a home-based temporary-employee agency, HomeWork. Businesses call me when they have a job to be done but no one to do it. I maintain a registry of people who work from their homes, doing computer programming, editing, word processing, sewing, desk-top publishing—anything, really, that can be done as easily at home as in the workplace. I put the business and the worker together." She stopped for a moment, embarrassed, and laughed. "I sound like a commercial, don't I?"

He laughed in return. "That's okay, I'll trade you your ad blurb for mine. We are a child-care provider, but we're also a training service. We work with you to make sure you understand how to get through the days and nights without neglecting the children to death."

Based on her track record with household poisons, that was a greater danger than he knew. "And just what is it you do to help me prevent that?"

"Everything, at least at first." He grinned at her, but this time she saw it coming and managed to keep track of the conversation. "I keep the kids out of trouble, get them where they're going on time, make sure they're clean and fed and dressed when they're supposed to be, make sure they're asleep when they're supposed to be that. And I slowly work you into the mix, so that by the end of our time, you're doing everything and I'm doing nothing." He looked around the kitchen. "Does your mother have any other help?"

Janet grimaced. "She used to. A woman named Mrs. Murphy cooks and cleans for her, but she quit yesterday. She said the girls made too many messes."

"Mrs. Murphy, huh? Give me her phone number, and I'll give her a call for you." He pulled out a battered notebook and opened it.

"She said she wouldn't come back." Janet spoke a little more vehemently than she'd meant to. She couldn't help it—he just sounded so disgustingly sure of himself.

He looked up. "Do you want her back?"

"Yes, I want her back. She's my mother's housekeeper. I don't know what my mother is going to say when she hears I ran her off." She arched a brow at him. "But if she comes back, I won't need you anymore, will I?"

His answering smile took most of the sting from his words. "You will if the only reason she comes back is because I'm here."

Janet gave him the number, but he seemed so certain of himself that she was half-tempted to call Mrs. Murphy herself and behave so abominably on the phone that the old battle-ax would never agree to work for her again. Then she remembered her mother and gave up on that brilliant idea.

"Who else is there besides Emma?" At the sound of her name, the little girl looked up from the key chain she was shaking and gave him a shy smile. He returned her smile, and she hid her face in his chest.

Janet couldn't believe it. Emma was at the height of stranger anxiety, but she was flirting with this man as if he were a member of the family.

Then again, Janet herself was having a hard time fighting the urge to flirt. *Not a good idea.* "There's also Carly, she's eight, and Heidi, she's four. They're both in school now. Heidi's in morning pre-kindergarten, Carly's in second grade."

He checked his watch. "When does Heidi get home?"

"Oh, my gosh. What time is it?" She craned her neck up to look at the kitchen clock, which said eleven-fifteen. "Oh, not again!" She jumped up and ran to the kitchen door and grabbed her keys from the wall. "Can you stay with Emma? I'm car-pool mom today. I'm supposed to be there right now. I'll be about three-quarters of an hour." She threw the words over her shoulder as she tore open the back door and ran down the walk to her car.

Gib watched her slide into the seat, shimmying her slender, curvy hips under the steering wheel. There was a flash of bare ankle between her leggings and the top of her sneaker as she pulled a trim leg inside, a swing of red hair as she checked behind her, and then she backed out of the driveway.

Oh, she was a looker, all right.

Well, he'd seen attractive women before. He'd even

worked with his share of them. He had a job to do, and he was just going to focus on that. No big deal.

He stood, Emma in a football-hold under one arm, and walked over to the door to push it shut. Turning, he looked around the kitchen. It looked as if a tornado had hit it.

He gave Emma a wry grin. "Well, Emma, I guess you and I can get started, anyway."

JANET PULLED UP in front of the house an hour later. The elementary school principal, Mrs. Higgenbotham, had been standing outside the building with Heidi and Heidi's classmates Michael and Jane. Poor little Michael looked suspiciously blotchy-faced, and even Heidi looked worried. After Mrs. Higgenbotham delivered a short lecture on the virtue of punctuality, Janet got all three kids buckled in. She swung by Jane's house and then Michael's. Michael's mother had taken one look at her son's mottled face and snapped, "Late again to pick them up?"

Janet could feel her nerves fraying.

She wanted to go home to her own quiet apartment. She wanted to sit by herself in some peaceful spot, someplace where no one was asking her for anything, doing something she knew how to do. She was no good at this parenting thing. For days, she'd been longing for her peaceful existence, sending hurry-home vibes toward Florida. And now she had another six weeks of this chaotic reality to look forward to. She'd never make it. How did other women keep up with this stuff?

She guided Heidi into the house through the garage, and as she reached to unlock the door, it swung away from her. Gib pulled the door back to let them in, and as she stepped into the room, a wonderful aroma met her nostrils. Soup?

Heidi smelled it, too. "I'm hungry!" She pushed past Janet to stand face-to-face with Gib, who had squatted down to her level to meet her. Janet tried not to notice that the muscles of his thighs strained the material of his jeans in a very interesting way.

Gib held out a hand to shake Heidi's. "You're Hungry? That's a funny name!"

She giggled. "No! I'm Heidi!"

He grinned. "Oh, you're *Heidi*. I'm Gib. There's a snack on the table for you, and lunch will be ready in a few minutes."

Beyond him, in the kitchen, Emma sat in her high chair, happily banging a wooden spoon on the edge of her tray. She gave Janet a grin and drooled. Clementine slept on the sunny window seat.

A small pink plate sat on a place mat on the kitchen table. It held an apple, cored and cut into quarters. A glass of milk stood next to it. Heidi clambered up into her booster chair and reached for a piece of apple.

Janet looked around the kitchen, feeling as if she'd never seen it before. It looked different. It was clean, for one thing. Cleaner than it had been since her mother left—even Mrs. Murphy didn't usually leave it looking this good. The sink was empty. The milk drips had been wiped off the cabinets. The little blobs of cemented-on Cream of Wheat had been chipped off the kitchen table. Even the crayon scrawls were missing from the refrigerator door. A pot sat on the stove, steam escaping from under the lid. Three soup bowls stood on the wooden counter, and a basket lined with a blue-checked cloth held an assortment of crackers.

"Well, I see you've made yourself at home."

"Oh, I just opened a couple of cans, no major effort. I did get hold of Mrs. Murphy, though—what a character. She said she'd be happy to come back and help out. She'll be here Monday, at the regular time. I promised her no more messes." He frowned slightly at a picture on the wall—a primitive print of a cat curled up on a hearth rug, with the caption "Contentment"— then reached out and adjusted it.

Janet frowned. It had looked fine to her.

Great. A perfectionist. She knew she was far from perfect. "Well, I guess you have things under control here, then. I really need to make a few phone calls. Business, you know. I guess that's what you're here for, huh? Call me when lunch is ready."

She practically ran up the stairs to her office. How could he have gotten things in order so quickly and easily? Of course, he'd only had Emma to deal with. But an after-school snack *and* lunch on the way *and* a clean kitchen! And as if that wasn't enough, Mrs. Murphy back on the job, too.

What an irritating man.

Janet threw herself into her chair, feeling about as inadequate as she'd ever felt. It was obvious that anyone with half a brain could handle three kids and a house and a business—women all over the country were doing it every day, and this guy obviously didn't have a problem with it, either. The problem wasn't the kids. It wasn't the house.

It was Janet.

Why had she ever agreed to take care of the kids, anyway? She could have just hired a sitter from the start. By taking them on, she had just set herself up for failure and taken her attention away from the one thing she'd ever been good at—her business. But, no, she had to prove she could do it all.

She'd proven something, all right. She'd proven she was her father's daughter—just like everyone always said. Her father, who had never been there for anyone but his clients—not for his kids, not for his wife. Her father, the brilliant businessman who'd had no time for his family.

He'd loved her and Georgie, she knew that. At least Mom had said he did, and he said it too, when he'd call from the office to say good-night. It had never seemed like enough, though. She'd always figured if he'd really wanted to, if it was a priority, he'd have been there for them. When he'd died—heart disease, probably triggered by stress and overwork, and undiscovered because he'd never taken the time to find out why he was always short of breath—it had felt like just one more desertion.

It was why she had been determined to take care of the kids herself while her mom was gone, why she'd wanted to give them what little continuity in their lives she could.

Well, enough was enough. Almost letting Emma poison herself had erased that silly desire from her memory. Maybe she *was* her father's daughter—and maybe he'd been trying as hard as she was trying. Maybe he just hadn't been very good at it.

Well, she was committed to her nieces, and she'd be here for them. But she was going to leave their physical care to the professionals and do what she knew how to do. From now on, she was going to focus on HomeWork. She reached for the phone.

GIB WATCHED Janet's back disappear up the stairs. Her hair bounced, alive, on her shoulders. He watched her round bottom, hugged by those close-fitting leggings, tighten and release as she climbed the stairs. He never thought he'd find leggings sexy, but her legs and bottom were damn near perfect, and the clingy material showed every curve, every muscle, every graceful line. It was almost hypnotic, sexuality in motion, and he found himself incapable of looking away until she'd disappeared up the stairs.

And incapable of controlling an immediate reaction from his body. He shifted his ground slightly, trying to rearrange things just a bit.

Okay. This was not a problem. He was a man of the world. He'd been around the block a few times. He'd had his share of fun with the opposite sex. He didn't need to possess every attractive woman he saw. Especially the ones who were clients. He could handle this, no problem.

All he needed to do was focus on her as a client, rather than a woman. No problem. No problem at all.

Maybe if he could get her to stop wearing leggings. Maybe he could run a load of laundry and accidentally throw bleach in with her leggings.

But she probably had another pair. Or two. Or ten. Maybe that's all she ever wore—tight leggings, hugging her bottom, fitting along her calves, clinging to her thighs....

"I'm hungry!" Heidi's piping voice brought him back to the here and now.

"You're still hungry? Okay, soup is the answer."

She giggled, and he ladled vegetable soup into a bowl for her as he forced his attention back to the job and the needs of the client. *A client, not a woman,* Gib told himself again.

He could tell already that this was not going to be an easy job. Most of his clients were at least aware that they didn't know everything. This one seemed to think the biggest problem she had was a lack of time.

Well, it was his job to make sure she found out what the real problem was. Her real problem was that she wasn't tuned in to these kids, and she hadn't figured out how to balance them with everything else.

Absently he caught the wooden spoon as Emma threw it at the cat. "No, no, Emma. We don't throw things at the cat." She reached for the spoon.

He leaned over to look directly into her face. "I'll give it back to you, but no throwing, understand?" She scrunched her face into a charming baby grin, and he returned her sunny smile and handed the spoon to her. He'd be taking it away from her in under a minute, but you had to start somewhere.

Right now, he really needed to start with Janet Resnick. *As a client, not as a woman.* It was his new mantra.

Emma threw the spoon at the cat again. He gazed at her reproachfully. "Emma, I said no throwing the spoon at the cat." He picked up the spoon and set it in the sink. Emma gave him a look of indignant disbelief and opened her mouth to howl. Gib held out a cracker from the stack on the counter, and instead of howling she said, "Ah!" and grabbed the cracker.

Heidi giggled.

He gave Heidi a tolerant smile and turned off the heat under the soup. "You sit right here for a few minutes while I get Emma changed, okay? If you want more milk, yell.'' He scooped up Emma, who was polishing off the cracker, and carried her toward the stairs.

As he reached the top of the stairs, he heard Janet's voice, talking to someone on the phone.

''Ms. Phillips, I cannot emphasize to you enough that you must learn to delegate. If you try to do everything yourself, you'll end up getting nothing done.''

She paused, and he wanted to hear her voice again. It was interesting, just husky enough but not too deep. A voice he could listen to for a while.

''You're absolutely right, they won't do it the way you would do it. You need to prioritize. Choose which projects really need to be done exactly the way you would do them, the ones which need your own personal touch. Then, for the others, let go.'' Janet's voice took on a persuasive, comforting tone. ''Find someone you can trust to do things well, if not exactly the way you'd do them, and then trust that person. I can help you find the right people.''

She sounded so different from the way she'd sounded just a few minutes ago that for a moment he wasn't sure he was listening to the same woman. The Janet Resnick he had met downstairs had been flighty, disorganized, forgetful.

The woman on the phone was a professional.

''Ms. Phillips, we can set up a plan for you. The key issue in formulating any plan is articulating the problem. If you don't correctly identify the problem, you can never hope to solve it.''

He looked into the room. Janet sat in a high-backed chair, her back half-turned to the door, dwarfed by the massive desk. Her hair looked as if she'd rolled straight out of bed and hadn't had a chance to brush it yet.

Something reddish stained the leg of her gray leggings. She looked for all the world like someone who couldn't explain her way out of a paper bag. But if he closed his eyes and listened to her voice, he could picture a navy-suited businesswoman, all that wild, curly, red hair pulled back, makeup perfect, ready to take on the world. As he pictured her, she developed a low-cut blouse, so he opened his eyes before his imagination could take things any further.

As the conversation seemed to be winding down, he waited for a moment. She said goodbye and replaced the receiver.

Gib shifted the squirming Emma to his other arm. "I'm impressed."

She jumped and jerked around in her chair. Her hand went to her hair, smoothed it back. "I didn't...what did you say?"

"You're a different person on the phone. You sound—" he searched for the right word "—bigger."

She looked confused. It didn't really make any sense to him, either. He cleared his throat. "Emma's fragrant. Based on the gander I took at her diaper earlier, I thought maybe you could use a refresher."

Up came the chin. "I don't know what you mean."

"Come on in here and I'll show you." Without waiting for her response, he turned and left the room. As he did, the phone rang. He glanced around, but she'd already turned toward it.

He waited while she spoke with her client.

As she finished, he cleared his throat. "Ready now?"

She rose, but as she did, the phone rang again. She shrugged at him and turned toward it.

"Let the machine pick up."

"This may be a client." She reached for it.

"Clients can wait. Babies can't." He leaned past her, brushing her shoulder ever so slightly—he felt as if he'd touched fire—and pressed a button on her machine.

Chapter Four

Janet's jaw dropped in disbelief as the machine clicked
on. Her blood pressure took a hike for the sky. For a
moment, she thought it was from the outrage, but at
least some of it was from the small brush of his arm
against her shoulder. She could feel the spot he'd
touched her, warm on her shoulder.

Her recorded message came on. "You've reached
HomeWork, your source for home-based temporary
workers. Please leave a message and we'll return your
call as soon as possible." Beep.

"Ms. Resnick, this is Sheila, from The Mommy
School. I'm looking for Gib Coulter. Would you please
ask him to call his office? Thanks!" Click.

Hah! The call was for him! Janet bit back a grin.
That would show him. Him and his diapering demonstration.

And she knew something else that would show him,
too. Her grin widened. Since the Vaseline incident,
Emma's diapers had been in rare form. Maybe she'd
just watch this little diaper disaster, after all.

She turned to him, an innocent smile on her face.
"You were going to show me something about a diaper?"

He turned away, and her smile transformed into a mischievous grin. She followed him across the hall into Emma's room, and when he started to hand her the baby, she held up her hands, palms out, as if to push the little girl back to him. "Why don't you show me your method first? Then, next time, you can watch me to make sure I'm doing it right." She schooled her face into what she hoped was an innocent, if slightly vacuous, wide-eyed gaze.

He gave her a suspicious look, but he set Emma on the changing table and pulled off her leggings. "All right, we'll pretend you know nothing. First, always keep one hand on the baby. Even a very young baby that's never rolled before may choose today to do it." As he talked, Gib peeled Emma's tights down over her fat legs. "And at this age, they have no common sense whatsoever. She'd happily roll right off this changing table. Wouldn't you?" He leaned down to grin into Emma's face. She cooed at him and kicked him on the chin.

Janet rolled her eyes. "Will you give me a break? I have changed a diaper or two before now."

He continued as if she hadn't spoken. "Get everything ready before you take the diaper off." He opened a fresh diaper and set it beside Emma on the table, and he pulled several wipes from the container and laid them next to the diaper.

Janet couldn't resist. "Oh, you're going to need more wipes than that."

He gave her a kind look and a smile that struck her as condescending. "I know what I'm doing."

Then he opened Emma's diaper, and his smile fell. "Good God." He picked up a wipe and swabbed at the baby. And another wipe. And a third. The mess just sort of smooshed around. Nothing seemed to be getting much cleaner, as far as Janet could see.

Janet felt like high-fiving the universe. But she managed to control her baser impulses and kept her voice casual. "Yeah, it's a real mess, huh? Been like that ever since she finished off that jar of Vaseline. Terrific demonstration, though. Thanks to you, I'm sure I'll know how to do it next time." She made a show of looking at her watch. "Gee, I'd better get some work done. In fact, don't bother calling me for lunch—I'll just make myself a sandwich later. I'd appreciate it if you didn't disturb me for a while." Janet turned and marched back across the hall.

Although he was up to his elbows in a slippery situation, Gib had to grin at her stiff back as she marched away. Boy, she was a prickly little thing. She got her back up just like a little red-haired cat. His smile widened at the image of Janet spitting and hissing at him.

Now, why was that so appealing to him?

Oh, he was in trouble, all right. She wasn't just gorgeous. She was intelligent and funny, too. And worse, from his point of view, she was single. He had a hard-and-fast rule—no dating clients. Even funny and intelligent and gorgeous ones.

So, no problem, right? So he just wouldn't think about her that way.

Yeah, right. He'd be the first man in the history of the world to be able to control those kinds of thoughts. No doubt about it, he was in trouble.

He gave up on trying to wipe Emma clean. He pulled her onesie over her head and, carefully holding her sticky-side-out, took her directly into the bathroom, where he deposited her into the tub. With enough warm water and soap, you could fix almost any mess.

JANET HEARD the water running in the tub and smiled. It had taken her two diaper changes and dozens of wipes before she'd realized that she might just as well put Emma right into the tub for each diaper change. He really was good, she had to admit it.

And he looked good, too. When she'd followed him across the hall, she couldn't help but notice again how he looked from behind, and her thoughts had gotten away from her. His shoulders and back were broad and masculine, his waist and hips narrow and sexy. For one wild moment, she'd felt a lurch deep inside, and he'd suddenly seemed about as appealing as any man she'd ever seen.

And then he had turned, and Emma had been in his arms, and everything had changed. What had seemed so blatantly sexual took on a new dimension, a tender, gentle, caring, nurturing dimension. Janet had ached to be in those arms, held tight and cared for gently.

Oh, this was never going to work.

Work, that was what she needed. She just needed to bury herself in the tedious details of day-to-day business. Work her plan. She could lose herself in paperwork and phone messages.

She reached for her in-basket.

And was interrupted by a knock on the door.

No way. She could not face the man right now. "Go away."

Silence, then the sound of footsteps fading down the stairs. What a relief.

And just as quickly, footsteps back up the stairs. Louder, this time. This time there was no knock. Janet felt a draft as the door swung open.

She turned. "What do you mean..." As she swung

her chair around to face the open door, she stopped short.

Gib stood there, a cold expression on his face, a tearful Heidi on his left hip. Janet took in Heidi's tear-stained face, but her gaze returned, reluctantly, to his. His face, all lines and planes, was tight.

But his voice, when he spoke, was calm. "I told Heidi I was sure you didn't mean it when you told her to go away."

His tone chilled her, and she barely caught herself before she rubbed her arms to warm them. She matched her voice to his. "I didn't realize it was Heidi knocking."

Heidi knuckled her eyes, and Janet's heart melted into a pool of guilt. She was supposed to be taking care of this little girl, and instead she was hurting her. Janet held out her arms, and Gib, his face a silent mask, handed her the child. She settled Heidi sideways onto her lap and hugged her close. "I'm sorry, Heidi. I didn't realize it was you. Next time, just open the door and stick your head in, so I'll know, okay?"

Heidi nodded and hiccupped, but she didn't look Janet in the eye.

Janet gently nudged Heidi's chin upward until the little girl was looking at her. "I'd never tell you to go away, not in a million years, do you understand? You are *always* welcome in here, any time you like, and I will *always* want to see you, no matter what I'm doing." Heidi leaned in against her shoulder, and Janet pulled her in tight so that the little girl's head was tucked under Janet's chin. Now that Heidi couldn't see her face, Janet transferred her gaze to Gib. "I thought you were someone else, someone who knew I was very busy working."

Gib curved his mouth into a not-quite-pleasant smile. "Sometimes we need to be reminded what's most important."

Janet returned his smile, though it almost killed her to do it. "Of course we know what's most important, but sometimes we have to get other things done, too."

Gib's face set. "Heidi wanted to tell you about the new gerbil at school, Mr. Rogers."

She sweetened her smile and her tone. "Didn't she want to tell *you* about Mr. Rogers?" Why couldn't Gib have listened to Heidi for a few minutes, and left Janet alone to get some urgent work done? That was what he was here for, wasn't it?

Gib took a deep breath. "Heidi, would you help me out and go see what Emma is doing? I'll be back down in a minute."

Heidi slipped down off of Janet's lap and padded out the door. Gib turned back to Janet as soon as the little girl was down the stairs.

"It's important that you spend one-on-one time with her daily. That's crucial for a middle child. They get ignored, especially when there's only one parent in the house—the oldest gets treated like a friend or a co-parent, the youngest gets all the hugs and physical affection, and the middle kid is left holding the emotional bag."

Janet bit her lip and looked out the door in the direction Heidi had gone. It was true. She tended to discuss things with Carly, even ask her opinion—what to have for dinner, when to go to the grocery store, what time to put the younger two to bed. And she also tended to touch Emma often—she held her on her lap while she read or watched television, patted her head or picked her up when she left the room, played with her. Where did that leave Heidi? She got to her feet to follow Heidi, but Gib held up a peremptory hand.

"Not now, she'll know you've been told to come after her. Kids sense these things. She'll know we argued, and she'll figure it's her fault. Wait a while, until she forgets we were talking about her when she left, then come down and talk or play with her. Better yet, just put some thought into interacting with her on a casual basis all day long. Reach out to touch her when you walk past, smile at her when you see her. Say 'hi' to her or mention her name first some of the time. Middle kids never get that. People always either go up or down the age progression."

He shook his head in exasperation. "And for God's sake, you're living in a house with three children. Think about that next time you just answer a door by saying 'Go away.' You can be rude to me if you really think it's necessary, but the kids sure don't deserve it." With that, he turned and left, and Janet sagged into her chair.

He was right. Everything he said was right. And, try as she might to blame it on lack of time, that wasn't the whole story. Other women, women whose schedules were just as full as Janet's, handled it.

Other men, too, if the paragon of virtue down in her spotless kitchen was any indication.

No, it wasn't Janet's lack of time. It was Janet herself. Face it, as a mother substitute, she stank. Sooner or later, she was going to do something that really hurt one of the kids.

At least she had Gib here to help. As much as he irritated Janet, his presence here was good for the kids. The social worker had been right—she wasn't a competent parent, not even on a temporary basis.

She straightened in her chair. Maybe, since she didn't have to worry so much anymore about things like feeding and bathing and actual physical safety, she could at least try to improve at the emotional part of parenting. Gib said she needed to spend some time with these kids—that's what she was going to do. Even if she found out she'd never make a good parent and that she'd better never have kids, she nonetheless needed to do her best with the bunch she was responsible for right now.

The problem was, she still needed to get some work done. It wasn't just a whim on her part—this business needed her energy and effort to stay afloat.

Okay, she had a problem. Half the answer was recognizing you have a problem, right? That's what she always told her clients. Once you recognize it, you can find a solution.

First, state the problem.

How was she going to keep her business alive while still giving the kids the attention they deserved?

Gib was here to make sure that the kids didn't come to actual physical harm. But she still needed to take care of them emotionally. He was the nanny, not the daddy.

Her mind took an unexpected detour at that thought, and she pictured Gib as a father, strong, gentle hands holding a baby of his own. What an excellent father he'd be. If he could be this good with other people's kids, what would he be like with his own? She pictured him, bare-chested, a sleeping baby clad only in a diaper cradled close in the crook of his elbow.

She shook her head. Those kinds of thoughts would get her nowhere. Or at least, they would get her nowhere she had any business going.

A plan. She needed a plan. All her life she'd been solving problems—her own and other people's—by organizing her way through them, making plans. This was no different, really.

She stood and paced for a moment, the germ of an idea forming itself in her mind.

A schedule was what she needed.

If she could just get on a schedule, and stick to it, she just knew she could get everything done.

She sat down again in her chair and pulled out a sheet of paper and a pen. She was going to find a way to make this work if it killed her. After a few minutes, she had a good start on a schedule—something that would allow her to get enough time for her business and also spend some quality time with both of the girls.

She stood up and frowned at the page. It would mean close timing, and she'd need help from Gib—he was the key to making it work. She walked to the door and jogged down the stairs.

She found Gib in the kitchen, standing at the counter, the three girls crowded near him. Janet stopped, transfixed by the scene.

Emma sat at his feet, chewing happily on the same battered wooden spoon Gib had given her earlier. Heidi was perched on a stool beside him. Carly, home from school, stood on his other side.

Unbelievable—this morning, when Janet had told Carly she'd hired a nanny, Carly had gone instantly anxious, full of questions about whether this meant Janet was going away. As Janet watched, Carly smiled up at Gib. She'd obviously been won over already, and with no help from Janet. He was three-for-three with the girls.

Gib and the two older girls leaned over a cookbook

on the counter. Canisters of flour and sugar, a tray of eggs, a carton of milk, and a stack of baking tins were scattered over the counter and tabletop. Heidi's hands were covered with sticky bits of dough, and Carly's with flour.

"Okay, after we knead it, we let it rise. We have to find a warm spot." Gib looked down at Heidi. "Where's a warm spot?"

Heidi screwed her face up, thinking. "Under the covers?"

From where she stood, Janet saw Gib's lip quiver. "Mmm, maybe. But it might get a little sticky under there. Then what would you do when you wanted to go to sleep?" Heidi giggled, and Gib turned his glance to Carly.

She thought for a moment. "Clementine always sleeps on the 'frigerator. It's 'cause it's warm up there." Janet glanced to the top of the fridge, and sure enough, there was Clem. Why hadn't Janet ever noticed her up there before?

Gib nodded at Carly, eyebrows raised in approving agreement. "Good thinking. Cats always find the warmest spot in the house. The top of the fridge it is." He opened a drawer and pulled out a tea towel, and Janet wondered how he'd known where they were. Already, he knew the kitchen better than she did. He and Mrs. Murphy ought to get along like a house afire. They could exchange tips.

She watched as he ran the towel under water, wrung it out, draped it over the loaf pan that held the bread dough. Then he pulled the cat down from on top of the fridge—he petted her head until she started purring, then deposited her gently onto the window seat, where she promptly went back to sleep—and then placed the pan on top of the refrigerator. His movements were slow and deliberate, almost hypnotic, and Janet couldn't figure out how he could move so slowly and yet appear so focused. The two older girls watched him as intently as she did herself, and suddenly she understood—that was the idea. Consciously or not, he moved that way so the children could follow his movements, understand what he was doing.

With a start, she realized he'd been doing the same thing with her, when he'd given her the diapering lesson.

He narrated the bread-making process with an ongoing patter, telling them what he was doing while he was doing it. "This damp towel will keep the dough from drying out. We'll leave it up here to rise for an hour. Let's set the timer so we don't forget." He smiled at the two girls. "And now, let's clean up this mess while we wait. Heidi, you put all the stuff away that goes in the bottom cupboards. I'll do the up-high stuff. Carly, you wipe off the counters."

Janet felt a wistful sense of loss. She wanted to be part of all this.

Well, next time, she'd just schedule things so she could be.

She cleared her throat. "Hi, guys. What are you doing?"

Carly looked up. "Aunt Jannie! We're making bread. Gib showed us how!" She held up the cloth she was using to wipe off the counters. "And now we're cleaning everything up." She giggled. "Even Mrs. Murphy wouldn't know we cooked. Gib said so." She turned back to her task, and Janet looked up at Gib. Her gaze went helplessly to his hands, which he was drying on a towel. They were large and strong. Competent hands. His movements were slow, and she had to tear her gaze away to meet his eyes again. He gave her an appraising glance.

She felt unaccountably nervous, and she picked up another cloth to help Carly. "I was just thinking that maybe we can solve this problem—that's one thing I'm good at, solving problems." She flashed him a grin, pulling the damp cloth through a pile of flour, wiping it carefully off the counter and into her hand. She poured it into the sink. "I'd like to be a part of all this—" she nodded at the busily working girls "—but I also have to get my work done. So, I was thinking. What if I schedule a certain amount of time to work, and a certain amount of time for the kids? I could have some Heidi time, and some Carly time."

She'd almost mentioned Carly first, but stopped herself just in time to remember what Gib had said, and she was rewarded with a sunny smile from Heidi. He was right; it worked! "And some time for everyone all together, to do stuff like this." She shook the cloth out over the sink, rinsed it, folded it carefully over the faucet. He still hadn't said anything, so she turned to look at him. "What do you think?"

His lips twitched as if he were fighting off a grin. "You might find it's more difficult than you think to schedule parenting."

Janet lifted her chin. He was probably a spontaneity-worshiper who didn't like to plan anything and couldn't stand it when other people were more organized than he was.

"Let's try it, shall we? I'm sure we can find a way to make it work."

She held up her schedule. "How about if we try it this way, at least during spring break—I'll start right after breakfast, at eight, and I'll work until nine. At nine, I'll do something with Heidi. Then, ten until noon, I'll work some more. From noon until one, we'll all have lunch together. From one until three, I'll work. Three to four, Carly. Four to six, work, then dinner. After dinner, I'm off until the girls go to bed, unless I've gotten behind. Then after they go to bed, I put in one more hour, on paperwork and stuff like that.''

She counted up the hours. "There, I get in a full eight hours of work, and I spend time with the girls, and we all do something fun together, and most evenings there's some family time, too." She looked up at him. "I'll put you in charge of finding something fun for us all around lunch hour each day, but I'll be responsible for the hour each morning and afternoon I spend with Heidi and Carly."

She couldn't decipher the look he was giving her, but he nodded, so she decided to assume he was agreeing with her. She looked at her watch. "Two o'clock. That means it's time for me to go work. Carly, come up and knock on my door at three, okay?"

Carly bit her lip and looked at Gib before she looked back at Janet. "Aunt Jannie, Brownies is today. It doesn't end until four-thirty."

Janet stopped for a moment, disconcerted, but not for long. Schedules were made to be flexible. "All right, then, I'll have Heidi at three, and Carly in the morning at nine. And if we find the three o'clock slot doesn't work for Heidi, either, we'll just find some time that does."

No problem! This was going to work out fine, she could just feel it. She'd get her work done, spend time with the girls, and not miss out on all the fun. She beamed and turned for the stairs.

GIB WATCHED her go, astounded. Did she really think this lamebrained idea was going to work?

Apparently she did.

He chuckled to himself. She didn't understand much about kids. Any parent could tell her that raising children was a little more complicated than just making a series of appointments.

Oh, well. She'd learn. And he had to admire her efforts at trying to get it right—she really did care about her nieces, that much was obvious. It wasn't that the kids weren't important to her—she was just having a hard time moving from one priority to the other. The stricken look on her face when she'd seen Heidi's tears earlier told it all. He'd felt almost as bad for Janet as he had for Heidi, and he'd had to stop himself from reaching out to touch her, to reassure her.

Bad idea. No touching allowed. If he touched her, he might not want to stop. And he shouldn't be starting in the first place. *She's a client, not a woman.*

Something Janet had said came back to him, and he looked at the clock. It really was two o'clock already! He hadn't called in to the office all day. He reached for the phone, listened to it ring twice.

"The Mommy School."

"Sheila, Gib here. Any calls?"

"Gib! I called hours ago! Yes, we had a call— maybe a new client. I think I almost got them talked into it."

He frowned. "What do you mean?"

"Well, when you didn't call me back, I had to call them myself. I know, I know, I'm not supposed to. Sheesh. You are such a control freak. But, listen, I told them all about the program, and they're really excited.

They want someone soon. I told them we were thinking about adding staff—"

He cut her off. "You know I can't do that."

"But, Gib, they want someone right now! We can find someone, I know we can. Or...well, I can do it."

He'd known she had an ulterior motive. "Forget it, Sheila. Just concentrate on school. Let me worry about the business."

"But, Gib, this is an easy client. One brand-new baby and a couple of parents who think they can't handle it. One week, two weeks, tops. I can do it, I know I can—"

"I said no."

Silence on the other end of the line.

He was losing his patience. "Sheila, did you hear me?"

"Fine. You said no. God forbid you should ever change your mind about anything, or acknowledge that anyone else can handle anything. No, you have to do it yourself. You have to make all the calls, you have to do all the work, you have to know all the details. You know, Gib, if you'd let someone help, maybe this job wouldn't seem so much like something you wanted to run away from for the rest of your life." She hung up.

He stood there for a moment, his jaw working, before he hung up.

AT THREE O'CLOCK, right on schedule, Janet placed a stack of signed, stamped and sealed letters into her out-basket. She pulled a presentation board from behind her desk and dug through her file drawers until she found a handful of markers. Then she turned her chair toward the door and waited for Heidi's knock.

After five minutes, she started to get restless. Maybe Heidi had misunderstood—after all, she was only four. Janet picked up the markers and the pads and headed downstairs.

As she approached the landing, the house echoed silence back to her. Where was everyone? Maybe they'd gone outside and lost track of time. She walked through the kitchen and peered out into the backyard. Empty.

Where could everyone be?

A note pinned up on the board next to the phone caught her eye. She walked over and pulled it down.

Had to run Carly to Brownies. Didn't want to disturb you, so I took Heidi and Emma. Back before 3:30.

                                                Gib.

They'd gone out and left her. Without even saying anything. The thought stung.

The phone rang, and she reached for it automatically. "Hello?"

"Ms. Resnick, this is Sheila again, from The Mommy School? Sorry to keep bothering you. Is Gib there?"

"No. Apparently he left. Without saying anything to me, by the way."

"He left without telling you he was going? What about the kids?" Sheila sounded shocked.

"Oh, no, he didn't leave them. He took them with him. But I was supposed to spend time with one of the girls this afternoon, and he knew that. Now I can't." Janet told herself she shouldn't be talking this way to someone she'd never met—someone who was probably Gib's lover—but she was irritated.

Sheila sighed. "That's my brother. Always thinks he knows best. He's the only one who can do anything right, you know." She laughed. "Of course, the rest of us would like to have a chance to try, too."

Her brother? Suddenly Janet felt better. "No kidding. I always get the feeling he's smirking at me. As if he's already tried all of my ideas and knows none of them are going to work."

"*Grr.* Or, why bother having ideas at all, when his are so much better?" They laughed.

Sheila harrumphed into the phone. "You wouldn't believe how stubborn he can be. I mean, I love my bro, he's a great guy, but he treats me like I'm still ten. I guess that's because he knows how to deal with ten-year-olds. He has no idea how to deal with me now that I'm twenty and have my own ideas about what I want to do with my life."

Janet dropped onto the stool by the phone. This was fascinating. "What do you want to do?"

"I want to teach kids to dance. I don't know if you've ever taken dance lessons...?"

"No, but my niece does." She knew her mother had signed up Heidi for ballet class. Actually, she'd missed it this week, she realized, wincing slightly.

"Well, then, you've probably seen what most dance teachers do to kids. It's all about pressure and discipline, when it should be about having fun, exploring movement, meeting challenges."

A teacher with that kind of passion was exactly what Heidi would get, if it was up to Janet. "So why don't you do it?"

"Gib, that's why! He won't let me quit school, or

even drop to part-time. At this rate, I'll never get a studio. Instead, I'll finish school and get some boring job doing something stupid, and I'll sit around wishing I could be teaching instead.''

Janet heard the frustration in Sheila's voice. ''Have you talked to your brother about it?''

''Only until I'm blue in the face. He doesn't even listen—he just goes into his lazy-boy routine. The more I argue, the more laid-back he gets. He never loses it, he just gets calmer and calmer. He starts to lean on things. When he's so calm he has to sit down on the couch and lean back, you'll know you've got him really nuts. Try it, you'll see.''

Janet opened her mouth to ask why she would want to make Gib nuts, but as she did, she heard the car in the driveway. ''Oh, here they come now.''

''Good. Pretend you didn't even know he was gone, then just watch him put the lid on his temper. It's quite a show.''

Janet laughed. ''Maybe I just will. Better run, then!''

''Call me later and tell me how perfectly I predicted it.''

Janet hung up the phone and dashed up the stairs as the key scraped in the lock.

Chapter Five

Gib, Emma in his arms, trailed Heidi inside the kitchen. He looked around. No Janet. He snorted. It was a good thing he hadn't sent Heidi up there. Janet had completely forgotten about the little girl.

He sat the two girls down and got them each something to drink, and then he headed up the stairs.

He turned the knob and opened the door to Janet's office. "We're back."

She slowly turned her chair to face him. "Oh?" She looked at her watch, smiling. "After three already! Is Heidi with you?"

He rocked back on his heels and crossed his arms. Janet didn't seem to have missed them. "She's having a glass of milk. Do you still want to spend some time with her?"

Janet raised her eyebrows. "Of course I do. Why would you think I didn't?"

He leaned over to rest his arm against the wall, and Janet turned her head away, but not before he caught a glimpse of a grin. What was she finding so damn funny? "You didn't even seem to notice we were gone."

"What makes you think I didn't notice?"

He stared at her. If he didn't know better, he'd think she was behaving this way on purpose, to make him nuts.

But that was crazy. This woman barely knew him. He straightened. "I'll tell Heidi to come on up. She's been looking forward to playing with you all day. What are you going to do with her?"

Janet showed him the dry-erase board and markers. "You can draw on it, then just rub it off with a tissue."

He had to admit it, that was pretty impressive. He looked at her, more intently than he really meant to. She met his gaze, anxiety in her big hazel eyes, and hopefulness. He softened. She obviously was working at this. "She'll love it. Any four-year-old would. You really put some thought into it."

Janet almost blushed with pleasure. As he disappeared down the stairs, she scolded herself for her foolishness. Who cared what he thought? The important person was Heidi—who just then flung herself through the door and into Janet's lap.

"Gib says we're going to play. What are we going to play, Aunt Jannie?"

"I thought we'd draw pictures. I have this special board that you can draw on and wipe it off, just like a chalkboard. See?" She showed Heidi how she could draw a picture and then erase part of it and change things. Heidi's eyes grew wide. "You mean I can color and if I make a mistake, I can fix it?"

"You sure can."

"But how do you hang the pictures up?"

Janet thought for a moment. "Simple—we'll just put it on the copy machine and take a picture of it when we're done."

Heidi and Janet drew happily side by side for long,

silent, companionable minutes. Heidi drew a dog, and Janet made a copy of it. She drew a house, and Janet made a copy of that. Then Heidi drew a row of people, their hands linked. As Janet was making a copy of the picture, she asked Heidi who they were.

Heidi looked at her as if she were crazy. "That's us!"

Janet looked closer. There seemed to be four tall people and three short people. And something extra with a tail and ears that Janet thought must be the cat, Clementine. "I think I see Clem, and here's you and Carly and Emma, but who are these?" She indicated the tall people.

"That's Grandma, and that's Mommy and Daddy, and that's you, Aunt Jannie."

Janet was stunned. "You drew a picture of the whole family?" And the family included Janet?

"Uh-huh." Heidi examined the picture. "Can we make another copy? I don't want Emma to forget Mommy and Daddy."

Tears stung Janet's eyes, and she made a copy for herself and her mother as well as one for Emma.

Four o'clock rolled around, and Janet couldn't bear to ask Heidi to leave. They were still coming up with things to draw and erase. After a while, they moved on to cutting the pictures apart and taping and stapling them back together. Then they made up stories about the pictures. Janet couldn't remember when she'd had so much fun. The next thing she knew, she heard a knock on the door.

Gib stuck his head in. "Aren't you guys getting a little hungry up here?"

Janet looked at the clock. Six-fifteen! She was horrified. She had promised Houston Whalen, her single biggest client, that she'd get back to him between four and six about an upcoming project he needed to staff. Maybe he was still in his office. She scrambled up from the floor and lunged for the phone. Clutching it, she punched in the numbers.

"Houston? Janet Resnick here. Sorry—I, ah, got into a project and just couldn't extract myself." She flicked a glance at Heidi, who was excitedly showing their creations to an apparently fascinated Gib. "Are you able to discuss our plans now?"

He sounded a little terse, but no more than usual when he was in a hurry. "Janet, I'm on my way out the door. I have a predinner meeting at Alhambra. But I'm free after that. We can discuss it over dinner. I have a reservation for seven. Ask for my table." Click.

"Houston, no, I—Houston?" Janet depressed the button, dialed again, then hung up in frustration after the phone rang and rang with no answer.

Gib still stood there. "Trouble?"

Janet shook her head. "Not trouble, just confusion. I'm going to have to go meet someone for dinner." She glanced at her watch. "And if I'm going to make it, I need to get dressed."

"So much for your schedule, huh?" His smile took the sting from his words, but Janet still felt defensive.

"It's just a minor glitch, that's all. So I won't have dinner with the kids tonight—we'll start doing that tomorrow night." She stopped, struck by a thought. "I am very grateful to have you here. I don't know what I'd do—with Mrs. Murphy gone today, I'd be in real trouble right now. Thank you for being here." She paused, but she needed to say the rest of it. "Thank you also for convincing me that having you stay was the right thing to do. You were right."

She looked up at him cautiously, expecting some variant on smugness. But she'd misjudged him. His smile was gracious and casual, holding no hint of self-congratulation. "I'm always right," he said, but his voice held only teasing warmth.

After Gib went downstairs, Janet took a quick shower. She slipped on her best power suit, psyching herself up for the confrontation ahead, and gathered her hair into a twist before finishing a quick makeup job. She tucked a manila folder labeled Whalen Marketing into her briefcase and slung it over her shoulder, clipping flat gold disks onto her ears as she clattered down the stairs. She needed to *look* like a two-hundred-dollar-an-hour consultant to convince Houston she was worth that much.

She stepped into the kitchen to tell the girls goodbye. They were sitting at their places around the battered oak table, waiting as Gib put the finishing touches on dinner.

Heidi saw her first. "Aunt Jannie, you look so old!"

Carly kicked her sister. "You aren't supposed to say that!"

Janet laughed. "It's okay, Carly. I'm trying to look old—and intimidating, and powerful, and competent. Like someone you'd trust with something important." Her eyes slid—she hated it, why did she care what he thought?—over to Gib, who was watching her from in front of the stove. "So, do you think I can pull that off?" She stepped back and held her arms out in a question.

He tipped his head at the kids. "Well, you already convinced your mother to trust you with something important, and I'll bet it didn't take a power suit." He looked her up and down, his eyes taking all of her in.

"But I'd say, in that suit, you're making a persuasive argument to get yourself just about anything you want."

Janet smiled uncertainly. What did he mean by that? She didn't have time to stick around and find out. Waving a quick goodbye to the older girls, she kissed Emma and dashed out the back door.

GIB WATCHED HER go. Damn, he'd been here less than twenty-four hours and it seemed he was always watching her go. Well, that was because she did it so well. She looked almost as good going as she did coming.

That navy suit, skimming her hips and nipping in at her waist, emphasized her curves and her slender figure, yet somehow made her seem more substantial than she was. Strong, like a force to be reckoned with. High heels—besides doing wonderful things to her legs—lifted her to almost average height. All that red hair wrapped into a smooth knot in back of her head emphasized her cheekbones, the shape of her eyes. And the flashes of gold at her ears caught matching flashes in the red-gold of her hair.

She looked incredible. And only fifteen minutes earlier, she'd been running around here in leggings and a sweatshirt, grimy sneakers on over slouchy socks, all that glorious coppery hair curling wildly around her face, great big hazel eyes flashing out at him, no makeup, no jewelry, nothing. Just Janet.

Actually, she'd looked pretty good then, too.

He watched her hurry down the back walk and lower herself into her car, sliding her hips under the steering wheel first with an unsettling shimmy, pulling a nylon-clad leg inside just before she slammed the door.

With an effort, he pulled his gaze back to the cook-top, but her image remained in his mind.

Normally, he went for a certain type of woman. Big and buxom, with an easy laugh and an easier style. The kind of woman you could share some good times with and then move on, with no regrets on either side.

Never a prickly little cat in stained leggings and shapeless sweats.

And for certain, never a power-suited career woman. The very idea would have given him shivers if anyone had asked.

So now, why was the idea giving him shivers of an entirely different nature? Why couldn't he just notice she was sexy, file her under Women Who Are Attractive, and go on from there? Just as he had any dozen times before? It wasn't as if the world wasn't full of pretty women.

But it wasn't full of women like Janet Resnick.

The smell of burnt food reached his consciousness, and he focused on the pot in front of him in consternation. A thin tendril of gray smoke curled up from the edges of the mushroom gravy he was supposed to be stirring. He stirred quickly and snapped off the gas beneath the pan. Pulling out a clean spoon, he tasted it. Hmm, not bad. An interesting smoky taste. He looked sideways at the kids, but they were busy straightening the place settings on the table. Good—he'd throw in a tablespoon of Worcestershire sauce, and once it was ladled over mashed potatoes, no one would notice.

JANET SLID into a seat across from Houston Whalen, one of Cincinnati's most influential business leaders. She'd been supplying him with home-based workers for six months now, but she'd sensed she was in a trial

period. He was testing her. She knew that if she passed
the test, if she convinced him she was on top of things,
what she'd been doing for him so far was only the tip
of the iceberg. She could double her entire business
just on the needs of his company alone. And once he
was a satisfied client, there was no telling how many
other new leads he'd send her way.

This was make-it-or-break-it time for HomeWork. If
she wasn't careful, if she neglected him just a little,
she'd blow this opportunity sky-high. She'd destroy all
the carefully crafted plans she'd been making for the
past five years.

If she hadn't already.

"I have to apologize again, Houston. I'd gotten myself caught up in a very complex project and managed
to lose track of the time this afternoon. I don't know
what happened—normally I'm punctual to a fault."

Houston nodded, a short, sharp jerk of his large
head. "No real harm done. I know you won't let it
happen again." His sharp, blue eyes glittered at her,
assessing, as always. Houston studied the world from
the vantage point of almost fifty years of business experience. Those who didn't measure up to his exacting
standards were dismissed without another glance.

"Never." Janet breathed an internal sigh of relief.
She was off the hook, but she had no illusions about
it—he'd just put her on notice. Make no mistake, she'd
used up her one freebie from Houston Whalen.

He picked up his menu. "Shall we order? Then we
can get down to business."

They discussed the growth of his firm over their
meal, and the complex direct-mail project he was planning for one of his biggest clients. It was a project that
would involve desktop publishing, hand-sewing, and

hand-assembly work, all accomplished by various of Janet's contract workers in their homes. By the time they were finishing their coffee, they'd reached an understanding of what each would do next.

Janet finished making a notation on her calendar and slipped everything back into her file. "Houston, I'll have that proposal for you by the first of the month. Along with the cost estimate, of course."

"And I'll discuss some preliminaries with my clients." He stood and extended his hand. "Nice to see you again, Janet. I predict that this little venture is going to be very profitable for us both."

Janet drove home too fast, the blood pumping in her veins. She knew exactly what she needed to do. Under ordinary circumstances, she could probably have had a proposal put together, along with all the related paperwork, within three or four days. In fact, Houston had been surprised when she'd told him it would take her over a week. In the past, she would have just worked around the clock, sleeping when she was exhausted, skipping meals, not leaving her apartment until she was done. But she had her schedule now, and she was sticking with it. She had eight hours a day to work, and the rest of the time belonged to the kids. She smiled in pleasurable anticipation—she couldn't wait to see them.

When Janet stepped into the darkened kitchen, she listened for a moment. The house was silent, but it didn't feel empty. "Carly? Heidi? Anyone?"

"Down here," came Gib's response, his voice gravelly, sounding as if he hadn't spoken a word in several hours. Or as if he'd just crawled out of bed.

Janet dismissed the picture that popped into her mind at that thought and stepped down the half flight into the lower-level family room, which was mostly in darkness. Gib sat in the pool of light spilling from a single lamp, an open book in his lap. He gave her a lazy smile, and her heart turned over once.

"The girls are asleep. It's past ten."

Janet's disappointment was palpable. She'd known it was late, past both girls' bedtimes, but for some reason she'd still half expected them to be up waiting for her. Maybe because she'd wanted so much for them to be.

"You could have kept them up for me."

"I didn't know what time you'd be home. You took off out of here like a bat out of hell. They were disappointed too, but you never called to say you were on your way back."

His calm voice grated on her. "I just wanted to say good-night to them," she muttered, turning away. Then she remembered something and turned back. "Do you know where you're sleeping?" When he shook his head, she jerked her head toward the door behind him. "C'mon, I'll show you. I wanted to be upstairs with the girls, so this room's empty. It's my old one."

She led him into the cozy bedroom that had been hers when she was a teenager, before she'd gone away to college. Before her sister Georgie had married and had kids.

Janet's posters, representing a series of high-school crushes, still hung from the walls. Emilio Estevez straddling a motorcycle, Tom Cruise bare-chested in faded jeans, Rob Lowe glaring down with a smoldering sexuality. Once she'd found that "I'm dangerous" expression irresistibly appealing, but now it seemed almost humorous.

The blue and yellow room, with its yellow-rose-print

bedspread and white wicker furniture, retained a poignant sense of naiveté that seemed so obvious to her, she wondered whether Gib would perceive it. She had thought herself so sophisticated, that she was about as ready to face the world as anyone could ever be.

She'd have laughed if it wasn't so painful still—her father's death while Janet was a freshman in college, and more recently the deaths of her sister and her brother-in-law, had forever changed Janet's idea of what the world was about. She'd realized she needed to seize the day, to accomplish all she could now, today, before...well, before anything bad happened. And she had accomplished a lot.

But she still had a long way to go. She shook her head and smiled at Gib, who was watching her with a bemused expression on his face.

The room had windows along only one wall, but they were deep and wide. Bookshelves built below the row of windows were topped with blue-and-white-striped cushions to make an inviting window seat, and Janet walked over to sit down. The windows looked out on the wooded side yard, dark now.

She rubbed one hand along the faded upholstery of the cushions as she stared out at the darkness. "I spent a lot of time on this window seat during bad weather, reading and looking out at the rain or snow or whatever." She looked up to find him standing near her, staring out into the same darkness. She smiled at him nervously, not knowing why she was nervous, then cleared her throat and got to her feet, which brought them even closer together.

She'd have to get closer still to walk past him to the door. "I guess I'd better get to bed. The bathroom's through there. Towels and everything are in the linen closet in the hall.'' She stepped around him, unable to avoid brushing against him in the crowded space, and once again she was excruciatingly aware of the spot on her upper arm that had touched his chest.

GIB'S HAND went unconsciously to the place on his chest that she had brushed against. He watched her slim hips sway as she danced away from him, her slender ankles rising, graceful, from ridiculously high heels— she'd kill herself on those stilts, but they sure did nice things to her legs—and carrying her up the stairs and out of sight.

He wanted her.

Stop it. Stop it right now. It was not going to happen. He needed to make sure it didn't happen. He'd never gotten involved with any of his clients before—not with them, and not with the kids, either—and he wasn't about to start now, not when he was almost home free.

A shower. He needed a shower. He turned and jogged up the stairs to fetch the carryall he'd brought with him. He took it back downstairs to the bathroom, turned the water on hot, and stood under it for twenty minutes, steaming up the mirror and the glass-block walls of the open shower stall and leaving trails of condensation coursing down the walls.

When he stepped out of the shower, he felt much, much better. He was a new man. He felt absolutely no desire to bed one of his clients. He hadn't really wanted to before, not that much, and he certainly wasn't feeling like it now. He was going to go into her bedroom, turn off the lights, fall asleep, and wake up sane in the morning.

Only it didn't work that way. When he walked back into her bedroom, those ridiculous flowers on her bed-

spread looked back at him, all pretty and open-faced
and endearingly sure of themselves and vulnerable, and
he felt it all over again.

He wanted her, all right.

Here, in her bedroom, with Emilio and Rob looking
down from the walls. On that bed, right smack-dab in
the middle of the yellow roses. Or maybe on the window seat. Or even on the floor. Or possibly all three
places, one after another. But he definitely wanted her.

This was not a good thing.

He turned again to look at the bed. How in the world
was he going to sleep there? He gritted his teeth and
walked over to turn down the comforter, cover up all
those roses.

And the sheets on that innocent-looking bed were
covered with tiny yellow roses, too.

Every time he woke up that night, and he woke up
over and over, he thought about those roses, and about
Janet.

It was not a comfortable night.

JANET SAT on the bed in her mother's bedroom, which
she'd taken over for herself, a level above her old bedroom. She picked at the lace trim on the bedspread.

She heard the water go on in the bathroom below.
Gib was taking a shower. Funny how some people
liked to take their showers at night.

Against her will, a picture of Gib showering entered
her mind. The water beaded up on his smooth chest,
trickled over his back, coursed down his legs. She
imagined him turning to find her watching him, faint
surprise and then welcome warming his features. He
held out his hand to her, palm up, beckoning. And
when she placed her hand in his, he pulled her, fully
clothed, into the shower with him.

The hot water molded her silk suit to her body, and the steam filled her lungs, and she kicked off her shoes as he crooked his arm, pressing her to him. He bent his head to hers, and she tasted his lips, wet and slick and hot on her own. Through the heavy, wet drape of her skirt, she felt him, strong, hard, urgent with desire. His hand ran up beneath the soft, dripping fabric, hiking her skirt, tugging at her panty hose. Janet gasped as he insinuated his fingers beneath her wet panties, his hands soapy, slippery....

One floor below her, the water shut off.

Janet opened her eyes, panting a little at the vividness of her fantasy. She looked down at her hands and uttered a little gasp of irritation; she'd torn the lace trim right off the edge of the bedspread. She dropped the shredded lace in exasperation.

What she needed was a nice, relaxing shower before she went to bed.

FOR THE NEXT COUPLE of days, Janet's schedule worked like a charm. Well, practically. Saturday, Gib took the kids to the park in the morning, so Janet pushed Heidi's time up to the afternoon. She got a little behind, but she managed to spend just about six hours working. She figured that was pretty good for a weekend. She could make up the time later.

Then on Sunday, Janet managed to get in almost seven hours of nearly uninterrupted work. She spent an hour with Carly in the morning and an hour with Heidi in the afternoon, had lunch with all three girls and Gib—that ran over a little because it was so much fun watching Emma feed herself spaghetti—and only had one minor glitch when Gib had to run an errand and wanted to leave Emma behind because she was napping. Unfortunately, she woke up just after he and the older girls pulled out of the driveway, and Janet spent an unscheduled but enjoyable hour playing on the family-room floor before Gib came home and took over. At six o'clock, when Gib called her for dinner, she turned off her computer with a sense of accomplishment and went downstairs to have dinner with the rest of the family.

After dinner, Janet felt so good about how well her schedule was working that she decided she could spend the next couple of hours with the kids, and then after their bedtime she could catch up for the hour she'd lost earlier today.

They played a couple of games of Don't Spill The Beans. Heidi won once and Carly won once. Emma happily went from Gib's lap to Janet's and back again. Then she found the picture Heidi had drawn for her and was happily crumpling it when Heidi looked around.

"Oh, no, Aunt Jannie! She's gonna tear it up!" Heidi jumped down and ran over to rescue her masterpiece. "It's Mommy and Daddy, and she's ruining it."

"She can't tell anything from that picture, anyway, dummy," said Carly.

"Carly!" Janet shook her head and gave a slight frown. "In this family, we don't call each other bad names."

"But she can't! She needs to look at real pictures!"

"But then she'll tear those up!" Heidi's voice was a whine, and she sounded near tears.

Gib put an arm around Heidi. "Heidi, that's how she learns, by crumpling things and tearing them up. We have to let her learn the way she learns best. When she gets bigger, she'll be able to look at pictures without ripping them up.'' Heidi quieted, but she didn't look convinced. Gib threw Janet a glance. "Bedtime?''

Janet nodded and stood. "Bathtime, girls. Run upstairs, and I'll come up in a minute to start the water.''

"And in the meantime I'll put this one down.'' Gib leaned over to pick up Emma, who had quietly fallen asleep under the table while her sisters were arguing about her. He slid strong, gentle hands beneath her, cradling her to his shoulder, and she made a little sound of tired contentment as she nuzzled into his shoulder.

Janet looked from Emma's perfect little face—could anything look more at peace than a sleeping baby?—to Gib's gentle, tolerant expression as he guided the two older girls to the stairway. It tugged at her heart, his easy mix of gentleness and strength, a rare and potent combination.

Janet watched the girls climb the stairs, followed by Gib, stepping softly so as not to disturb the sleeping Emma. Watching them, so like a family, tugged at her heart. She listened as the girls giggled while they got ready for their bath, and she heard Gib's footsteps overhead in Emma's nursery. She reached to flick off the light over the table, leaving a single light to help Gib find his way to his room. Then she headed up the stairs after them.

After she gave the girls their bath, she spent a couple of hours working. As she turned off her computer, she decided she'd better get started an hour earlier from now on. That would make room for the minor emergencies of everyday life, like babies waking up early from naps. But other than that, the schedule was working.

That night, Janet listened once again as the shower

ran in the downstairs bathroom. She thought she'd stay safe this time by keeping her hands away from the lace trim on the bedspread. But when she slept, she dreamed of Gib. He carried her into his bedroom and laid her on the bed, and he made strong and gentle love to her until dawn.

At seven, her alarm went off, and she frowned at it in confusion. She was disoriented to find herself in her mother's bed, alone. The dream had been that real.

How embarrassing. Surely Gib would take one look at her face and realize she'd been dreaming about him all night long. Maybe she could make it downstairs for her coffee without running into him. She pulled on a pair of leggings and a sweatshirt and ran down the stairs.

Chapter Six

No such luck. She stepped down onto the kitchen landing, and there he was, his back to her. She wondered if, under that shirt, his back was as broad as she'd dreamed it.

He looked around as if he heard her thoughts, and she blushed furiously.

To cover it up, she started to chatter. "Oh, bless you, you made coffee. And what's that, eggs?" He had about a dozen in the pan, it looked like. "You're expecting an army?" Janet seldom ate breakfast herself, and she usually just poured cereal for the kids.

He gave her a sideways glance. "Not a breakfast-eater?" She shook her head. "Ever offer the kids a big breakfast?"

She wrinkled her nose. "Who could eat that much food that early in the morning?"

"Most kids will, if you give them a chance." He slid the eggs onto a plate and set it inside the oven. "What time do they usually get up?"

"On spring break? I don't know, really. Emma's always up by seven-thirty or so. Heidi can sleep in. Carly's usually up, made her bed, dressed herself, and is down here by now."

Right on cue, Carly clattered down the stairs and into the kitchen. "Wow! Eggs! I love eggs!" She climbed into her chair and picked up her fork, waiting while Gib spooned eggs onto her plate.

Janet was relieved to have another person in the room, even if it was an eight-year-old. There was something too intimate about breakfast. Especially after an all-night lovemaking session. She sneaked a peek at Gib from the corner of her eye. Well, she apparently wasn't wearing a sign reading I Slept with You in My Dreams. Either that, or he was ignoring it.

In fact, he almost seemed to be consciously ignoring *her.* He chatted with Carly while Janet poured herself a cup of coffee, and when she announced she was going back upstairs to start working, he barely looked around.

Apparently, her crush on him was not reciprocated.

Janet trotted back upstairs with the steaming mug. If she wanted to spend time with Carly, she needed to get in a good two hours' work before nine o'clock rolled around. She reminded herself to put breakfast bars on the shopping list—she was never going to be able to work on just coffee, and she wasn't going to have time to plow through Gib's idea of a real breakfast in the morning.

She tried to concentrate, but her mind kept jumping to the upcoming time she'd spend with Carly. She had a great idea in mind.

At eight-fifteen, she started to wind down. At eight-thirty, she recorded a new message for her answering machine, telling callers she'd be in regular one-hour meetings each day at nine and three o'clock for the next week. At eight forty-five, she couldn't stand it any more, and she put her work away, even though she'd barely managed to get an hour in, and that hour less productive than usual. She dug through her wallet and her drawers until she found everything she needed. At nine, when Carly's timid knock sounded on her door, she was ready.

"Come in!"

Carly poked her head around. "Are you too busy?"

Janet grinned at her from the floor where she was sitting. "Honey, I'm never too busy for you." She held out her hand to her niece. "Come here and let me show you something we can do, if you want. You can decide whether you want to do this, or something else."

Carly sat down next to Janet, cross-legged on the floor, and pointed at a small machine Janet had dug out of one of the boxes she'd brought from her apartment. "What's that?"

"That's a laminator. It seals things in plastic. I use it for presentations. But we're going to use it to make a photo album for Emma."

For the next hour, Janet and Carly pasted pictures of the family, which Janet had found in her wallet, onto index cards. Carly wrote the names of each family member pictured on the cards beneath the photos. Then Janet sent the cards through the laminator. When they were finished, they had a stack of six cards, each with a picture of someone in the family, each encased in plastic.

"Let's see, we need some way to put them together, like a book." Janet thought for a moment, then reached for her purse. She pulled out her key ring, and one by one worked the keys off the ring. "Why don't you punch a hole near the top left corner of each of those cards, honey?" She showed Carly which corner she meant, and handed her the hole punch.

When Carly was finished, Janet snapped the ring through the holes in the stack of cards.

"Neat!" Carly picked up the album. "But what if Emma chews on it?"

"Won't matter. The plastic will protect the pictures. Want to go see if she likes it?"

"Yeah!" Carly jumped up, and Janet smiled at her excitement and got to her feet. She was thrilled at Carly's reaction. The eight-year-old hadn't shown much enthusiasm for anything in the past year. Maybe Carly was finally starting to come out of her shell.

Just then the phone rang. Janet looked at her watch. Quarter past ten! How could it have gotten so late? She waited while the machine picked up.

"Janet?" Janet sighed as she recognized the voice. "This is Houston. I have a couple of questions that I need answered ASAP. I'll be in the office for the next ten minutes, and then out for the rest of the day, so if you can get back to me right away, I'd appreciate it." Click.

Carly gazed up at her, disappointment clear in the little girl's open face. Janet bit her lip. "Honey, I'm sorry. I'll have to call him back. But why don't you go find Heidi, and the two of you can give the album to Emma? I'll come down as soon as I'm finished, okay?"

Carly nodded and reached for the door. With her hand on the knob, she turned back. "Aunt Jannie?" Her voice had dropped again to a low whisper. "I had fun. Thank you very much." She pulled the door closed behind her, and Janet heard her start down the stairs.

Janet felt guilty and torn. But what could she do? She reached for the phone.

The questions Houston had for her were important ones, and she needed to get the answers for him right away. Finally she pulled it all together. As she fed the last of the information he'd requested into her fax machine, she hit the ''send'' button and was out the door in the same movement.

Music and giggles floated up to her as she ran down the stairs, and she stopped on the landing to push open the door into the kitchen.

The radio was playing a California Raisins commercial. Heidi and Carly, each carrying a cup and a plate, danced a ragged conga around the work island in the center of the kitchen. Gib, Emma slung under his arm like a sack of potatoes, pretended the wooden spoon in Emma's hand was a microphone. He sang into it.

''I heard it through the grapevine, ooh, ooh,'' Gib sang, his eyes screwed shut. He swung his hips from side to side in time to the music. Janet pulled her eyes away before she was actually staring, but not before she noticed how good he looked in well-worn khakis.

Carly swung her hips in imitation of Gib. ''Ooh, ooh,'' she echoed.

Heidi tried to swing her hips too, but only managed to slosh milk onto the floor from the cup she was carrying. She giggled as it hit her shoe.

''Raised in the California sunshine, ooh, ooh.''

Carly pulled the dishwasher open and stacked several plates into it. She swung her hips. ''Ooh, ooh.''

Gib walked across the kitchen to the sink, scooped up a sponge in his free hand, and followed Heidi along, wiping up the spilled milk. As he bent down, Emma hung upside down over his arm, and she squealed with delight.

Janet felt a twist of mixed emotions. Mostly, she told

herself, it was happiness, with maybe a tiny sprinkling of lust. But there was also a little wistfulness—she'd missed the fun stuff again. And, if she used a little insight into her own less-than-appealing character flaws, there was also a measure of jealousy. She'd known these kids all their lives, and she didn't have this kind of easy rapport with them. How did he do it? She'd have felt stupid, dancing around the kitchen, singing along with a commercial on the radio. But the kids loved it.

But she concentrated on her more positive feelings, and she leaned up against the doorjamb to enjoy the show. As the song ended, she applauded.

He turned and gave her a slightly sheepish grin, and she realized with a shock that maybe he *did* feel a little stupid.

"How do you do it?" She reddened, realizing she'd blurted the question out with no explanation.

She lowered her voice, so the kids, who were squabbling over who rinsed and who loaded, wouldn't easily hear. "I mean, the dancing, the kid stuff. I might be able to pull off the dancing, the singing, the playing. But you seem so comfortable with it."

He kept his voice low and casual, too. "Being comfortable with it is the only thing that really matters, to the kids. They don't care if I can't actually sing or dance. But if they thought I was faking the fun, they wouldn't enjoy it. You just have to go with it."

Well, duh. Suddenly, Janet felt about as dense as she ever had. Why was that such a revelation to her? She stared at him for a long moment, amazed at the obviousness of the idea, and at her own obtuseness.

Carly came over and tugged on Janet's arm. "Aunt Jannie, can we can give Emma the picture book now?

Gib said we had to wait." She ran over to the china cabinet and pulled the booklet off the second shelf.

"Why don't we all sit down and show Emma?" Gib carried Emma into the living room and dropped down cross-legged in the middle of the floor with the baby on his lap. Heidi and Carly plopped down on either side of him. Gib looked up at Janet. "C'mon, let's see how she likes it."

Janet walked over and dropped to her knees beside Heidi.

"Emma? Emma?" Carly got the baby's attention, then held the plastic-covered pictures out in front of her. "Look, pictures! And you can chew on them, if you want. Look, here's my school picture from last year, and a picture of you and me and Heidi, and here's a picture of Aunt Jannie, and here's..." Her voice faltered as she came to the picture of her mother.

"That's Mommy!" Heidi flashed her eyes, obviously indignant that Carly didn't remember.

"I know it's Mommy!" Carly looked at Janet. "But maybe Emma forgets." Her eyes shone bright with the threat of tears.

Emotion tugged at Janet's heart and tears sprang to her own eyes. She smoothed Carly's hair. "She won't forget, honey, not if you keep reminding her." She remembered Heidi, and touched her, too. "You, too."

"I'll remind her every day." Carly's hand tightened on the booklet of pictures, and she held the picture of their mother up again for Emma to see. "That's Mommy, Emma. And this one's Daddy." Emma pulled the plastic-coated picture of her father into her mouth and bit down.

Janet glanced up at Gib. He raised his eyebrow and

nodded in a silent salute, and she felt a thrill of warmth at his approval.

And the picture of him she'd been forcing from her mind came back full-strength, the picture of him bending over her nearly naked body, reaching for her with desire in his eyes. She blushed, hot and deep, and turned away, hoping he hadn't noticed her discomfort. She tried to come up with something to say to provide a distraction. "Well, I guess I better get a sandwich and get back to work, if I want to stay on track today."

GIB SIGHED as he watched her go. Yet another pair of leggings. This pair was red. He decided red was a particularly good color on her.

She was really something. He'd thought he was an old master at understanding people, but this woman was managing to surprise him at every turn. Who would have thought she'd have this drool-proof photo album up her sleeve? When he'd first walked in here— was it only four days ago?—he would have sworn she couldn't have managed her way out of a paper bag. But here she was reassuring an anxious eight-year-old as if she'd been doing it all her life.

She kept showing him new sides of herself. And he kept finding something attractive about every one of them. He was a hopeless case. If he was smart, he'd get out now, while he still could.

Maybe he should talk to her about just hiring a nanny, which was what she'd said she needed.

He felt a strange sense of reluctance. Maybe he should give her at least a few more days. For the kids' sake.

He pushed aside a little voice that told him he was making excuses. After all, what possible reason could he have for that? It wasn't as if he was actually going to do anything about his feelings, so sticking around was really just an exercise in self-torture for him. He was getting nothing out of it. Except for a heck of a lot of long, cold showers.

JANET WAS FEELING pretty good as she walked back toward the kitchen to make herself a sandwich. Then she pushed open the door, and there stood Mrs. Murphy, her back to Janet, rinsing dishes and stacking them in the dishwasher. Janet stopped dead. She really didn't want to get into it with Mrs. Murphy this morning. Maybe she'd get her sandwich later.

She turned, trying to push back through the door silently, when she realized Mrs. Murphy was... humming? Janet had never heard Mrs. Murphy hum. She'd never heard her make any noise not associated with disapproval. But Mrs. Murphy was humming. "Oh, What A Beautiful Morning," if Janet was making it out correctly.

She turned back. "Mrs. Murphy?"

Mrs. Murphy half turned, her hands continuing to rinse a bowl. "Oh, Janet, hello, dear! Can I do something for you?"

Dear? "Ah, no, I'm so glad you decided to come back. I wanted to thank you."

"Oh, that nice Gib! He talked me into it, the rascal! Tsk-tsk. When he first called, I told him I just couldn't do it, I couldn't come back. But then he told me he'd worked with Margery Rawlings, and she's an old friend, dear, and she keeps house for Mrs. Stevens, and he told me I should call her and ask her how things had gone while he was working at the Stevenses'. So I did, and Margery just couldn't sing his praises too highly.''

Janet didn't think she'd ever heard Mrs. Murphy put together more than six words at a time.

And she still wasn't finished. ''So I told him I'd give it another chance, and you know, he was right! He's kept the children out of my way all morning.'' Mrs. Murphy paused for a breath.

Janet gave her a weak smile. ''So you'll stay?''

''Well, as long as he keeps everything running even half this smoothly, I'd be happy to.'' She smiled fondly at Janet, as if she'd never had a smidgen of a problem with her, and turned back to the dishes, humming again.

Janet told herself it was just luck—besides, she'd had Carly for over an hour this morning, herself. But somehow she wasn't convinced. Gib's record was perfect—he'd won over everyone important in Janet's life. It was really too much.

But she pushed aside the feelings of inadequacy that niggled at her, made herself a cold sandwich, and trudged back upstairs to her office.

Houston's emergency this morning had thrown her schedule out of whack. She was going to have to work double-time. Working feverishly for a couple of hours, she managed to get through most of the emergencies that had cropped up during the morning. Just as she turned to her computer to get started on the proposal for Houston's project, a knock sounded on her office door. Before she could answer, Gib stuck his head in. ''Three o'clock—time for Heidi. But since it's ballet-class day, do you want me to just take her? It's only five minutes away, and she's already dressed.''

Janet looked at her watch. ''No, I'll take her. I, um,

forgot about it last week, so I'd like to go this week, maybe meet her teacher.'' After her conversation with Sheila, she also wanted to observe the class.

Throwing a regretful glance at the computer, Janet got up and followed Gib out the door and down the stairs.

She called back over her shoulder. ''Come on, Heidi, or we'll be late.''

Heidi, dressed in a black leotard, ran out of her bedroom door and followed her downstairs and out to the car. ''Miss Rita doesn't like it if we're late.''

''Well, we'll hurry, then.''

Just before three, they pulled into the parking lot of a small strip mall and parked in front of one of the storefronts. The sign said Miss Rita's School of Dance, and through the glass window, they saw six little girls in matching short-sleeved black leotards standing in a ragged semicircle around a pink-chiffon-clad woman. Her chignon was snowy white, and her parchment-thin skin was as pink as her chiffon skirt, but she held herself erect and her legs could have belonged to an extremely fit thirty-year-old woman. As Janet watched, the woman curtsied to the little girls, who, as one, curtsied back.

Janet pushed the door open for Heidi and followed her in. ''Is that Miss Rita?''

Heidi nodded. ''Uh-huh, and it's time already!'' She handed Janet her sneakers, then ran to join her class, sitting down to tug on her ballet slippers after she had crossed the room.

Miss Rita said something to Heidi that Janet couldn't hear, and Heidi scrambled to her feet and curtsied.

There was no one sitting at the receptionist's desk

immediately inside the door, so Janet plopped down on the pink bench to wait.

As Janet watched, Miss Rita demonstrated a position for the girls to imitate, her face stern. She walked along the line of preschoolers, changing the tilt of an arm here, the position of a foot there. Then she demonstrated another position. After a few minutes of this, Miss Rita flipped a switch on a tape player by the wall, and the girls ran through a short choreographed routine, Miss Rita calling out sharp instructions as the little girls followed each other in a winding line. All the little girls watched Miss Rita's face intently, almost worriedly.

After class, Heidi walked over to where Janet was sitting. Janet handed Heidi her sneakers, and Heidi sat down on the bench next to Janet to change into them.

"Did you have fun?"

Heidi shrugged. "Uh-huh."

"Do you like dancing class?"

Another shrug. "Uh-huh."

Janet frowned. "Do you want to stop taking dancing, Heidi?"

Heidi looked up, eyes wide. "No!"

"It didn't seem like you were having much fun." Indeed, none of the girls had been smiling much.

"Miss Rita says we're working, not having fun."

"But you still want to do it?" Heidi nodded. "But why, honey, if it isn't fun?"

"'Cause you can't be in the 'cital if you don't be in class. Miss Rita says so." Heidi stood and clutched her ballet slippers. "The 'cital is in two weeks. I'm the Lammender Princess. I'm wearing a purple dress. Everybody else has to wear *pink*." She screwed up her nose to illustrate her opinion of that fate. "But Miss

Rita says I gotta come to class every time from now on, or I can't be in the 'cital.''

"Oh, don't worry, honey, I'm sure you'll get to be in the recital." Janet reminded herself to check the time and date of the recital and write it on her calendar.

The pink-clad woman crossed the floor to where Janet and Heidi were standing, and Janet introduced herself. "I'm sorry Heidi missed class last week—it was my fault. I forgot all about it."

Miss Rita arched penciled eyebrows at Janet. "Heidi has assured me it won't happen again."

"Oh, no. It was just a nutty time for us, with my mom being on vacation and all." For some reason Janet felt compelled to continue to explain. "And now she's had surgery, and won't be back for six more weeks, so things are even more up in the air than they were. But we'll try to keep on top of things from now on." She finally ran down.

Miss Rita smiled. "Of course, the show must go on, with or without Heidi. But if she wants to continue as the Lavender Princess, she must not fail to attend any more classes." She nodded her head and smiled, and sat down at the receptionist's desk and started to shuffle papers around.

Janet watched her for a second, considering. Miss Rita's style bothered her, but maybe she was just a little paranoid, after her conversation with Sheila. She wondered what Sheila would think of this place.

She wondered what Gib would think.

She turned and pushed the door open for Heidi. As it swung shut behind them, she checked her watch. "Hey, it's only three-forty-five—shall we go get an ice-cream cone?

"Yes, ice cream!"

Janet laughed and held out her hand to Heidi and they walked a couple of blocks to Mrs. Goody's ice-cream parlor. While Heidi and Janet ate their ice cream, Mrs. Goody told Janet how well the HomeWork temp she'd hired was working out. "She even showed me a way to defer part of my quarterly taxes."

Janet couldn't keep from beaming. "I'm glad it's working out so well."

As they drove home, Heidi gazing sleepily out the window, Janet felt great. She'd gotten as much pleasure from knowing she'd helped Mrs. Goody as she'd gotten from the ice-cream cone.

Well, almost as much. That Rocky Road had been pretty darn good.

Heidi fell asleep in the car on the way home, and Janet carried her inside just as the clock struck five.

Gib stood at the stove, tasting a spoonful of whatever heavenly-smelling stuff was cooking in a big white enameled pot over a low flame. His lips touched the spoon carefully, and he blew a little, then tried again. With an effort, Janet tore her gaze from his mouth as he dropped the tasting spoon into the sink and turned toward her.

"How was ballet class?"

"Well..." Janet checked to make sure Heidi was still asleep. "I'm not sure I liked what I saw. I was thinking of maybe asking your sister to attend a class with me. It seemed to me like Miss Rita is a little hard on these preschoolers."

He stared at her. "My sister? You mean Sheila?" Janet nodded. "When did you meet Sheila?"

"Oh, we met on the phone. We've talked a couple of times."

"Oh." His face creased into a vague scowl.

Janet bit back a smile. If Sheila was as forthcoming with all his clients as she had been with Janet, he had reason to be uneasy. Absently, he plucked a wooden spoon from the spoon rest. The movement of his broad wrist was circular, graceful and unhurried as he stirred the pot.

She was staring again. With an effort, she switched her gaze to the clock. She couldn't believe it. When was she going to get her proposal done for Houston? Time had slipped away from her again. "I cannot believe it's five o'clock. I'm going to have to work straight through 'til midnight to catch up!"

"Either that or rearrange a few things." Gib tapped the spoon on the side of the pot and set in back in the spoon rest.

She stiffened. "What do you mean, rearrange them? You mean the schedule? I know you think it's stupid, but it's working fine for me."

"I just mean prioritize. Decide what really needs to get done. Then concentrate on that."

"I know what prioritize means. I teach other people how to prioritize, not the other way around."

He gave her a not-so-gentle smile. "Then maybe you should take some of your own advice and figure out what's important to you."

Janet gritted her teeth. How dare he criticize her, when she was doing the best job she could? She was only one woman. She set Heidi down in a chair, carefully holding the little girl's shoulder for a minute as she stirred awake, using the distraction to calm herself. She was saved from having to answer when Heidi raised her head and opened her eyes to look at Gib. "I'm hungry." The little girl yawned.

"Dinner in about half an hour."

"But I'm hungry now."

"Then you can set the table now." He picked up a stack of place mats and handed them to her.

Janet turned and made a quick exit while he was distracted. As she climbed the stairs, she asked herself if he might be right. Was she just trying to do too many things? And which things were most important to her? She pushed the thought away and sat down at her computer. For the next couple of hours, at least, she needed to give all her attention to this proposal. She needed to pretend that *it* was the most important thing to her.

The next thing she knew, it was ten o'clock. *Damn!* She'd missed the kids' bedtime again.

Gib had called her for dinner a few minutes before six, and she'd told him she'd be down in a few minutes and then promptly forgot all about dinner. She had so much to do. Now her stomach growled impatiently. She was going to have to eat—and face Gib—eventually.

It might as well be now.

She stood and stretched, and groaned. Her whole body ached from sitting for so long. She turned off her computer and headed for the stairs.

And for Gib.

GIB WATCHED as Janet stepped down the last stair from the landing into the kitchen. A split-level above him, he saw her walk to the refrigerator in the semi-darkness. She opened the door and leaned over to peer in, and the tiny light from within lit up her face. He almost gasped at the picture she made, her features outlined in the darkness by the weak light. She looked like a painting, impressionistic, perfectly composed, somehow distant and unattainable, untouchable.

He swallowed.

She reached in and pulled out a block of cheese, and turned, pushing the door shut with the swing of her hip. As the light went out, the spell was broken. She was a woman again, standing in a darkened room. A beautiful woman, a real woman.

A woman he wanted, very badly, to touch.

No, a client, whom he should under no circumstances be thinking about this way.

She caught sight of him and walked down the half flight of stairs toward him, a plate of cheese and crackers and carrot sticks in one hand, a glass of milk in the other. She set them on the coffee table and dropped down next to him on the couch.

"I missed the kids again. I am the world's worst excuse for an aunt." She chomped morosely on a carrot, and he tried to think of something to say to make her feel better.

"So you'll see them tomorrow, right?" He eyed her, enjoying the opportunity to ogle without seeming to. "They'll get over it." Would she buy that? It wasn't strictly true—they'd get over it as long as it wasn't always happening, as long as the norm was otherwise—but she might not know that.

"I know, but..." She flicked a glance his way. "I was thinking about how it felt to me when my dad said stuff like that. I didn't understand that kind of reasoning, even when I was older than Carly is now. I have all these memories of Dad not being there. He might have been there a lot more than I remember. Maybe I'm just remembering the times he wasn't."

She frowned, obviously working to articulate her reasoning. "*I* know I'm trying, and you may—or may not—" a little twinkle in her eye, there, that was good, she was keeping a sense of humor ''—know I'm trying, but do *they* know it? Do they even care? Can they understand the idea of delayed gratification—let Aunt Jannie work now, and later we'll go outside and play and have even more fun than we would if I read you the book this very minute? They want attention now *and* later, today *and* tomorrow. Does telling them I'll make up for not seeing them today by seeing them tomorrow make any sense to them?''

He stared at her, amazed. She was getting it, really getting it. His gaze skimmed over her face, fascinated by the play of concern and earnest emotion, by the transparency with which her thoughts showed on her features.

He was amazed at himself, too. He should have been telling her those things, not the other way around. But she was being too hard on herself. ''You don't have to meet every expectation of every child. Just because a child believes she's the center of the universe—and they all do—doesn't mean you have to behave as if you believe it, too. Of course you don't want their most consistent memories to be the absence of the adults in their lives, but someday they do have to learn that you have your own life.''

She shook her head, not ready to listen to that. ''But if I just get my act together better, I can be there for them and have my own life, too.'' She sat forward. ''Okay, if I get up an hour earlier, say at six, I can get in three hours before I see Carly at nine. Then at ten, I'll get in another couple of hours just before lunch from twelve to one. At one, I'll work for another couple of hours until it's time to go to dance class or whatever with Heidi. We'll just have to stick to our schedule and come right back her after class, no stopping for ice cream, so I can get a couple of hours in before dinner at six. Then I'll stop working for the day and we'll all spend some time together.'' She counted back. ''Okay, that's three, five, seven, nine hours. If I plan for another hour's work after the kids go to bed, I'll get in ten for the day, if all goes well. Which of course it won't, but if I plan for ten, there's a little extra built in for the usual chaos, and maybe I'll actually get eight hours of real work done. I'll have to get to bed earlier to make it work, but it'll be worth it.''

She paused, narrowing her eyes. ''And, of course, once spring break is over, everything will have to be rearranged again.''

He tried to cover his laugh with a cough, but she saw through it.

''What's so funny?''

''I'm not laughing at you. I'm more...'' He leaned forward, searching for the word. ''I'm commiserating—raising kids is hard work. It's tempting to think that if you just try a little harder, work a little faster, you can do it all. I'm wondering when you're going to learn that you can't.''

''Look, I know it won't be easy, but if I put a little effort into it, I'll make it work.''

Fascinating. She was fascinating. He couldn't take his eyes off her. She looked so earnest, sitting there planning out everyone's day for them, counting up the hours on her fingers. A thick strand of hair curled over her cheek. She shrugged it back impatiently, but it kept falling into her eyes.

He couldn't help himself. His hand reached out of its own accord, his finger slipping beneath that red-gold strand, pushing it out of the way, back behind her ear. The coppery curl insinuated its silky way around the tip of his finger, and the soft edge of her ear felt like warm velvet.

What was he doing?

He stopped, confused, and his eyes met hers. She looked as uncertain as he felt, her hazel eyes hesitant. She bit her lip, pearly teeth digging into soft pink flesh, and her gaze traveled to his lips and back to his eyes.

His fingers trailed along her ear and traced a slow path along her delicate jaw, and as her eyelids drooped, he tilted her chin and bent his head to cover her lips with his own.

A shock ran through him as he touched his lips to hers, and he felt as if she weren't nearly close enough to him. He wove his fingers into her hair, pulling her to him, and she leaned into his embrace. He drank her in, learning the smell of her and the taste of her and the feel of her, and a small moan escaped her and lit him on fire.

She slid her tongue between his lips to meet his, and he thought he would lose his mind if he didn't have her, now, here on the couch.

"Aunt Jannie?"

He froze, then lifted his head, and Janet scrambled to her feet. At the top of the flight of stairs, hair all rucked to one side, stood Heidi, rubbing her eyes. "I'm thirsty. I yelled, but nobody came."

Janet moved first, which was a good thing, because Gib wasn't sure he could move until things settled down a bit.

He watched as Janet climbed the stairs, poured Heidi a cup of water, and murmured to her for a moment before sending her back to bed.

Janet paused for a moment with her back to him,

then turned to face him. "I guess I'd better be going to bed, too." She didn't meet his eyes.

"Janet, I'm sorry. I shouldn't have…"

"No, it's not…it's just not a good idea, really. Not with the kids and you living here and all." She still wouldn't look at him. "Let's just agree to pretend it never happened, okay?"

No, not okay. But she was right. He sighed. "Okay."

She finally looked at him and smiled, a half smile that seemed more perfunctory than sincere. "Okay, then." Then she turned, and he watched as she disappeared up the stairs.

He threw himself back down onto the couch, stunned dismay warring with frustrated desire. Was he completely nuts? What had he thought he was doing?

What more would he have done, if he'd had half a chance?

This was not a good thing. Janet was not a good woman for him to get involved with. Not right now, when he was so close to unshackling himself from all obligations. She wasn't the type to go for just a bit of uncomplicated fun—that much was obvious. For one thing, she'd probably have a plan for any relationship she got into. The plan would not include her lover jaunting off to New Zealand or the Amazon for three weeks at a time.

For another thing, as things went along, her plan would insidiously become his plan, and he'd find himself happily putting off his life again. One thing would lead to another, and pretty soon he'd have another set of college tuitions to provide for. And he'd be saying to himself, *See, things turned out for the best after all, even though I never did get to live life for myself, not even once.* Trying to convince himself that he didn't mind. That he was happier that way.

No way. He wasn't going down that road, not now. Not until he got a chance to be on his own, for once in his life. It was too bad he'd met a woman like Janet just now, but he wasn't taking that route any time soon.

Luckily, it looked like she wasn't any more interested in following it up than he was.

She was right, the whole thing had never happened. He was going to forget all about how her lips had tasted. How she had fit in his arms so perfectly. How his body had responded to her smallest sound, her least movement.

He groaned.

Chapter Seven

When Janet's alarm went off at 6:00 a.m., she was right in the middle of an amazing kiss. The world's most perfect kiss ever. Which, unfortunately, was being rudely interrupted by reality.

Morning already? It couldn't be. She'd only just hit the pillow, hadn't she? She groaned and groped for the snooze button.

She hated getting up early. She'd always set her own hours. They'd always been late hours. Even when she was just starting out, when she was offering her own services as a home-based worker, before she'd actually come up with the idea for HomeWork, she'd done most of her work after 10:00 a.m. Since she'd started farming out the actual work to be done, she'd needed at least to be capable of answering the phone by nine every morning. But she'd never had to be up and ready to function by six.

For a moment she snuggled back into her pillow and considered going back to sleep. Back to that kiss. But then she remembered the kids.

And Gib. She opened her eyes. Had that part actually happened?

It was too real, too fresh in her mind, to have been

part of the dream. Her body reacted to the memory in a way that told her it was remembering an actual event. She felt a little warmer just thinking about it. The man could kiss.

And if she didn't get up now, she'd definitely run into him in the kitchen. She wasn't ready for that yet. Not after last night. She needed to think how she was going to handle this one.

She stumbled down to the kitchen and stumbled back up with her coffee. She took a quick shower, gulping coffee and blinking under the hot water, before she sat down at her computer.

At nine, she and Carly decided to go for a bike ride. As they passed through the kitchen on their way to the garage, Emma watched her from the floor where she was playing while Gib loaded the breakfast dishes into the dishwasher. Janet smiled at Emma, who held her hands out to be picked up.

"Oh, I'm sorry, baby. I can't right now. I'll have to play with you when..."

She stopped dead, dismayed. She hadn't scheduled any time for Emma. She hadn't really thought about it—the older girls seemed to need her more, and Emma was completely infatuated with Gib. But of course Emma needed some time, too.

Why hadn't Gib brought it up? She hadn't spoken to him since last night—really, she'd been avoiding him, if she wanted to admit it. They'd both been getting into this whole idea that nothing had happened, and she hadn't exchanged six words with him all day. Now she shot him a glance, and the expression on his face told her why he hadn't brought up the fact that Emma needed attention, too.

Because he'd been waiting for her to figure it out on her own, that was why.

Boy, she really hated it when he was right.

"Okay, from now on, Emma from ten to eleven. What's the difference between 6:00 a.m. and 5:00 a.m.?"

THE NEXT MORNING at 5:00 a.m., six o'clock seemed a luscious lifetime of tempting sleep away. But Janet pried herself out of bed. She'd managed to almost stick to her schedule yesterday and she wasn't going to blow it today.

At nine, she and Carly made muffins. Emma sat in her high chair watching them, so Janet wondered if she could count both girls at once. But when they'd finished cleaning the kitchen and Carly had proudly taken a plate full of muffins downstairs to Gib and Heidi, Emma reached up her fat little arms to Janet, and she couldn't resist. Janet spent the next hour with Emma in her lap, looking at picture books. At eleven, she reluctantly handed Emma to Gib, who made gobbling noises on the baby's stomach that elicited delighted squeals in return. Even more reluctantly, Janet marched herself back upstairs to her office for an hour's work before lunch.

At noon, ravenous and aching for company, she sailed down the stairs to a strangely silent house. On the fridge she found a piece of folded notepaper marked with her name. She grabbed it and unfolded it, already feeling more lonely than before.

The kids wanted a picnic. There's leftover soup in the fridge.

Janet reread the note. No mistaking it, they were gone. They were going to be gone for lunch. She might as well go back upstairs and finish up the invoices she'd interrupted.

She'd never interrupted invoices before. That was one job she always followed through to the end. It was too important to risk not being on top of. Maybe this was an omen, telling her to get back to work.

Or maybe he was avoiding her, too.

Suddenly, she wasn't very hungry.

She grabbed a handful of crackers, an apple, and a can of diet pop and trudged back up the stairs. No matter what, she was going to have a talk with Gib about this unplanned picnic of his. And a few other things, too. They obviously needed to talk, to clear the air. If they were avoiding each other, it was time to stop. Nothing had happened, right? Or at least, they'd agreed to pretend that way. So why were they acting as if something had happened?

As the clock ticked toward three, she listened for their return. Heidi didn't have a ballet class today. Surely Gib wouldn't let her miss her time with Heidi.

Sure enough, a few minutes before three, Janet heard Heidi's feet race up the stairs. She fell into the room, panting a little, full of news about the picnic she and Emma and Gib and Carly had gone on.

"And I went on the big kids' slide! Gib helped me! I went down two times!"

Janet bit her lip. Her mother had told her how scared Heidi was of the high slide—the big kids' slide, as Heidi called it—when Janet had promised to take the kids to the park.

But she hadn't taken the kids to the park, not even once.

And now Heidi had gone down the big kids' slide, and not only had Mom missed it, Janet couldn't even tell her about it. Well, nothing to do about it now. Heidi was still waiting. "So, what do you want to do today?"

Heidi considered for a moment. Then, face sober, she looked up at Janet. "What I really, really want is to make a pie."

Janet stared at her. "A pie?" After making muffins, Janet didn't feel like facing the kitchen again. She started to tell Heidi to pick something else, but the expression on the little girl's face stopped her. Suddenly Janet had a moment of revelation—Heidi needed to spend time in the kitchen with Janet *because* Carly and Janet had made muffins. She smiled, giving in. "What kind of pie?"

"With cherries. Like Grandma makes. With ice cream on it, not whip cream. And it has little stripes on top."

"Little stripes? You mean, a latticed piecrust? You don't mean we make it from scratch, do you?" At least with the muffins, she and Carly had used a mix.

"We just make it."

Heidi took Janet's hand and tugged it until Janet followed her downstairs and into the kitchen. A pie? Janet had no idea even how to start. "Well, I guess first, we need a recipe." She looked vaguely around the kitchen. "Where does Grandma keep her recipes?"

Heidi shrugged. "Sometimes she uses a book, I think."

A cookbook. Of course. Janet looked around the kitchen and spied a shelf full of thick, colorful books.

"Well, thank goodness for *Joy of Cooking*." Janet pulled the cookbook down. Even she couldn't mess up its foolproof instructions.

WHEN GIB AND CARLY came home from running errands, Heidi and Janet were sitting at the kitchen table waiting for the buzzer to ring. On the counter behind them sat all the accoutrements of pie-baking, and then some. *And then some, with a vengeance,* thought Gib. It was a good thing Mrs. Murphy had left early today.

Janet had a little smudge of flour on her nose, and his fingers itched to brush it off. He clenched his hands to keep them under control. Somehow, he had to figure out a way to stop wanting to touch her.

He just needed to concentrate on something else. He took a deep whiff of the cooking aromas. "Mmm, smells good in here. What are you making?" He walked toward the oven.

"It's a surprise." Janet stood and blocked his path, all five-foot-zip of her. "You'll just have to wait until it's done." She brushed her hair back with one flour-covered hand and looked behind her at the oven door.

"You look like you're expecting it to explode."

"Well, we didn't have all the right ingredients. And we didn't find that out until it was already too late to go back to the store, so we had to substitute. I'm sure it'll turn out all right. After all, it's just pie-baking, not magic."

The buzzer rang, and Janet pulled the pie out of the oven and set it on the counter.

Heidi frowned at it. "That's not how it's supposed to look!"

Gib walked over. The cherries had bubbled up inside just fine, and the smell was delicious, but the cross-hatched piecrust did look a little odd. It was dark brown, for one thing. Not burnt-looking, exactly. Just brown. It looked more like—

"It looks like brown Play-Doh." Carly stared at it,

then at her aunt. "That doesn't look like any pie I ever saw."

Heidi wrinkled her nose. "It doesn't look like Grandma's."

To be honest, it didn't look like any pie Gib had ever seen before, either. But he decided to keep his mouth shut.

Janet dismissed their lack of confidence with a wave of her hand. "Oh, don't worry. I'm sure it'll taste just fine. We probably just baked it a little too long. We'll let it sit here to cool, and by the time dinner is over, it'll be cool enough to cut."

But after dinner, when Heidi brought the pie to the table, it wasn't so easy to cut the crust. Gib watched Janet try to slice through it. Then she sawed at it. It finally gave way in hunks. She scooped a piece onto a plate and handed it to Heidi, who put it in front of Gib on the table.

He poked at the crust with his fork. The crust didn't move. He smiled at Heidi, who was watching him. "Mmm, this smells good!" He gave Janet a sideways glance. "So, ah, what substitutions did you have to make?"

"Nothing major, I told you." She served up three more pieces, and everyone sat down with a piece. "We didn't have enough pastry flour, so I had to use whole wheat." She squinted at the brown crust. "That's probably why it looks so brown. That and the brown sugar, of course."

Gib coughed.

She looked at him sharply. "I couldn't find the white sugar!"

"Your mother keeps it in the tea canister."

"Do you know where she keeps the butter? I couldn't find that, either."

He raised an eyebrow. "In the freezer. What did you use instead?"

"Canola oil. I'm sure it's much better for you, anyway."

Gib coughed again. He and the two girls looked at her expectantly, their hands at their sides.

Janet gave them an exasperated look. "Oh, for heaven's sake. It won't bite you back! It just looks a little odd, that's all." None of them moved, so she picked up her fork. "Fine, I'll take a bite first, if it'll make you happy." She sawed the tip off her pie and stuck it in her mouth.

Her teeth felt like they were chewing leather. Hard leather. Hard, slightly brittle leather. She gnawed at it for a few minutes, then took a furtive look at Gib. He was watching her. Neither he nor either of the girls had taken a bite yet.

She slowly raised her fork to her mouth and deposited the little corner of piecrust on it. "Okay, you win. We should patent the recipe and use it to repair driveways. It's like little crosshatch bricks." She thought for a moment. "But the filling is really good. Why don't we scrape it out of the crust and pour it over ice cream?"

Over ice cream, it was very good indeed. While they were eating their ice cream, the phone rang. Gib reached behind him for it.

"It's your mother."

Janet's heart jumped. Her mother! It couldn't be her mother. Her mother only called when Janet was stressed out.

Well, come to think of it, she *ought* to be plenty

stressed now. She still had a lot of explaining to do—about the Vaseline, and the houseplants, and the ink. About Gib, and of course about Mrs. Murphy. But it was funny, until this very moment, she hadn't felt nearly as stressed as she probably should.

Okay, now she was stressed out.

Feeling the anxiety settle around her, she took the phone. "Hi, Mom, how are you feeling?" Her voice cracked, and she cringed. Her mother's ears were razor-sharp. She waited for her mother's alarmed questions.

"Oh, I'm coming right along, honey. How are things going there?"

Janet blinked. Maybe the connection wasn't good, and her mother hadn't heard the tension in her voice. "Oh, fine. These kids'll keep you running."

Her mother chuckled, which amazed Janet. Her mom seldom laughed, and certainly never indulged in anything more than a refined titter. "They'll do that, all right. How are my babies?"

Janet pulled the phone away from her ear and stared at it. Maybe she had someone else's mother on the line. She put it back to her ear. "Oh, they're fine, just fine. Uh, we've had a little excitement around here, though. Ha ha!" Even to her own ears, Janet's laugh sounded sick, and she waited for her mother to glom onto that and probe until she dug out the truth about the poison-control hotline, the social worker, and the fact that Mrs. Murphy had quit and then been lured back.

But instead, she heard her mother speak to someone who was in the room with her.

"Oh, Morris, how sweet! Yes, just a moment—I'll be right out, as soon as I finish talking to my daughter and granddaughters." Her mother's voice fairly tinkled.

"Mom? Who's with you?"

"Oh, just a friend of your Aunt Mary and Uncle Al's, someone we play bridge with in the evenings. It's a very friendly place down here. I especially wanted to talk to the kids—are they around?"

Janet handed the phone to Carly and went over to the couch and sat down on it, feeling slightly battered.

"You look poleaxed."

She looked up to see Gib watching her. "I *am* poleaxed. My mother, who treats life as if it were an unfair test, is behaving like she hasn't a care in the world."

"Well, that's good, isn't it?"

Janet frowned. "This is a woman who had her gall-bladder removed two weeks ago. She's spent a longer time recuperating from a bad perm. But instead of telling me all the particulars of her convalescence in agonizing detail, she barely mentions it. She behaves as if...as if she's having *fun!*"

"So, you're happy for her, right?"

She gaped at him. "You don't understand. When I spoke to her, she behaved as if she didn't hear the undertones in my voice. She acted as if she believed everything was fine here. She didn't pick up on a cracking voice. She didn't pick up on a fake laugh, for heaven's sake!"

"Maybe it was a bad connection."

"Bad connection, my fanny. This woman has been known to detect a fake laugh in e-mail. She's picked up on her loved ones' painful experiences from the signatures on Christmas cards. I've seen her look at a picture of a laughing couple with their arms around each other and murmur, 'Oh, dear, and after twenty years of marriage. Such a shame.'"

"So you're saying exactly...what?"

"That there's something wrong! There is something very, very wrong." What wasn't her mother telling her?

Unfortunately, Janet had too many things to worry about herself to devote much time to divining her mother's troubles.

After she bathed the three kids together and read to them before tucking them into their beds, she marched back downstairs to where Gib was closing the dishwasher. Now that the kids were down for the night, she had a bone to pick with him.

She opened her mouth to speak, but hesitated for a moment, watching him move around the kitchen, his back turned to her. He wiped down the counters, leaned over to wipe a glob of applesauce from Emma's high chair. Physically, he looked so out of place, like a half-tame wolf navigating a child's dollhouse. But he seemed so comfortable with himself. She watched as he stepped around the high chair and slid it back into the corner effortlessly. He bent, his back turned to her, and retrieved a fallen napkin, and Janet watched helplessly as the muscles in his thighs and buttocks flexed beneath the material of his faded jeans. She couldn't help herself; she could watch him move for hours. Forever.

She shook her head to clear it and took a breath. "I was upset this afternoon when you took the kids on a picnic to the park without telling me."

He glanced over his shoulder. "What?" Her complaint barely seemed to register.

"You could have at least told me first, found out if I wanted to go."

He rinsed out the cloth and hung it on the faucet before turning to look at her.

"As I recall, your specific instructions on interruptions were something like, 'Don't bother me unless it involves fire or blood.'" Folding his arms, he leaned back against the counter.

He leaned back. Just as Sheila had said. Just as he'd done before, when he was upset.

She could read him like a book, and he was pushing away his irritation with her. Men! And this man especially—always needing to be in control. She was getting to him.

And that meant she was right. He *had* done it on purpose. "Oh, don't think I don't know exactly what you're doing. You're intentionally doing fun things so I'll miss out. And you're doing them on my time, which is really inexcusable!"

He walked over to the table, where he draped himself over one of the chairs. Surely he couldn't be aware of how sexy he looked, ranged over the chair. With an effort, she ignored his physical presence and concentrated on what he was saying.

He frowned at her. "I don't think I'm following you. What exactly are you trying to say?"

He'd done it on purpose, all right. She moved in for the kill.

"You had a one-hour time frame to work in while I was upstairs. One hour between the time I stopped playing with Emma and the time I was due downstairs for lunch. What you're telling me is that the kids clamored for a picnic to the point where you gave in, packed them all up, decided not to wait for me, wrote me a note, and took off—all within the same hour? Give me a break. I think you hustled them out the door before I could get downstairs to join you. And it's the last real day of spring break, too." After this weekend, Carly would be back in school full days, and Heidi half days, and it just wasn't fair!

She jutted her chin up at him. "And here's what else I think. I think you did it just to prove some point. So why don't you save us both some time and yourself some trouble and just come right out and say whatever it is you're trying not-so-subtly to tell me about how messed-up my priorities are and how ridiculous my silly schedule is?" She thrust her jaw toward his face and leaned out over him, hands on her hips.

Gib bit back a grin. Boy, she was cute. How could a woman look so cute when she was so mad at him? Hazel eyes snapping, making herself just as big as she could be—she was practically standing over him on tiptoe. Made him want to grin all over.

Made him want to kiss her again. Maybe several times. Definitely for an extended period.

How could he possibly be wanting to kiss someone who was lighting into him like nothing he'd ever heard before—outside his sister, that is.

Better not grin, though. Then she'd really get mad.

On the other hand, he'd like to see that. He gave her a lazy grin, just for the fun of seeing her hit the roof.

She didn't disappoint him.

Janet couldn't believe it when he slowly raked her up and down with his eyes, then leaned his head back and grinned at her.

She stiffened, then straightened. Okay, she was going to let him have it with both barrels. Was there no limit to this easygoing act of his? "From now on, I'd appreciate it if you'd at least act like I'm the boss. If you're going to take the kids out, tell me first." She spun, but not quickly enough.

His hand snaked out to catch hers, and she gasped

at the thrill that went through her. He slowly pulled her around to face him, and for a moment, she thought he was going to kiss her. And for a moment, she wanted so badly to lift her face to his that she thought she wouldn't be able to stop herself. "The children," she whispered, dropping her gaze, and he released her wrist.

He cleared his throat, but his voice still came out husky. "I would never do anything to hurt your relationship with those kids." Janet wondered wildly whether he was talking about kissing her or about taking the kids out without telling her. Or both.

He turned. "I'll be sure to let you know before we go anywhere, from now on." He hesitated a moment, then walked down the half flight of stairs, crossed the family room, and disappeared into his bedroom.

Turning to climb the stairs to her own bedroom, Janet heaved a sigh—whether of relief or frustration, she wasn't sure. She felt a little of one and a lot of the other.

It was going to be another uncomfortable night, full of ridiculously vivid dreams. She just knew she was going to be confused again when she woke up in her own bed.

THE NEXT MORNING, Saturday, Janet dragged herself out of bed at 5:00 a.m. She worked like a dog until nine o'clock, then waited for a few minutes for Carly to appear before going looking for her.

She found Carly in her room, standing in front of the full-length cheval mirror her parents had given her just before they died.

She had a pink ruffled dress on, and two other dresses lay on the bed. As Janet watched, Carly turned before the mirror, frowning at her reflection in a way that reminded Janet of Georgie—flirtatious, knowing, just a little self-critical. Georgie hadn't been able to pass a mirror without checking her hair, her makeup, whether her slip was showing. She'd always looked perfect, but she'd always checked. Carly clearly took after Georgie that way. It did Janet good, a bittersweet kind of good, to see her niece show so much of her sister.

Janet smiled at her. "What are you doing?"

"Trying on my dresses. I think this one makes me look nine, don't you?"

A sudden fear clamped on Janet's stomach, and she felt the blood drain from her face. The mirror, given almost exactly a year ago, had been an early birthday present. "I do. I really do. Excuse me for a minute, honey." She forced herself to walk calmly from the room, but as soon as she was out of sight, she bolted down the hall to her office to check her calendar.

March twenty-third?

Carly's ninth birthday.

Janet dropped into her desk chair. What was she going to do? Carly was expecting a party, and Janet didn't have any guests. She also didn't have a cake, decorations, games, or a present.

The present! What had her mother told her? *Get her a Baby Talks A Lot. She's been talking about it for weeks.*

She closed her eyes for a moment as a twenty-year-old image flooded into her brain: her father, shrugging his coat on while he grabbed his briefcase, forgetting to say goodbye to her or her sister. She stood in the doorway, watching him through the flames from the candles on her sister's birthday cake, which she held clutched to her chest. Ten candles flickered in the breeze. How was she going to tell Georgie that Daddy had left before they even opened the presents or had cake and ice cream?

Janet shook her head to clear it of the unwanted image.

Could she fix this?

She had to.

Well, then, she'd better get cracking. She sat up and pulled her desk calendar to her—what did she have today? Just an appointment with Mrs. Goody. She could reschedule that.

And while she was at it, maybe she could order an ice-cream cake.

Luckily, it wasn't a busy day. Saturdays seldom were, even in a business that operated primarily in workers' homes. She could completely ignore HomeWork today and no one would be the wiser.

But still, she was going to need some help.

She went ahead and called Mrs. Goody, who was happy to reschedule and even happier to sell an ice-cream cake. "I happen to have one all made up, dear. I'll just write Happy Birthday Carly across the top, and you'll be all set. Pick it up any time after noon."

Okay, that was the cake down. Gifts, decorations, guests to go. *Take a deep breath.*

Janet trotted downstairs to the kitchen, and then to the family room, looking for Gib. Where was he? She needed him.

She didn't want to, but she did. She also didn't want to have to ask him for help, not after last night, but she had to.

She found him in the backyard, pushing Emma in a swing while Heidi played in the sandbox. She abso-

lutely, completely ignored the fact that those same
hands that had pulled her to him, so sexual, so powerful, could so easily turn to gentle play with a toddler.

Janet kept her voice down so it wouldn't carry to
Heidi. She didn't need Heidi repeating this conversation at some inopportune time. She struggled also to
keep her voice calm. "Today is Carly's birthday. My
mom promised her a party before she left on vacation,
and I forgot all about it. I don't have a present or any
decorations. None of Carly's friends have been invited.
I need some help." Her heart beat slightly fast, but she
felt strangely calm. Together, they could handle this.
No matter what their personal problems, she knew she
could count on Gib.

He let the swing slow for a moment, then pushed it
again when Emma opened her mouth to shriek a protest. "The invitations are the crucial thing. Put Emma
down for a morning nap and send Heidi and Carly
across the street to the Jenkins, then get on your office
phone and start making calls. Tell exactly what happened—every parent can understand something like
this—and tell them the important thing is that their
daughter be here, not that she bring a gift. In fact, I'll
pick up several gifts, in case any of the moms can't
get one on such short notice."

Janet laid her hand on his arm, near the elbow.
"There's one special present—it's called Baby Talks
A Lot. It's a doll, I guess. My mom practically promised it to her." He looked down at her hand, and she
hurriedly removed it from his arm, and when she
looked up at him again, he was staring at her. She
looked away.

He cleared his throat. "Right, Baby Talks A Lot, got
it. I'll also get decorations and favors, we'll need those

for eight- and nine-year-olds. I'm out of here." And he was turning away, digging in his pocket for his keys, striding across the yard to his van before Janet could thank him.

Janet got busy on the phone. "Is, uh, Monica's mom there?"

"This is Melanie, I'm Monica's mom."

"Ah, my name is Janet Resnick. You don't know me, but I'm Carly's aunt, Monica's friend? And it's Carly's ninth birthday, and I forgot—"

Understanding laughter. "Last-Minute Party Planners?"

Janet smiled in spite of her chagrin. "I'm afraid so."

"What time do you want us?"

"Three o'clock?"

"Do you need help getting ready?"

Janet almost wept in grateful relief. "Would you?"

"I'll be there a little after noon."

Janet called five more of Carly's friends' mothers, and four of them could make it. They were all very understanding, and a second woman offered to come and help out. Janet took her up on it gratefully.

Gib made it back home just before eleven, a stack of packages under one arm. He glanced around quickly. "Carly here?"

"No, she's downstairs. Why?"

He shook his head. "No Baby Talks A Lot. Just this one—Baby Wets A Lot. I guess he's Baby Talks A Lot's little brother, or something. I went to three different stores. There isn't one to be had. It's the big toy this year." He looked into Janet's face. "I'm sorry."

It hit Janet right in the pit of her stomach. If she'd planned ahead, if she'd shopped when her mom had told her about the party, if she'd even written it on her calendar, she'd have a Baby Talks A Lot right now. She'd have a real birthday party, instead of this thrown-together-at-the-last-minute sorry excuse for one.

And now Carly, so anxious about her birthday party that she'd nagged her grandmother to the point of distraction, wasn't going to get the one single thing she'd asked for. And it was Janet's fault, foursquare.

She bit her lip and looked back at Gib. His face held only sympathy, when what she really merited was some well-deserved contempt. *Janet, the deadbeat aunt, does it again.*

She reached for the Baby Wets A Lot and upended it—gingerly, given the doll's name—to find the name of the manufacturer. PlayCo Toys. That was up in Columbus. The manufacturing plant was on the Olentangy River.

So, where was the distribution center?

She looked at him, hope dawning. "Can you manage things here for a while—the decorations next, probably? I have a couple of calls to make."

He frowned. "Business calls? Can't they wait?"

"Not HomeWork business. Toy business." She stepped into the kitchen and picked up the phone.

Her first call was to PlayCo Toys, at their Columbus number.

A recording. "You have reached the offices of PlayCo Toys. If you know the extension of your party, please enter it now. If you wish to speak to customer service, our hours are nine to five, Eastern Standard Time, Monday through Friday. Thank you."

Grr.

Her next call was to Ronnie's Toys, the nearest toy store.

"Ronnie's Toys." A teenaged voice that sounded like she was chewing gum.

"I'd like to speak with the manager, please."

A pause. "This is Bobby. How may I help you?"

"I'm looking for a Baby Talks A Lot."

Bobby laughed. "You and ten dozen other people. Sorry, ma'am, we're out."

"I know, but have you checked to see if the distribution center has any?"

"That would be Rossiter's, over in Covington. Naw, we just take what they bring us each week. They're due back first thing Monday morning. If you get here early, you can probably get a Baby Talks A Lot then."

Monday was too late. Maybe she could get the doll direct from the distributor. She looked up their number, and dialed one more time.

Another recording. "Hello, this is Rossiter Distributors. Your call is very important to us. Our office hours are eight to six, Monday through Friday. Please try again."

Grrr.

She hung up the phone, slowly. If toy stores were open on Saturdays, the trucks might be out then, too. Maybe the warehouse was staffed, but the front office wasn't.

Covington was only a fifteen-minute drive. It was worth a try.

She grabbed her keys and called in to Gib. "I'm going out for a few minutes. I'll be back as soon as I can."

Down in the warehouse district in Covington, Janet drove slowly along the loading docks. There it was! And there were two men with dollies loading pallets onto a truck.

Pallets of shrink-wrapped boxes of Baby Talks A Lot. Dozens of them. Hundreds.

She screeched to a stop and jumped out of the car, and both men turned to look at her. She gave them her best trust-me smile. "This is going to seem odd, I'm sure, but my niece's birthday is today, and she's been asking for a Baby Talks A Lot, and I've, well, I haven't been on top of things, exactly, and I just can't stand to let her down one more time." She paused expectantly, and the two men exchanged a puzzled glance before looking back at her.

She nodded at the pallets full of Baby Talks A Lot boxes. "Please, can I buy one of those dolls?"

The larger of the two men shook his head. "Ma'am, we can't sell it to you. I wish I could, but it's worth my job. If my bill of lading says one hundred Baby Talks A Lots to Ronnie's Toys, that's what I gotta show up with first thing Monday. If I have ninety-nine, they ask me where the other one went."

The other man piped up. "They'd think it fell off the back of the truck, if you know what I mean. They'd look at us."

"Can't you just tell them you sold it, and give them the money?"

"No, ma'am. We aren't even allowed to buy them ourselves. We have to go to the store."

Janet's shoulders sagged. She turned, started to trudge back to the car. Baby Wets A Lot it was. Carly would just have to understand. She could get it for her first thing Monday, when the truck made its delivery.

She stopped, struck by an idea, and turned. "Is there any rule against delivering early?"

The two men looked at each other, shrugged. "Nope, I guess not."

"Look, if you'll drive over to Ronnie's Toys now, and make this delivery of Baby Talks A Lot, I'll give you each twenty-five bucks."

A quick glance at each other, a short whispered conference. "Make it forty each?"

Janet nodded, holding her breath.

Another glance between the two, a nod, and the shorter man looked back at her. "You want to go now?"

Janet almost collapsed in relief. "Yes, right now, please."

When she walked back into the house and described her success to Gib, his eyes almost popped out of his head. "You got one? How?"

She told him the whole story, and the amazement in his eyes turned to respect and admiration. She warmed under it. "I thought I was going to have a problem with the store manager—he didn't want to unpack the pallet right that very minute. I told him I had three kids under the age of ten, and he was the nearest toy store to my house. He thought about it for a minute and decided a happy customer was worth a little inconvenience."

Gib laughed. "So you spent ninety-six bucks for a sixteen-dollar doll?"

Her smile was wry. "It was the only thing she asked for. And it's worth every penny, if it teaches me a lesson."

He shook his head. "I'm thinking you ought to be giving lessons, not learning them."

Janet shot her gaze to him, and his eyes were full of sincere admiration, and she felt herself redden as she dropped her flustered gaze away from his.

Now, why was she behaving like a teenager with a

crush? She was an adult—she ought to be able to behave herself, even after the kiss they'd shared. She wasn't doing a very good job pretending it hadn't happened.

To cover her confusion, she said, "Well, I'd better get cracking on decorations."

"Right. I'll go wrap." He took the Baby Talks A Lot from her, his fingers brushing hers as she handed it over.

Unbidden, the physical memory of their kiss came flooding back to her, the feel of his lips on hers, the taste of him. His hand on her cheek. Her body vividly remembered how it had felt to be in his arms. Enthusiastically remembered it, even.

She looked back up at him, trying to hide her feelings, and he was still watching her, his face serious. She tried to smile casually, as if she weren't standing there fantasizing about kissing him again, and after he finally turned away, she sneaked a glance at him as he disappeared up the stairs.

Oh, this was not working.

AT ONE, Monica's mother, Melanie, came over, and they sent Carly outside to play with Monica.

"I can't tell you how much I appreciate you coming over to help us out. I almost had a heart attack this morning when I realized it was Carly's birthday."

Melanie stuck a strand of long, dark-blond hair behind an ear and leaned in close. "Every parent has a birthday horror story. Last year, for my niece's fifteenth birthday, my sister sent fourteen teenagers on a scavenger hunt that took them all straight through a patch of poison ivy."

Janet winced. "Ouch!"

"It gets worse. The prom was the next day. They all ended up accessorized with calamine lotion. Awful! But they all laugh about it now."

"Okay, now I feel better." As they laughed, Gib stepped into the room, arms full of wrapped gifts, and Melanie gaped at him and went suddenly silent.

"Where do you want these?"

"On the hall table?"

He held up a largish package. "This one's the Baby Talks A Lot, by the way."

"Gib?" She wanted to tell him how much she appreciated everything. She wanted to ask him if he thought Carly would notice the party had been thrown together at the last minute, and whether she'd be very upset, and if she'd get over it, and whether she'd feel even more anxious. But she would seem so pathetic, so desperate for reassurance. Especially in front of Melanie, who stood silently at Janet's side, still staring at Gib. Janet felt some sympathy—wait until he smiled at her. She'd be catatonic.

So, instead, Janet just said, "Thanks for everything."

He smiled, as if he understood all that had just gone on inside her head, and carried the brightly wrapped packages out into the hall.

As he left the room, Melanie grabbed Janet by the arm, her fingers tight around Janet's elbow, her lips close to Janet's ear. "Who *is* that man?"

Janet feigned a casual attitude. "Oh, that's the nanny."

Melanie craned her neck, watching after Gib. "The nanny? That's the nanny? How come mine always look like Mrs. Doubtfire?"

They strung a few streamers from the chandelier,

twisting them out to the corners, and then Janet handed Melanie the rest of the decorations and left to pick up the ice-cream cake. She was back by one-fifteen, and when she came in, Melanie was supervising Gib and Linda, the other mom who had offered to help. Janet joined them as they finished hanging balloons.

Melanie wiggled her eyebrows at Janet every time Gib had his back turned, and Linda made arch remarks about "letting the nanny do it" whenever a balloon needed to be hung or a streamer attached up high. Janet kept a carefully schooled expression of innocence on her face whenever Gib glanced her way, but she had to admit, he looked pretty good up on a ladder.

Emma wrapped herself in streamers and shrieked in alternating fits of delight and frustration. At two, the other women went home, promising to come back to help with the party.

At two-thirty, Heidi came back home from the Jenkins', and Janet got the two girls and herself dressed. Gib took the baby upstairs to dress her. At three on the dot, the doorbell rang, and Monica and Melanie came in, dressed in flowery party dresses.

Janet took their coats and whispered a quick thank-you to Melanie. "I'm so glad you showed up right on time. About five minutes ago, Carly started getting nervous that no one would come. I didn't think she'd be able to stand it much longer."

"I know—we once had no one show up for ten whole minutes. Monica was in tears! I vowed to show up right on time for kids' parties after that."

They exchanged a smile, and the doorbell rang again, and Janet turned to answer it.

Within fifteen minutes, five little girls and Linda had arrived, almost all with gifts in hand.

"How did you manage to get a present on such short notice?" Janet kept her voice low as she took Linda's coat.

"Oh, I always keep a few things around, just in case. You can never tell when someone's going to forget to mail the invitations." She winked at Janet.

Well, they had a party. What now? The little girls were chasing one another from room to room, screaming and giggling.

Gib walked up behind her and whispered in her ear, a warm brush of breath that sent a shiver through her. She took a deep, controlled breath to help her concentrate on what he was saying. "First, games. The more physical, the better. They're all keyed up from being at a party and all dressed up. They need to let off some steam before they can settle down and watch Carly open her presents."

Janet breathed a sigh of relief. She'd had no idea what to do first. "Okay, everyone, let's all go downstairs and play pin-the-tail-on-the-donkey." In a shrieking rush, all the little dressed-up girls ran out the door and down the stairs. The adults followed them.

They played Twister, and duck-duck-goose, and then Gib, who had been sitting in the corner holding Emma and watching the fun, leaned forward in his chair. All the little girls quieted and turned to look at him.

So did both mothers, Janet noticed.

"Time to open presents?" He made it a question, but Janet knew it was a suggestion. She smiled and nodded, and the little girls gathered around Carly while Janet handed her one shiny, beribboned package after another.

Carly laughed and squealed as she opened her gifts, but she kept eyeing the one large gift. She looked over at the brightly wrapped package every time she finished opening one of her other gifts. Baby Talks A Lot. Janet could see the knowledge in her eyes.

Because she knows exactly what it should look like.

And the Baby Wets A Lot came in a box the same size.

Janet threw a glance at Gib, and he was already looking at her. "She can tell by the size—" she whispered, and he whispered back, "I know. Baby Wets A Lot would have been a mistake. She would have been even more disappointed once she'd opened it." He shook his head. "I just didn't think."

Janet widened her eyes at him. The man who was always right—who always knew just what to do—was admitting he'd made a mistake? Amazing. And very appealing, too. Not that it was important that she found it appealing, she reminded herself. It was just interesting that she did.

Carly was thrilled with Baby Talks A Lot, and she came over to hug Janet. "I thought maybe I wouldn't get it, because I heard it was all sold out, and nobody could get it. But you did! Thank you, Aunt Jannie."

Janet would have felt like a hero, except she'd caused the crisis herself. And, besides, how heroic can you feel when it costs you ninety-six bucks to save the day?

After they'd opened the presents, Gib suggested one more game of Twister before having cake and ice cream. "Carly's all worked up because she's the center of attention. The other kids are all worked up because they just gave away a bunch of stuff they'd have liked to keep for themselves. The best thing to do is let them work off a little more steam, then eat."

Janet and the other women, seeing that Gib had everything under control, did a fade into the kitchen, mumbling things like, "I guess I better see about the cake," and "Gee, someone better check to see if there's enough juice made up."

Janet went to the freezer and pulled out the cake. She opened a box of candles and pulled out nine. She had just lit a match when someone screamed down in the family room, the high-pitched, earsplitting scream of a little girl having too much fun. Janet jumped, and the match went out, and Janet closed her eyes for a minute, then opened them and looked over at Linda. "I am getting just the tiniest bit of a headache."

"Better take something for that, right away." Linda reached into a grocery bag she'd brought with her and pulled out a bottle of wine. "I've found this particular remedy very effective in similar situations." She uncorked it, poured the three of them a glass each, and they took a minute to enjoy the relative peace of the kitchen and a sip of wine.

The giggling and shrieking transferred itself to the dining room, and Janet lit the candles and picked up the cake. When the other women didn't stand up to follow her, she grimaced at them. "Cowards! I'll be back as soon as I cut this and make my getaway." She shouldered open the swinging door and stepped into the dining room.

Carly and three other little girls were chasing each other around the dining-room table, shrieking. A fifth sat under the table, holding a burst balloon and crying. Heidi, an anxious expression on her face, knelt by the crier and patted her shoulder. The sixth party guest was nowhere to be seen.

Janet set the cake on the table. "Okay, where's Monica?" No one answered her. Not one of the children even paused in what she was doing. Janet raised her voice to be heard above the screaming. "Where's Monica?" Nothing.

Gib stepped into the room, Emma in his right arm, a squirming Monica under his left. He looked at the four little girls running and screaming, at the two under the table crying and patting, and at Janet, standing next to the fast-melting ice-cream cake. He set Monica down, leaned against the door frame, held up his free hand and said, "Okay, that's enough. Time to eat cake. Everyone sit down."

The screaming stopped, the crying stopped, and as if by magic, seven little girls sat in seven chairs and allowed Janet to set seven pieces of cake in front of them. Janet gave him a helpless smile and shook her head. How did he do it?

The doorbell rang. It was obvious that Gib had everything under control in the dining room, so Janet went to get it.

A young woman in uniform handed her a large box wrapped with red-white-and-blue tape. "FedEx, ma'am. Can you sign here for me, please?"

Janet juggled the box and signed the ledger. She carried the box inside and turned it to read the address— HomeWork wasn't expecting any shipments, as far as she could remember. And, besides, this was hand-addressed.

Carly Granger
10039 Churchill Downs
Cincinnati, OH 45242

The handwriting was Janet's mother's.
Her mother, the woman with the crystal ball. The

package was the exact same size as a Baby Talks A Lot. Apparently, her mother had known that Janet would somehow screw up the present.

"Carly?" Janet called as she walked into the dining room. "Look, one more package for you! It just got here, from Grandma."

Carly looked up from her cake, and she spotted the package. The size wasn't lost on her, either. Or on Gib, whose sharp gaze hit the package and immediately bounced up to meet Janet's as she handed the package to Carly.

Carly pushed her plate to one side, and she tore into the brown paper wrapper, and through the beautiful purple-flowered paper beneath that, and when the words Baby Talks A Lot were exposed, Janet looked up at Gib. "My mother has superhuman powers. Did I ever tell you that? She senses things. She knew we'd need this."

He looked straight at her. "Well, she was wrong this time, wasn't she? Her powers must be fading."

They finished eating cake and ice cream, and then Janet handed a little bag of party favors to each of Carly's guests, and the party was officially over.

As Linda and Melanie herded their daughters out the door, Janet clutched their elbows and leaned near. "I literally could not have done it without your help. Thank you both, so much. I just can't thank you enough."

Linda laughed. "What are neighbors for? Besides, now we own you, body and soul."

Melanie nodded. "One day, when you least expect it and cannot possibly manage it, we'll be calling you for help."

Linda threw a glance over her shoulder at Gib, who

was occupied helping a little girl take her party hat off without removing her glasses. "And we'll expect you to bring the nanny, too. We can always use *his* kind of help." She winked, and they left.

Janet felt a quick stab of regret as she watched them go. She wouldn't be here to repay the debt. She wouldn't be the one drinking wine in the kitchen with these women while they all hid from a pack of screaming kids during some future pool party or cookout. She'd be back at her own apartment, alone with her fax machine and her computer. Wasn't that what she'd been looking forward to for almost three weeks now? The prospect didn't seem very appealing anymore. No Carly, no Heidi, no Emma.

No Gib.

After the party, when all the mess was cleaned up and all the presents admired once again and three tired little girls were fed and bathed and in bed, dead to the world for the next ten hours, Janet and Gib collapsed side by side at the kitchen table.

Janet groaned and slumped forward, resting her elbows on the table and her head in her hands. "I am too tired to move."

"I am too tired to breathe. Next time one of the kids has a birthday, let's just do it at Mickey D's."

Her heart gave a little skip, and she looked over at him, wondering if he'd heard himself. He was either too tired to guard his words, or too tired to realize what it was he'd just said. His eyelids drooped, the eyelashes throwing shadows over his cheekbones. He stretched, reaching up to rub his neck, and she watched his fingers knead the muscles in his shoulders.

Almost without conscious thought, she reached over to him, sliding her hands under his, tugging until he turned slightly to expose his back to her. She kneaded where his own fingers had been a few moments before, pressing hard, deep, and he groaned in happy agony.

His groan, the sound arising from deep within his throat, sent a shot of lust rocketing through her. She could swear she *felt* his groan, felt a physical response so immediate that it seemed simultaneous, as if she were somehow hard-wired into his senses. She barely caught herself before she gasped in response.

What was she doing?

She took her hands from his shoulders and stepped back, confused by the strength of her reaction to him.

He turned, and his gaze met hers, and the thickness of desire in his eyes made her catch her breath. He reached for her hand, pulling her toward him with gentle pressure. He watched her closely, but she only gazed back at him, wide-eyed, silent, neither pulling back nor moving forward of her own conscious volition.

She could stop him with a single word.

But she knew she couldn't stop herself.

Chapter Eight

As he pulled her nearer, her breath caught, and with a little whimper of relief—or despair, she wasn't sure which—she bent her mouth to his, and he pulled her down into his arms.

She knew it for relief then, because she felt as if she'd been waiting for this forever. As if this man, this moment, had been drawing her all her life, and she'd finally found the spot she'd been seeking, the place she belonged. As if she finally understood where she'd always been headed.

His hands clutched at her shoulders, and he ran his fingers up her neck and dug them into her hair, gently deepening the kiss. He slid his tongue into her mouth and she met it with hers, and she groaned again as she felt him harden against her hip.

She'd never wanted anything as much as she wanted this now, and when he tugged her around to straddle him, it seemed like the most natural thing in the world.

She tilted her hips forward to increase the pressure of her body against his, and he clutched at her, pulling her into his embrace.

He kissed her with desperation, his mouth fastening hungrily on her cheek, her ear, her neck, and his hand brushed down her shoulder to her breast and lay there, warm and heavy and solid, as her breast swelled toward the weight of his fingers. She threw her head back and rocked again, her breath catching with the aching pressure she felt as she rubbed against him.

She felt herself moisten.

Through the silky fabric of her blouse, his thumb found her nipple, and he rolled it between the pad of his thumb and forefinger. A sharp wave of desire shot through her. With his knuckles he nudged open her blouse, and he slid his hand inside her bra, pushing the strap off her shoulder to expose her breast.

His eyes darkened with pleasure, and her desire fed on his, spiraling until she panted helplessly. She didn't trust her voice to speak, could do no more than simply watch her hand as it caressed his shoulder, his neck, ran down his chest.

He bent his head to her nipple and caught it with his tongue and lips and nibbled with gentle teasing. She rocked forward again, and he gasped as she pressed against him. He tugged the zipper of her jeans down, and slid his hand inside to caress the swell of her hip, to cup her bottom within the palm of his hand.

She fumbled at the buttons of his shirt, tugging harder until one button flew off and skittered across the kitchen floor, making a little scraping sound against the tile. The other buttons slipped through their holes, and she placed her hands on his bare chest, feeling the heat. The heat was for her, and she felt a surge of power, an answering heat of her own.

His muscles shuddered as she brushed her fingers over them, and his chest rose and fell as he breathed deeper, faster. With her nails she raked upward to encircle his neck with her arms, running her hands down the muscles of his back beneath his shirt. She pressed her cheek into his rough, dark mane of hair and breathed deeply, filling her lungs with his clean, musky scent.

He moved his head to nuzzle her other breast, and then to circle the nipple with his tongue, sending jolts of electricity through her with every flick. He took the nipple into his mouth and sucked hard for just a moment, and her back arched as heat shot through her, and her hips tilted forward to press up against him again, an almost involuntary reaction. She gasped, and trusted her voice for a bare moment. "Oh, please."

Her whisper galvanized him, and he pulled her hips into him, held her there for a moment, and his body shuddered from the strain. The muscles in his neck tightened beneath her palms, and she realized how strictly he was controlling himself and reveled in it.

His hand released her bottom and slid around to caress her belly, to slip inside the waistband of her panties. Her breath came harder as he dipped his fingers deeper. His tongue flicked over her nipple again, and she bit her lip to keep from screaming at the pleasure of the sensation, at the spike of desire it evoked.

The pressure of his hand against her felt slippery, and when his finger slid inside her, she felt as if she were falling over the edge. She groaned and bit his neck, a light brush of teeth, and he raised his head and reclaimed her lips with a desperate pressure.

With a heave, he set her up onto the table. He pulled her jeans and panties from her, reaching around her to pull her hips toward him, toward the edge of the table, until her bare bottom came up against the roughness of his jeans. The coarse texture against her sensitive skin sent her senses spiraling, and she gasped and pulled him closer, a subconscious jerk of her hands against his hips.

She reached for his belt, his zipper, then inside it. He clasped her to him, and her hand dipped to find him, hard and round and pressed up against his flat belly. She took him in her hand and tugged with light pressure, and he dipped his head again to taste her nipples.

He paused for a moment to prepare himself, and she kissed his forehead, his cheek, his neck, hungry for him. And when he raised his lips again to hers, she pulled his hips to her.

And as their lips met, he entered her, smooth and sure, and she pressed forward to meet him. And he pulled his head back for a moment to stare into her eyes. "Janet," he whispered, and then reclaimed her lips, her jaw, her throat.

And they moved together, as one, in a rhythm at once new and ancient, until they reached their peak and spun off into the melting place.

AT FIVE O'CLOCK Sunday morning, Janet's first perceptions were of the secure feeling of strong arms wrapped around her, the arousing scent of nearby male body.

Boy, she had to hand it to herself. These dreams were getting better and better.

She gradually became aware of an insistent far-off buzzing sound. She tried to push it away—it didn't belong in this sexy dream. It sounded just like her alarm, only far, far away. Like in her bedroom, upstairs.

She shot straight up in bed. Her old bed.

Gib's bed, now.

Where he'd carried her last night, after...

After she'd slept with the nanny.

Her eyes slowly traveled over the quilt, covered with yellow roses. To the edge of the sheet, also yellow roses. And pulled up against a shoulder. A naked shoulder. A naked, very broad, very male shoulder.

Really, it was an incredible shoulder.

What if the alarm woke Carly or Heidi? Or both? What if they came down here, after not being able to find Janet in her own room? What would seeing their aunt lying naked in bed with Gib do to them?

It was doing something to her, right now. She better cover it up, before she gave in to temptation and uncovered it altogether.

She pulled the sheet up over his shoulder, and started to slide out of bed. Gib mumbled a protest in his sleep, and reached for her.

She leaned down to whisper in his ear. "I have to go, the alarm upstairs in my bedroom..."

He opened his eyes, blinked a couple of times and a slow smile spread over his face. And that smile did it to her again. She almost got right back into bed with him. She steeled herself, and smiled back at him. "Not that I wouldn't like to stay—I could stay here forever."

Then his face changed, as if a shutter had closed over it, and she felt a tiny niggle of remorse.

He looked at her, then away. "We need to talk, about what this means." He didn't say it, but she knew the rest of the sentence was: *and what it doesn't mean.*

She pulled back. Was it going to be like that? Janet felt the heat creep over her, and she felt suddenly naked and vulnerable. Then her pride asserted itself. "Oh, don't worry, ha-ha. I'm not going to go all weird on you. *Fatal Attraction,* or something. No big deal, right?"

He frowned a little. "It's not that. I think you're... well, I think you're really incredible. It's just that I wouldn't want to lead you on. I have obligations, plans I made before I came here. They don't really allow for ongoing relationships right now." He was watching her intently, so she made sure to put a casual smile on her face. "I really enjoyed being with you, Janet. It was... It was incredible."

It certainly had been that.

She watched his face, and she saw no signs of any macho garbage. He wasn't saying she'd been a notch in his bedpost and now, *sayonara*. He was simply being honest with her. She really ought to appreciate it—a lot of guys would just have said, "I'll call you." So she smiled, a sincere smile this time, though she still felt about as rotten as she ever had. "Gib, it's okay. I enjoyed myself, too."

She turned away then, and pulled her clothes on in awkward silence. At some point during their conversation, the alarm had stopped sounding overhead, but she still felt a certain urgency about getting out of his bedroom. Finally, dressed again and feeling less vulnerable, she turned and met his gaze. "I guess I'll get upstairs before the kids wake up."

He was watching her as if he had some major regrets, as if he had things he wanted to say. But she really didn't want to deal with any more honesty from him right this very moment. So she pulled her gaze away. "Well, I better get a move on." And she turned and left.

Upstairs, she brushed her teeth, pulled on fresh clothes, and ran a brush through her hair.

She got herself down to the kitchen while it was still dark out, poured herself a thermos full of coffee, and took it up to her office. When she heard Gib banging around in the kitchen, she went to the top of the stairs and called down to him. He came through the kitchen door holding Emma and a bottle of juice.

It almost took her breath away, how he looked holding that baby, but she gritted her teeth. She tried not to look quite straight at him. "I'm in the home stretch now—I can finish this in the next few hours if I can just get some uninterrupted time. Can you figure out something to do with the kids for a few hours? Then this evening we can all relax together." She blushed, thinking of how relaxed she'd felt in his arms last night, how her concept of "together" had changed in just a few hours' time. And then changed right back.

"Of course." He smiled tentatively, and she smiled back as if it were the most casual encounter in the world. But she still wanted to touch him, to follow him down the stairs and get right back in his bed. *Stupid.*

Avoiding him as much as possible seemed like the only safe bet at this point.

Janet worked well, but she was aware of the sounds of the house coming awake around her, dressing and eating and laughing and then, with a sudden final rush of activity as Gib got them all packed up and out the door, silence.

She sighed, and kept working.

AT THREE O'CLOCK, she stood and stretched. She was finished. She picked up the fifty-page proposal and took it over to the fax machine, where she hit Houston's number and fed the pages in one by one. It was done. The biggest, most important proposal she'd ever written in five years of nurturing this business along, five years of planning and working.

As the last page slipped through the fax machine, and the green light told her the entire document had been successfully transferred, she opened her door and walked down the stairs into the silent house.

Feeling at loose ends, she wandered through the house, picking up a small lacy sock, a puzzle piece. She stuck them into her pockets.

She supposed her life could go back to normal, now. Well, as normal as it could be, with the three girls still here. A normal schedule right now meant plenty of time to spend with the kids, plenty of energy to deal with their problems. Like were Emma's shots due this month, and how was Carly doing in school. Whether or not Heidi's ballet class was really good for her.

The ballet class. She'd wanted to ask Sheila about it. That was something she could do now. She stepped back into the kitchen and picked up the phone.

"The Mommy School, this is Sheila."

"Sheila, hi! This is Janet Resnick."

"Janet! Don't tell me he went out and left you again?"

Janet laughed, but it sounded forced to her. "He did, but it was at my request, so I could work. But now I'm done, and I'm itching to spend some time with the kids, and of course they aren't here."

Sheila made appropriate sympathetic noises.

"But thinking about the kids, and especially Heidi, made me think about you. I'm a little concerned about her ballet class—the teacher seems very autocratic, almost harsh. Would you mind visiting the studio with me, maybe seeing what you think?"

"You mean, like, I get to be a spy?" Sheila's voice rose in delight.

"Well, sort of, if you want to think of it that way."

"I'll disguise myself! I'm a good actress. We'll have to come up with some reason I'm there asking questions, or she'll get wise that you have some ulterior motive. Like, maybe it's because I'm considering opening a tattoo parlor across the street, and I want to know what the traffic is like in the area, so I'll know if there's a clientele."

Janet cleared her throat to hide her laugh. "Or we could just tell her you want to open a studio of your own. You can ask her about her studio, and she won't be suspicious at all."

"Hmm, okay. But it would have been a lot more fun if we could have come up with a reason I needed a disguise."

"Heidi's lesson is at three-thirty tomorrow. Corner of Cooper and Montgomery. Meet me there?"

"You got it."

Janet hung up, hoping Sheila wouldn't show up in her version of a Mata Hari outfit.

At five, Gib and the girls came ripping home, talking ninety to the dozen as they all tried at once to tell Janet about their day. Janet tried to focus her attention on the kids, tried to keep her voice and gaze casual when she looked at Gib.

"Aunt Jannie, and then I rode a camel, all by myself."

"The elephant took a peanut right out of my hand!"

"But Gib had to take Emma on the camel ride, because she's too little." Janet had to look at him then. She found him watching her, his face serious. As if he were still concerned that he'd hurt her feelings. She didn't want to deal with his pity, so she smiled brightly and looked back at Heidi. "And then what?"

"And there was a big chicken, only it wasn't a

chicken, and it thought Emma's buttons were something good to eat. She almost got scared, but Gib made it go away.''

"And we went on the little train, and there were lions there!''

Janet laughed and looked up at Gib. "The zoo, I take it?''

"The zoo, and then the library for books about the zoo.''

"I'm hungry!'' Heidi climbed into her chair. "What's to eat?''

Janet groaned. She could have at least started dinner. She glanced at Gib, schooling her face carefully into a mask of casual unconcern. "Pizza?''

He nodded, silent.

Carly beamed. "Oh, goodie. We didn't get pizza since Gib got here!''

After dinner that night, Janet tucked Heidi in and turned to the bookshelf. "What story do you want?''

"*Gobble, Growl, Grunt.* But Gib has to read it to me.''

Janet called for Gib. "She wants you to read her *Gobble, Growl, Grunt.*''

He seemed to take special care not to brush up against her as he passed her in the doorway. "I'll be getting good and sick of this one in the next few days.''

Janet watched as he pulled out the book of animal sounds and seated himself on the bed beside Heidi's pillow. He leaned back against the high, painted headboard and held out an arm, and Heidi crawled out from under the covers to sit in the crook of his arm, her short blond curls resting on his shoulder as he held the book out in front of them.

Gib opened the book and pointed to a picture on the first page. "Who's that?"

"Turkey. He says gobble-gobble." Heidi pointed to another picture. "What's that?"

"The rooster. He says cock-a-doodle-doo." Gib ran his finger over the words as he read them.

Janet watched for a moment from the door, the light of the single bedside lamp playing over features soft with a padding of baby fat and features lean and hard. If Gib let her, Heidi could read that book for hours. Any book, really. Heidi had pulled that one with her father enough times.

Janet frowned and bit her lip, then turned away and headed down the stairs. Of the three kids, Heidi seemed to be the one who was becoming most involved with Gib.

Too involved.

Janet worried about it. Gib would be gone soon. Would Heidi have trouble with that? Would she feel deserted when he left? Would she wonder if she'd done something wrong? Janet had just finished a book on grief in children—Gib had suggested it to her, and she'd found it in the library—and it seemed that many children Heidi's age blamed themselves when they lost someone important.

She chewed over it for a while, and later, when Gib came down the stairs to the family room, Janet looked up at him, then back to the fireplace. "Gib, we need to talk."

"Okay." He sounded cautious.

"I'm worried. About Heidi. I'm afraid that after you leave, she'll have a hard time dealing with it."

"Every other child I've taken care of has dealt with it. That's one of the reasons I always keep my time short." He sat down across from her. "If I don't stick around, no one gets too attached. That way, no one gets hurt. I'm careful that way—I'm always very careful. And if I thought a problem was developing, I'd leave right away."

Janet wondered if he was still talking about the children, or if he was talking about her. Which was another whole facet of the problem. "And what about us? I think that if what happened last night happens again, the children will eventually catch on. They'll think we have a relationship. They'll think we're becoming a family. They'll think you're staying."

"Well, I'm not staying." He spoke a little louder than strictly necessary, and Janet flicked a glance at him.

"I never said you were."

"I have things to do, places to go, and I'm not interested in a ready-made family or even a steady relationship. I'm only planning to be here for a short time." He sounded stilted, as if he'd rehearsed saying these very words to her.

"Well, fine, because I don't think it's a good idea, either. Especially now, with these three kids here. They're liable to get the wrong idea. The last thing they need is to see another relationship end."

That surprised him, that she would see the connection between death and breaking up. That she would realize the kids wouldn't see much difference between the two, that they'd see just another adult who was leaving them. "You're right. They've seen that already. To see it again could affect how they deal with the world, whether or not they're able to form lasting relationships of their own someday. Whether, when they find a good relationship, they'll decide to stay in it, rather than running from it. Whether they'll repeatedly choose bad relationships instead of good ones, rejecting the good ones and pursuing the ones that can't possibly work out."

He stopped, suddenly confused by what he'd just said, by how familiar it sounded. He looked at Janet. She was saying something. With an effort, he focused on her words.

She was nodding as she spoke, agreeing with what he'd said. "I think that's what Carly's doing. I think that's why she's been so tentative, so fearful. She's afraid to believe anyone she loves is here to stay. I want her to get beyond that, to heal. I don't want her to spend her life pushing people away."

Her words struck him with the force and clarity of manifest truth.

Was that what he was doing? If so, he'd been doing it...well, since he was eighteen or so. Since he lost his parents.

He'd always found himself most drawn to women who weren't interested in more than a good time. He'd always thought that was because he wasn't interested in any more than that himself. But maybe there was something more at work. He'd spent a lot of time and effort gathering insight into the kinds of things his brothers and Sheila were going through after their parents died. Had he been that dense about his own reactions?

Was he avoiding something he was afraid of?

The thought rankled, made him feel irritable.

Janet was watching him, and he realized she was waiting for a response. He struggled for a moment to find his place in the conversation. "Ah, so, what should we do?"

She turned her face away, to stare once again into the fire. "I think it's best if we stop this now. The kids don't need it." She took a breath and turned back, looked straight at him. "To be quite honest, I don't, either."

He nodded, still caught in his own thoughts, and finally, unable to come up with an answer to that, he rose. He just stood there for a moment, nodding slowly, rooted to the floor, staring at her, until he felt about as idiotic as he ever had. "Well, then, I guess I'll turn in."

He left her sitting there, watching the dying fire. In his room, he listened, trying to hear when she went up to bed, but he never did, though he tossed and turned most of the night.

Chapter Nine

Monday afternoon, Sheila and Janet walked into Miss Rita's studio. Sheila looked around as they entered the small reception area and shook her head in amazement. "Boy, is this place pink."

"Wait 'til you see the proprietor."

Miss Rita came through the curtains at the back of the studio, her pink skirt flowing behind her, a pink scarf dangling down her back. Her nails were pink. Her makeup was pink. Even her white hair had a pinkish cast to it.

Janet introduced Sheila. "Miss Rita, Sheila's interested in eventually opening a ballet studio here in town. She wanted to talk to someone who'd been in the business here for a while."

Miss Rita nodded, a single vigorous, positive movement. "Oh, yes, I've been at it forever. It's time for me to retire. I've been meaning to for over ten years now, but I can never seem to let go. My knees, though, they aren't what they used to be. It is difficult for me to even demonstrate the positions any more, much less the movements." She sat perfectly straight, serene and graceful in a position Janet would have found awkward to maintain, and Sheila mirrored her, sitting across from her. Janet could picture Sheila forty years from now, looking just as Miss Rita did now. Only less pink. "But the point is moot—I haven't been able to find a buyer. It's a business that requires so much of your own time and energy that only another dancer would want to own it."

Sheila sighed. "It's perfect. I'd *love* to own it." Her eyes were shining. Janet felt a tiny bit of alarm. Maybe she should have let Sheila pretend to be a tattoo-parlor owner, after all.

Miss Rita eyed Sheila speculatively. "Spoken like a true lover of the dance. And, believe me, I'd love to sell it to you. But you're young—you're probably looking to start from scratch, aren't you? I remember when I started out—I didn't have two nickels to rub together. Luckily I, er, had a patron to help me during those early years." She eyed Sheila for a moment, looking up and down, as if she were weighing the merits of some idea. "Are you really interested in a studio?"

Sheila nodded, her eyes very wide. Janet sat up straighter and looked from one dancer to the other. They mirrored each other in posture and in the dawning excitement in their faces. This wasn't going the way it was supposed to at all.

Miss Rita nodded, as if she'd come to some sort of decision. "This may sound a bit impulsive—well, more than a bit, really—but I've learned that life's too short to waste time on the niceties." She leaned forward, focussing her intense gaze on Sheila's face. "I don't suppose you'd like to work here, and bit by bit buy the place, maybe over four or five years?"

Janet tried to think of something to say to get Sheila off the hook—this was all happening way too fast.

And what in the world would Gib say when he heard about this?

But when she threw Sheila a desperate glance, Sheila's face was so alight with hope and astounded joy, that Janet couldn't bring herself to say anything negative.

"Yes, I would!" Sheila hesitated, and the light in her eyes dimmed a little. "But you might not like my, er, teaching philosophy."

Miss Rita looked at her out of the corner of her eyes and leaned over to pull open her desk drawer. "Oh, you have some of those, do you? Well, to each her own." She rummaged around in the drawer for a moment and pulled out a lighter and a pack of Marlboro Lights and lit one.

Sheila gaped at her. "You smoke? That's impossible."

Miss Rita exhaled. "Only since I turned sixty. I figured, once my knees went, what was the harm? I figure it'll take years to cause major damage—and I always wanted to smoke, back when it was glamorous. I always wanted to be blond, too, but that never worked out." Sheila threw a sideways glance at Janet, but it didn't escape Miss Rita's sharp eyes. "Oh, don't worry, I don't smoke around the kids—I don't have another class for twenty minutes. But I have to tell you, I am really starting to enjoy this nasty habit. It's so ritualistic, don't you think? All the little props. And it gives you a minute to think. I think that's why it seemed so glamorous to us, back when we thought it did nothing worse than cut our wind."

Sheila laughed. "You know, I think this might just work out. What exactly did you have in mind?"

While Janet watched in silent bemusement, Sheila

and Miss Rita discussed the idea. If Miss Rita's accountant and her attorney could work out the details, Miss Rita thought Sheila could work half-time for four or five years, with her entire salary going to buy the business. She could move into the tiny studio apartment above the studio, which was empty now, and live there free. And at the end of the time, Sheila would own half the business. Then she could use her business equity as collateral for a loan to buy the building and the other half of the business, and Miss Rita would retire.

Sheila would have to get another job, at least part-time, to manage her living expenses until she owned the business, but hard work was fine with Sheila.

Fifteen minutes later, as a car pulled up and let out a couple of preteens, Miss Rita stubbed out her second cigarette and slipped her pink ashtray into her desk drawer. She rose. "I'll talk to my lawyer about drawing up some papers. If he can get it to work, I'll give you a call right away, and we can start whenever you're ready."

Sheila bit her lip. "I'd have a few things to take care of first—how about if we start in three weeks?"

"Three weeks it is. Keep in touch." With a flounce of pink chiffon, Miss Rita turned and crossed the floor to where the girls were warming up.

Janet waited until they were out the door. "Don't you want to see the class?"

Sheila smiled. "Don't need to—I know exactly what kind of a teacher she is, just by talking to her. She's autocratic, maybe a little harsh, and the Dance must be the most important thing in her pupils' lives. Especially older girls, but even the young ones are expected to toe the line. I had a dozen teachers just like her. She's doing everything exactly the way I don't want to do it."

"Then why..." Janet was confused.

"That's just how it is—or, how it always has been. For generations, probably. It's not that it's wrong, really—it's just not how I want to do it." She grinned. "But if she can put up with me, I can put up with her. I can't believe it—I'm going to have my studio!" She gave a series of graceful spins, exuberant, across the parking lot. Then she stopped. "Janet, please don't tell my brother anything about this—he'll be furious."

Janet felt uneasy. She started to shake her head.

Sheila put her hand on Janet's arm. "Please? Just until I can figure out a way to tell him, okay? Please?"

Janet bit her lip. "Okay, but tell him soon, all right? I hate keeping secrets from people." She didn't like it, but she supposed it was Sheila's right to tell her brother in her own time.

Besides, it certainly wasn't Janet's right. Gib had made that perfectly clear. He may have been pretending to talk about the kids, but his message came through loud and clear. *Don't expect me to be around for you, because I don't plan to be around for anyone but myself.* This man was not sticking around any longer than the kids were, and Janet was not going to set herself up for any extra pain.

Oh, she could pretend they'd agreed to cool it for the sake of the kids. And it was true enough—it wouldn't be fair to the kids to see Aunt Jannie forming a relationship with Gib when the girls were going to lose both of them so soon. But Janet knew that at least part of her was also protecting herself—because it wouldn't be just the girls he was leaving when he left.

SO WHEN GIB called her for dinner that evening and asked her what Sheila's opinion of Miss Rita had been, Janet cut her eyes from his and just told him that Sheila had said Miss Rita was no different than any other dance teacher.

Then she hurried over to settle Emma into her high chair before he could ask her anything more. "Everything smells great! Wow, biscuits! Are these homemade?" Dropping into a chair, she picked one of the warm golden disks out of the basket and broke it open. A fresh wave of yeasty steam escaped, and she closed her eyes and breathed deeply, the tantalizing aroma making her mouth water. "And lentils and rice! My favorite." Gib eyed her suspiciously, but he just pushed Heidi's booster in for her before seating himself.

After a few moments, as if he were just remembering it, Gib pulled a piece of folded white note paper from his shirt pocket. He pushed it across the table with two fingers. He probably didn't want to risk the possibility he'd touch her—she might take it wrong or something. Think it meant they were engaged. Couldn't have that. *Oh, stop it. He's being completely honest with you. Give him a little credit.* Janet was exasperated with herself. If something didn't happen to cut this tension, she wasn't going to be able to stand having him around.

She picked up the paper, then looked at him, raising her eyebrows in a silent question.

He nodded toward Carly. "Carly's principal sent it home."

Janet looked at Carly, who was engrossed in her food. She unfolded the note and read it.

Dear Ms. Resnick,
Recently, one of Carly's fellow students, Jeremy

Cooper, has been becoming upset each day at lunchtime. Apparently a group of students has been depriving him of part of his lunch. We have determined that Carly is somehow involved. Please give me a call once you've had a chance to discuss this with Carly.

Thank you for your attention to this matter,
Genia Higgenbotham

Carly? In trouble at school? Janet looked at Carly, who was staring into her soup bowl. She threw a questioning glance at Gib, but he shrugged and shook his head. She refolded the note and set it beside her plate until the meal was over.

She stood, her plate and the note in her hand, and walked over to the counter to set the plate down. "Carly, would you help me clear the table? Heidi, why don't you go get ready for your bath, honey? And after you guys get your jammies on, we'll play some games before bedtime."

"I get to sit near the spigot!" Heidi jumped up and pounded up the stairs.

While Carly, head down, carried plates from the table to the sink, Gib got a damp cloth and started to wipe up Emma and the mess around her high chair.

Janet made her voice casual. "Carly, Gib showed me the note from your principal today." She put a little question mark on the end, but Carly just stopped and sat down. She huddled her shoulders into herself.

"Can you tell me what happened?"

Carly put her forehead down on her folded arms on the tabletop.

Janet reached out and placed a comforting hand on Carly's back. "Honey, Mrs. Higgenbotham says she thinks you might have been taking part of Jeremy's lunch. Is that true?''

A nod.

"Don't you get enough lunch for yourself?''

Carly raised her head. "No, I get enough.''

"Then why, honey?''

"Well, I just put the ketchup in to gross him out, not to make him cry. He never cried before.'' Carly sounded indignant.

Janet felt confused. "What did you put the ketchup into?''

"In my chocolate milk.''

"Ketchup? In your milk? Doesn't it taste funny?''

"The ketchup goes to the bottom. If I drink off the top, I don't get any ketchup, just chocolate milk.'' Behind Carly, Gib had his head down, and his shoulders shook up and down. Oh, great, he thought it was funny. *Butthead.*

Janet stared at the little girl, mystified. "But if you don't want the ketchup in your milk, why do you put it in, in the first place?''

"I did it once to gross him out. He's pretty easy to gross out. But he got so upset about it that I kept doing it. He gets so grossed out he gags. Then can't drink his own chocolate milk, so then *I* get it.''

Gib had a sudden coughing fit.

Janet gritted her teeth. *Men's idea of humor.* Come to think of it, this *was* like something out of the Three Stooges. Janet ignored him. "But, honey, why would you want to gross him out?''

"Because he's such a dweeb. He follows me around all over the playground, and he grabs the back of my shirt and says he's snapping my bra strap.'' Carly's eyes sparkled with tears of remembered humiliation. "I don't even have a bra yet! It's so weird! I hate him!"

Gib turned, and there was anger in his eyes. *Not so funny anymore, eh, Mr. Rambling-kind-of-guy? Don't tell me you aren't letting yourself get involved with these kids.*

Janet held up a hand to quell his reaction. She took a deep breath. "Carly, he was wrong to do that. But I think you know that what you did wasn't the best way to handle it. Please don't do it again. Do you understand me?"

Carly nodded, obviously embarrassed, and Janet hugged her. "Don't worry, honey, I'll call Mrs. Higgenbotham, and we'll get things straightened out." She placed a gentle hand under Carly's downturned chin, nudged it upward so Janet could look her in the eye. "I can understand exactly why you were mad. I'd be pretty mad about that myself. Next time something like that happens, you come to me." Except she wouldn't be here, Janet reminded herself. "Or to Grandma. Understand?"

"Yes, Aunt Jannie."

Janet hugged her tight for a minute. "Why don't you go on upstairs and get ready for your bath? I'll be up in a few minutes."

As soon as Carly was out of the room, Gib gave Janet a steely look. "I'll kill the little harasser."

"Gib, he's just a kid. He probably doesn't know that what he did was wrong. He probably likes her, and that's how an eight-year-old mind tells him to show it. Think how many forty-year-old men think that kind of thing is acceptable."

"Yeah. Right." Gib wasn't cutting the kid much slack. "Well, then, we'll just have to make sure he learns the lesson now, rather than when he's forty. Do him a big favor, probably save him from a sexual-harassment lawsuit thirty years from now.'' He had a proprietary look in his eyes.

A fatherly look.

Janet pushed those thoughts away—they'd do her no good, and he'd made himself clear on the point that they were only the product of her imagination.

She tried to refocus on the problem at hand. How should she approach Mrs. Higgenbotham? And Jeremy's parents—they might well scoff at the idea that what Jeremy had done was something to be discouraged. After all, little girls had been putting up with that kind of stuff—and worse—since schools were invented. Janet could remember getting her own bra strap snapped a few times, and how mortified she'd felt. Good for Carly for not putting up with it.

A picture of Carly, grimly intent on vengeance, pouring ketchup into her milk, formed in Janet's mind. She laughed.

Gib cut his eyes to her. ''What?''

''Actually, I think Carly's solution was a darned good one. Hit the kid where it really hurts—in the lunch box. I wonder how long she's been getting his chocolate milk from him?''

He tried to frown, not quite ready to see the humor, but then Janet laughed again. ''He's lucky she didn't decide to squirt ketchup over her whole lunch. He could have gotten darned hungry.''

He laughed then, and Janet joined him, and then she couldn't stop. Janet laughed until her sides ached, and she leaned over the kitchen counter, gasping. Each time she got herself under control, she met Gib's eyes, and saw the tears streaming down his face, and it would start her off again. After a while, Janet wasn't sure whether they were still laughing about Carly, or to release the tension between them.

But when they finally stopped laughing, she felt as if they were back on the same team, and Gib seemed to feel it too. She still felt a constant undercurrent of tension, but it was closer to being tolerable.

That evening, after the girls had their baths, they all spent some time together in the cozy family room. Janet and Gib shared the newspaper while the girls played games and colored.

"No, Emma." Heidi pulled her coloring book away from the toddler. "Aunt Jannie, make her stop."

Janet looked up at the two little girls, struggling in a battle of wills a couple of feet from her. Carly sat looking through the photo album they'd made for Emma. Gib was sitting on the floor beside Janet's chair, newspapers spread about him. He leaned over the pages, and Janet smiled to see his lips occasionally move slightly as he read.

"Aunt Jannie! She's ruining everything."

"Why don't you give her a page to play with? She'll be happy with that."

"No!" Heidi pulled at the coloring book, but Emma was clutching it in her strong little hands. She wavered back and forth on her unsteady feet.

Then, as Janet watched, Heidi turned and reached her hand out to push Emma away. Janet jerked her hand toward Emma and opened her mouth to cry out— Emma was standing next to the fireplace, and if she fell the wrong way, she'd be hurt. But just as Heidi made contact with Emma's back, just as Janet reached for the little girl, Gib was already there. He steadied

Emma with one hand. He turned his head to look at Heidi, his face serious, and she pulled her hand back.

"Heidi, what have we said about pushing Emma?" He gave her a solemn look.

Her face crumpled. "She could fall, an', an' get *hurt*," she sobbed. She sat down on the floor and started to cry.

Gib pulled Heidi into his lap. He cradled her against his shoulder, and as Janet watched, he wrapped his arms around her, so that the little girl seemed to fit into the curve of his shoulder as if she'd been made for that space. Or as if he'd been specially formed to comfort a little girl her age. His big, square hands patted and smoothed her tiny back, delivering silent messages of comfort.

"Heidi, you've had a long day, haven't you?" His voice was so low that Janet almost missed it.

Heidi hiccuped through her sobs.

"I think maybe it's time for bed. C'mon, we'll go up now, and we can read a book together, okay?" With no apparent effort he stood, and Heidi transferred her head to the ridge of his shoulder, and when Janet looked into her face, the little girl looked worn-out.

"Are you okay, honey?"

Heidi just cried.

Gib looked at Janet and mouthed the words, "Just tired." He and Janet shared a wry, sympathetic smile.

"Do you want me to take her up?"

Gib shook his head. "I've got her."

"I'll come up and say good-night in a few minutes."

Janet watched Gib's steps as he carried Heidi up the stairs, the soles of his soft shoes making no sound as he climbed, his arms comforting around the little girl. As they disappeared from sight, Heidi's sobs quieted to little tired sounds. She'd probably be asleep before she hit the pillow.

Janet walked back over to the fireplace and sat down in the wing chair, pulling Emma up into her arms. Emma gave a contented sigh and snuggled into Janet's lap. She'd be asleep before long, too. Even Carly, still turning the pages of the homemade photo album, was fighting back yawns.

Janet sat there by the fireplace, holding a child, and watching another, and felt a sudden ferocious longing for a family. For a loving little family, with normal kids who fought sometimes and normal parents who made mistakes sometimes. For a simple, tender family who generally got along and always, no matter what, loved each other.

She felt a strong sense of peace along with that realization, and she leaned back in her chair, holding Emma to her and listening as the toddler's breathing grew deeper and slower. She watched Carly by the light of the fire, the way the glimmers of the flames danced in the little girl's hair, the way the face of her mother shone through the translucent eight-year-old features. When Carly looked up, Janet held out her free arm, and Carly climbed into Janet's lap beside her sister and laid her head on Janet's shoulder. And for a few minutes, as Janet sat in her father's old wing chair, a child in each arm, listening to the sound of Gib's footsteps above her as he tucked Heidi into bed, she felt as if she had everything she could possibly want out of life.

All she had to do was ignore the fact that it wasn't real.

UPSTAIRS, Gib got Heidi to bed just barely in time. She was asleep practically before he got her teeth brushed.

He pressed a kiss to her forehead and turned off the light. When he got to the door, he turned and watched her breathe for a moment by the light from the moon.

He was becoming too attached to this child, to all three of these children. Who were, by the way, someone else's responsibility, someone else's joy.

And even if they weren't, this was not what he wanted at this point in his life. He wanted to move about on his own schedule. He'd raised three of someone else's children once already, and though he had no regrets, he was done with that.

Abruptly, he turned away from Heidi's doorway, shutting her image out of his line of sight. He pulled the door gently closed and started down the steps to the family room.

When he stepped into the family room on silent feet, he stopped to stare at Janet, her face in three-quarters profile to him. She held a sleeping Emma in one arm and a sleepy Carly in the other. She and Carly gazed together into the firelight, and as he watched, Janet pulled Carly a little tighter and Carly tipped her face into the hollow where Janet's neck curved into her shoulder.

Carly was the same age Sheila had been when their parents had died. It wasn't that he hadn't realized it before now, hadn't seen the similarities, but suddenly, it all reminded him too much of his feelings twelve years ago. His breath caught, and he couldn't get it back. He was suffocating. He coughed, and Janet and Carly both looked at him, two golden heads, one red-gold and curly, the other golden brown and silky-straight, side by side in the firelight.

He cleared his throat. "Bedtime, Carly." Anything to break the spell.

She looked up at her aunt, and Janet raised one hand to brush Carly's cheek with her knuckles.

Carly gave her aunt a convulsive hug. "I wish you could stay here all the time." Then she rushed away before Janet could answer, past Gib and up the stairs. Gib avoided Janet's stunned gaze as he took Emma from her and followed Carly up the stairs.

When Gib came back down the stairs, he stood across the room for a moment. And although it took a supreme effort not to watch Janet as she drowsed by the fire, the flames flickering fascinating silhouettes, he wanted to avoid any conversation.

He was not going to get involved with this woman, with these three little girls. He was going to free himself of all encumbrances as soon as possible and spend blessed years alone with no one but himself to worry about. He hated himself for having made the emotional connections to them that he already had—it wasn't fair, not to Janet and definitely not to the girls.

He stretched. "I'm for bed."

"Me, too." Janet also stood.

She took a slight step toward him, or maybe she was just heading for the stairs behind him. When he finally couldn't resist meeting her gaze, she pulled her eyes away from his. She looked down at the fire, as if it was something fascinating she'd never seen before. "Well, good night. I guess I'll get some work done."

He cleared his throat. "Janet, I..."

She looked up at him. "Yes?"

He looked away. "Never mind. Good night." He turned and walked into his bedroom.

Gib heaved a deep sigh of regret as he crossed to the window to stare out at the darkness. He had wanted to apologize, once again, for overstepping the bound-

aries of good judgment. But maybe it was better to
leave things as they were, rather than to get into a
dangerous area. It was better to try to get things between them back on an even keel, get them back to a
professional level. And keep them there.

THE NEXT DAY, Janet almost managed to keep strictly
to her plan. Now that her proposal had gone out to
Houston, she was able to get everything done that she
needed to. Well, close to it, anyway.

She started to feel pretty good. Heidi and Carly were
back in school, so she rearranged her schedule to reflect
that, and she spent some serious one-on-one time with
Emma in the morning.

Gib took Emma with him to pick up Heidi from
preschool, and while the house was silent and empty,
the phone rang. Janet picked it up. "HomeWork."

"Janet? Houston Whalen. Here it is, this is it. I've
got a meeting set up for us with my client, and we've
got three days to prepare. I'm faxing you the prelimi-
nary changes to your proposal." Janet turned, and sure
enough, papers were starting to slide out of the fax
machine. "Fax me the updated document as soon as
possible—but tomorrow at the latest. We'll turn it
around for you A.S.A.P., and you can have it all back
to revise a final time, and back to us by Thursday. The
meeting is Friday at four o'clock. We'll have dinner
with the client afterward. Congratulations, Janet. This
could turn into a big contract for both of us."

Janet hung up the phone and pulled a few pages out
of the fax. As she read them over, she felt beads of
sweat break out on her forehead. These were major
changes—hours and hours of concentrated work. She
sat there for a moment, numb. She felt as if she'd

jumped out of an airplane. She just hoped her parachute would open.

She sat frozen beside her computer for a moment, paralyzed by the sheer enormity of the task in front of her. There was no way she could get this plan done in time. All of this to Houston by tomorrow? And there were sure to be more changes to come.

She felt suddenly hot, and she couldn't breathe. She rose and stumbled to the window, threw it open, and stuck her head out for a moment to gulp in the cool air.

She'd never missed a deadline in her life. Her father had taught her that, one of the things of value she'd learned from him. "No matter what," he'd always told her—usually while he was explaining why he wouldn't be able to make it to the school picnic or the father/daughter dance or some other event Janet wanted him to attend—"if you've told someone you'll do something, you do it. No excuses." The irony hadn't struck her until she was in college and he was dead, and by then the lesson had been hard-wired in.

She'd just have to work all night. Too many people were depending on her.

When Gib returned home with Heidi and Emma and found Janet in her office poring over faxes, she told him what had happened. "I'm going to need long periods of uninterrupted time over the next few days if I stand any chance of getting this done." She bit her lip, eyeing him warily—although the tension had eased between them since the Ketchup Solution, as he'd taken to calling it, she didn't know how he'd react to her abandoning all her responsibilities for a few days and barricading herself in her office. Would he make things hard on her?

He shrugged. "So cancel the schedule for the day and I'll take the kids to the zoo, then out for pizza."

He could have thrown up roadblocks—he could have given her a hard time about the kids, her work, her priorities, or a hundred little failings. But he didn't. He just picked up the ball and ran with it, and safe or not, she could have kissed him. Now she could get to work without worrying about the kids, or about Gib's disapproval, or anything.

She reached out to touch his arm. "Thank you. I really appreciate this." He looked into her eyes, and for a moment she felt warm in his gaze. Then the discomfort returned—not in full force, but it was back. She needed to stop thinking of this man as...well, as a man. He was here to do a job, and he was agreeing to do it. Nothing more. His approval or disapproval was irrelevant to whether or not she needed to work.

And she did need to. She forced her eyes back to the fax in her hand, knowing that as soon as she allowed herself to concentrate on that, she'd be able to stop thinking about Gib.

So she tried to focus her attention on it, while he narrowed his eyes for a moment, thinking. "I can pick Carly up at school—I'll call them and tell them not to put her on the bus. Emma can nap in the car—she won't mind. And we'll just meet up with you later."

Janet nodded, following him downstairs absentmindedly, only half listening as he continued to talk.

Gib stuffed a stack of diapers and a fresh box of wipes into the diaper bag. "We'll just plan to spend the whole day, then. Heidi, do you have your shoes?" Heidi turned and ran barefoot back up the stairs. "Get socks, too," he called after her, before turning to Janet again. "Just don't forget this recital thing."

Janet nodded, her eyes still on the papers in her hand. "Yes, yes, the recital." The recital wasn't for several days, she didn't have time to think about that now. She shook her head over the changes Houston had suggested. What he was asking was ridiculous— didn't he see that there was a much easier way?

Gib checked Emma's diaper one last time before they left. "Emma's bottle is empty. Let me just fill another one for her." Heidi appeared at the bottom of the stairs with her shoes on the wrong feet. Gib stooped to help her. "So then, we'll see you later. I'll call if anything comes up."

Janet nodded. "Anything, just call." She frowned in thought. Maybe if she re-estimated the hand-sewing portion of the project, she could show Houston what she meant.

As Gib herded the girls out the back door, Janet picked her way up the stairs, still concentrating on the fax she held in her hand. It was going to take some work, but she could do it.

Chapter Ten

Janet jumped when the door to her office swung open and hit the wall.

"Where were you?" Gib thundered at her. His eyes sparked at her, hard black stones, dangerous.

Janet blinked at him. She'd never seen him lose his temper. He usually kept it under such a tight rein. He was out of control now.

She almost couldn't respond, she was so surprised. "What do you mean, where was I?"

He gave her a look of pure incredulity. His gaze traveled to her desk, which was three inches deep in paper, and to the fax machine, from which curls of paper hung in crazy corkscrews. His expression became one of contempt. "You really don't know, do you?"

She stared at him. What was she missing? The dawning of understanding brought horror. "Not the recital— the *practice* for the recital." It was tonight. She jerked around to look at the clock. Ten o'clock.

She'd missed it.

"I called five different times. Don't you pick up your phone?" His hand closed on the door frame as if he wished it were her neck his fingers were clenched around.

Janet bit her lip. "I was only answering the business line. I'm sorry."

He shook his head. "Don't apologize to me. Apologize to Heidi. Not that it'll do much good tonight—she's crushed. She thinks you don't care. What's worse, she thinks somehow it's her fault—that you did it because she pushed Emma the other night. Good work, Janet. Just when she needed you most, too." He gave her a look of pure disgust—it shook her to her very core—and then he turned and walked out.

Janet sat for a moment, frozen with regret. Then she jumped to her feet and hurried out into the hall.

"Heidi?" She leaned over to listen down the stairs, but the first floor was dark. Gib must have put the kids to bed before he gave her her dressing-down. Janet turned and padded down the hall to Heidi's room. The door was ajar, and there was a faint light from a night-light shining within. Janet pushed the door open and listened for a moment. Quiet sniffing sounds told her Heidi was still awake, and probably crying. Janet's own throat threatened to close; tears burned in her eyes. She wiped them away angrily; she had no patience with herself right now.

"Heidi?"

No answer.

"Honey, may I please come in?"

A pause. "Okay."

Janet walked over and sat down on the edge of the bed. Heidi watched her through wide wet eyes, and when Janet reached for the little girl's hand and squeezed it, it lay unresponsive in her palm.

"Heidi, I am so sorry. I know that doesn't help, but

I can't tell you how sorry I am. Something came up...something happened today that really got me upset. I got so upset that I forgot I was supposed to come see you in the practice tonight. I forgot what day it was, even. Did you ever forget anything before?''

Heidi picked up her stuffed dog and pulled at its ears. She was silent for a long time, and when she spoke, her voice was so low that Janet had to strain to hear the words. "Not if it was important, I didn't."

Janet winced. "Heidi, you're right."

Heidi stopped fiddling with the stuffed dog and looked at her. "I am?"

"Yes, you are. I promised to do something, and I should have found a way to make sure I remembered it. I let you down, and I was wrong. I'm very, very sorry, but that doesn't make it better. It's important to say it, though."

She squeezed Heidi's hand again. "Something else is important to say, too. Heidi, I don't want you to think I missed the recital on purpose. Gib told me you thought it was because I was still mad because you pushed Emma. Is that what you thought?"

Heidi looked down and nodded.

"Oh, honey, come here." Janet pulled Heidi into her lap, and Heidi pressed her cheek down on Janet's shoulder. "Heidi, there is nothing in the world that you could possibly do that would make me want to hurt you like I hurt you tonight. I don't care what it was. I'd never, ever, hurt you on purpose." She leaned down to look in Heidi's face. "That doesn't mean I was happy about you pushing Emma, or that sometimes I don't have to punish you for something you do. But I would never lie to you or try to trick you or embarrass you. Do you understand the difference?"

Heidi nodded, but Janet wasn't sure she understood, herself. Her thoughts went back to a day when her father had told her he wasn't getting her a dog after all because she'd forgotten to give him an important message and therefore she wasn't responsible enough to have a dog. Janet had been twelve. Was that punishment, or was that an attempt to destroy?

Or was it simply a basic ineptness, without malicious intent?

For the first time, Janet felt sorry for her father. Given his inadequate parenting skills, he might have been doing the best he could, most of the time.

She looked down at Heidi again. "I wish I could come up with some way to make this up to you, Heidi, but I don't know how. Can you think of anything?"

Heidi thought for a moment, then shook her head.

"If you think of anything, you tell me, okay? And I'll do it, if I can."

Heidi nodded.

"I love you, honey." Janet hugged her tight, then laid the little girl back down on her pillow and snugged the blankets up around her. She tucked the little stuffed dog under the covers next to Heidi's shoulder. "Here, don't let Goggie get cold." Heidi smiled, and Janet touched her cheek for a long moment, loathe to leave her. Finally, Heidi's eyelids drooped, and Janet rose from the bed.

As she stepped through the door, Heidi called her. "Aunt Jannie?"

Janet turned back. "Yeah, honey?"

"Gib says I'm gonna be the best Lammender Princess ever."

Janet smiled, bittersweet. "Well, honey, I've never known him to be wrong."

She pulled the door not quite closed after her, and when she turned, she almost ran smack into Gib, who stood leaning against the wall in the hallway outside Heidi's room.

"You were eavesdropping!"

He snorted. "I was keeping track of what happens in these kids' lives. Someone around here has to do it."

"I apologized to her."

"And you think that's enough?"

She looked him straight in the eye. "No, I don't. But it's the best I could come up with right now." She started to turn away, then turned back. "I feel terrible, Gib. I really do. If I could take it back, I would, sale or no sale. I wouldn't hurt her for the world." Again tears burned her eyes.

He looked at her and his face softened. He took a deep breath, and finally he spoke. "You did a nice job. You apologized, and you didn't try to downplay the importance of the practice recital in her life. I was impressed." He turned and walked down the stairs, leaving Janet standing with her mouth open.

She went into her own bedroom, unsure of her reactions. She'd tried to fix some of the damage, and Gib's approval warmed her. Slightly.

But it still didn't change the fact that after almost three weeks of dealing with the kids, she didn't feel any closer to being able to do it right. And she still had another month or so to go. Another month in which to screw up three little psyches. She sat down on the bed and pulled her shoes off. She'd never get it. She'd never be able to do it right. *Stop that—it's a self-fulfilling prophecy.* Of course she'd never be able to do it right, if that's what she kept telling herself.

She wondered what new disaster loomed tomorrow.

THE NEXT DAY, Wednesday, Janet faxed off to Houston all the changes she'd made. Things looked good—or, at least, not disastrous. The meeting was set for Friday afternoon. Houston's people had just over two days—barely enough time, as far as Janet could see, but Houston laughed when she expressed concern. "Janet, my people are very well paid, and I expect them to perform that way."

Janet wondered how much she'd have to be paid to perform the miracles she knew Houston's people were expected to pull off in the next forty-eight hours.

Other than a final meeting late Thursday, Janet didn't have anything pressing for the next couple of days, so she—and Gib, of course—worked on spending as much time as possible with the kids. They went back to the zoo, and to the Museum of Natural History, and to the park, where Janet finally got to see Heidi go down the big kids' slide.

Gib watched Janet coax Heidi once more down the slide, catching her at the bottom. Janet laughed as she scooped Heidi up into her arms and threw her over her shoulder. "You did it!"

Heidi screamed in delight. "I'm a big kid, now, huh?"

"You sure are. Next you'll be going off the high dive this summer." Heidi's hair blew into her face, and Janet reached down to tuck it behind an ear, and Heidi giggled and flung herself into her aunt's arms. Janet hugged her close. She threw Gib a glance and whispered something into Heidi's ear that made the little girl giggle.

He smiled to himself. Janet was really good at this. She'd make a terrific mother. Even though she had trouble separating from her work, she was good with the kids. He'd been too hard on her the other night. He knew he'd been overreacting. He'd lost his temper—something he never did. Something he'd always been careful to avoid.

And he suspected he knew the reason why. He'd stopped being objective about these kids and about Janet.

Especially about Janet.

He needed to get out, and now. He really should have left before this. Why was it so hard this time?

Maybe it was just that this was his last job—he was feeling nostalgic about seeing this part of his life end. It was natural, really, to confuse his feelings about giving up his work with his feelings about this family. Maybe that was why he kept finding reasons to stay on.

Yeah, maybe that was it.

He watched as Janet turned to look for him. Her big hazel eyes widened as she saw he'd been watching her, and she smiled before she reddened and turned away.

Or maybe he was just plain full of bull.

As Gib watched Janet race Heidi back around to the ladder, a woman standing on the other side of the playground equipment called to him. "Gib?"

He turned, and he almost didn't recognize the woman. In fact, it wasn't until he looked at the baby in her arms and recognized Lissa that he could place the mother. "Laura?"

This was Laura Jason? He smiled in amazement at the change in her. Laura's hair, which had always looked like it couldn't decide whether it was blond or brown, curly or straight, now fell in honey-colored waves. She smiled, a relaxed, confident smile, and walked nearer.

"I thought that was you!" Laura's face beamed her happy confidence. Gib bent his head to smile at Lissa, who hid her face in her mother's shoulder.

"Oh, she's going through this S-H-Y thing." Her mother hugged her close. "Even in just a few weeks, she probably doesn't remember you."

"No, I guess she doesn't." He'd always felt he'd touched his clients' lives, helped them, and then moved on. He'd never minded before that once he left, he was no longer important to them. He looked down at Emma in his arms, and over at Janet, where she was pushing Heidi on the swings. He thought of Carly, who would soon be home from school, looking for a cookie and an enthusiastic listener to hear about her day. How soon would these four forget him, these females who were too fast becoming too important to him? How soon would he be no longer very important to them?

He needed to concentrate on the goal at the end. His freedom would soon be here, and he was leaving. As soon as possible, as a matter of fact. Before he could get any further entangled with these four.

Gib introduced Emma, who pulled her own shy act, and they walked over to the swings, so he could introduce Janet and Heidi, too.

Heidi craned her head around. "I want Gib to push me!"

Gib handed Emma to Janet as she paused between pushes, then stepped into place as Janet stepped away. He took up the rhythm of the swing, smoothly transferring the beat from Janet to himself, an easy team. They shared a smile as she moved away.

Janet and Laura walked a few steps over to the sandbox to deposit the two squirming tots. They sat on a nearby bench to watch the two little girls squabble over the available digging toys, and to watch Gib pushing Heidi.

"Higher, higher," Heidi demanded, watching the older girl next to her, who was pumping herself high enough to kick at the leaves on a nearby bush.

"Do you think you're high enough? Remember what happened last time?"

"I fell off and skinned my knee."

"That's right. But you're getting bigger every day. Maybe by summer, you can go higher."

"Okay, when summer comes."

Laura rolled her eyes at Janet. "Right again, as usual. You know," she told Janet, her voice low. "I never thought I'd get along without Gib, but he was right—he left at exactly the right time. I cried when he left, but he was right. He really was."

Janet grimaced. "Don't you just hate it?"

They laughed.

Janet lowered her voice. "I hate the thought of it, too. He's better with the kids than I am. He's better with everything. He can just walk into a room and take it all in—where everyone is, who's going to get into trouble next, what I need help with. When he says something, everyone in the room listens, did you ever notice that? And when you talk to him, he really listens to you. Not like some men." She broke off, as she noticed Laura watching her with a curious smile. "What?"

"You're in love with him." Laura smiled, but Janet could hear an undertone of sympathy. And perhaps of yearning.

Janet shook her head, definite. "Nope. I know he's leaving. Oh, I'm not saying he wouldn't be an easy man to fall in love with." She sneaked a glance at him, her eyes straying over dark hair whipped back by the wind, strong hands that reached to help a toddler onto a swing. "But it's not going to happen. He's leaving. He's made that clear. And I'll probably feel the same as you. Right now, I feel as if I won't survive without him. But a few weeks later, just like you, I'll look back and realize he was right to leave." She laughed. "After all, he's always right. Right?"

Laura nodded, but a bit uncertainly, and Janet looked from her to Gib. When she met his eyes, a small shock of longing went through her, and she knew she didn't believe herself, either.

ON FRIDAY, as Janet was dressing for her four-o'clock meeting with Houston and Tri-State, something niggled at her brain, and she glanced at her calendar. Meeting w/ Tri-State. Dinner after.

Dinner after.

Heidi's recital was tonight.

Houston was expecting her to have dinner with the client's representatives tonight, after the meeting. She swallowed hard, but there was no question in her mind at all. The recital came first.

She finished dressing and walked down the stairs to the kitchen.

Heidi sat there in her booster chair, already in her costume even though the recital wasn't for another four hours. Gib had wrapped a large towel around her and clipped it in back to protect the precious dance costume from the peanut-butter-and-jelly sandwich she was eating. Heidi's eyes shone with pride and excitement. Around a bite of sticky sandwich, she said, "I'm the only one who gets purple!"

If Janet missed this recital, if she even asked the question, she'd break this little girl's heart. Janet knew exactly what she was doing—she was letting Houston Whalen down. And when she did, not only would she lose her chance with him, and this particular client, but she'd lose the rest of her chances, too. Once she was on the outs with him, no one else would touch her.

So be it. Her father had taught her never to let people down, had he? Well, that could cut two ways.

She stood there for a moment, waiting for it to hit her. The fact that she'd decided that the main, unifying goal of her life for the last five years—building her business—was perhaps not the most important thing she could be doing with her life right this very minute. Was not, perhaps, the number-one priority she'd always thought it was. She'd been working so long and so hard to make her business a success that the means had become the end. The plan had taken on a life of its own.

Now suddenly, she was deciding to put something else first. Deciding something else was more important.

How did she feel about that? Like a failure? Like a loser? Like she'd been wasting her time?

She examined the feeling, poked at it a little to see if it smarted.

Not even a twinge.

A slow grin crept over her face. She didn't feel like a loser at all. She didn't feel as if she'd failed at anything. And she hadn't been wasting her time—the work had been important to her, and she had enjoyed putting it first, for a very long time. But, at least for now, it wasn't the most important thing in her life. Maybe it would be again. Maybe soon, even, maybe as soon as she was back in her own place. She wondered if she'd regret her change of priorities then.

She looked down at Heidi's jelly-smeared face, at the towel wrapped so carefully around her. At Gib, standing there watching her, as if he was aware of exactly what was going on in her mind. He gave her a smile, a smile that took her breath away.

She didn't think she'd regret a thing.

Suddenly, Janet felt just great.

She reached down and grabbed one of Heidi's chips.

"Hey!" Heidi grinned at her. "Those are mine!"

"Can't you share?" Janet grinned right back. "Besides, I'm going to miss dinner because of you and this Lavender Princess thing. You sure you want to do this? Because we could all just go to Chuck E. Cheese instead."

"No!" Heidi giggled, pretending she didn't know Janet was kidding.

Gib was watching them, smiling as he put another sandwich together. Janet threw him a wry glance. "Houston was expecting me to have dinner with the clients after the meeting. I never really told him I'd make it, but when he mentioned it, I forgot it was the same night as the recital."

"What will he do?" He'd stopped spreading peanut butter on the slice of whole-wheat bread dwarfed by his palm.

Janet shrugged and stole another of Heidi's chips. "He'll either deal with it, or he won't. It's up to him." She said it with a great deal more bravado than she felt, and when she flicked her eyes back up at him, he was giving her a glance of sympathy. And something else. Admiration?

That, and Heidi's shining gaze, almost made her feel prepared to face Houston.

Janet turned to follow him, raising her voice slightly.

"Houston, I can't. I have—a family obligation."

He looked puzzled. "I didn't know you had a fam—"

"I'm taking care of my sister's kids temporarily, and I couldn't ... " her voice trailed away. Fund of her lip, knowing it hurt, but ... there would ... It ... ...

Chapter Eleven

An hour later, Janet sailed through the meeting. Houston's marketing department had done some amazing things with Janet's proposal. Janet almost felt impressed with herself as she listened to them describe her business and the proposal to the vice president of Tri-State, Hildegarde Thomas, a serious-looking woman in a tailored suit and horn-rimmed glasses.

As the meeting ended, everyone stood. Houston, obviously elated by how things had gone, issued his invitation to dinner, to general agreement. As the rest of the table packed up their briefcases, Janet pulled Houston aside and lowered her voice to a whisper.

"Houston, I can't make it to dinner tonight."

"What do you mean, can't make it?" He frowned. "Janet, this is a very important client to me—and to you, too. You may feel things went very well today, but this isn't over, not by a long shot. On Monday, Tri-State meets with our competition. We need this face-time with them, we need to make sure that when they're deciding who to award this contract to, they're thinking of us as 'those nice people over at Whalen Industries, who we don't want to disappoint.' This isn't an optional dinner, Janet, this is part of the deal." He started to walk away, argument over.

Janet turned to follow him, raising her voice slightly. "Houston, I can't. I have a...a family obligation."

He looked puzzled. "I didn't know you had a family."

"I'm taking care of my sister's kids temporarily, and tonight is my niece's ballet recital." Janet bit her lip, knowing a four-year-old's dance recital wasn't going to cut it. But she wasn't going to back down—wild horses couldn't keep her from this.

Houston opened his mouth to give her a pointed retort, but he was interrupted by another voice as Hildegarde Thomas came up behind them. "A ballet recital?" She gave Janet a sharp look. "You need to miss dinner because of a ballet recital?"

Janet's heart sank. From the corner of her eye, she saw Houston's face darken. "Yes, a ballet recital. My four-year-old niece is the only one who gets to wear purple." Now, why had she said that?

Hildegarde Thomas sniffed. "Well, I can understand perfectly how that could cause a conflict. I have seven-year-old twins of my own. Believe me, when I even miss a Little League game, there's hell to pay. From the kids, from my husband, and from myself."

Janet allowed herself to hope. Surely if Hildegarde had children of her own, she could understand how important these things were?

Hildegarde sniffed again. "I've found that it's simply a matter of scheduling things better. Of setting certain priorities. If you knew this recital was scheduled, and it was a priority, we might have planned our time differently. We could have met earlier, or later."

Janet felt a little defensive. She had tried to schedule

things. She'd tried to schedule everything, in fact. She hadn't set up the meeting—Houston had. She hadn't even had any control over it.

Hildegarde gave one last sniff. "Well, it's a problem, but surely we can come up with a solution, no? Some sort of plan?"

Janet started to get some insight into what her own more irritating personal idiosyncrasies might be.

Hildegarde pursed her lips together in thought. "Well, recitals don't last forever. Why don't you go to your recital, then meet us at the restaurant afterward?" She loosened up enough to give Janet a wink. "You can schmooze with us then." She slung her briefcase over her shoulder and nodded at Houston as she brushed past them on her way to the door.

Houston still wasn't happy—he glared at Janet as he followed Hildegarde out to the reception area.

It wasn't his fault he didn't understand. He was the product of a time when work—and especially the work traditionally done by men—took precedence over the needs of family. By his lights, he wasn't being inflexible or harsh, just realistic. Given the traditions he'd grown up with, he was probably doing pretty well just accepting women as equals in the business world, much less making concessions for family needs.

Well, he couldn't fire her at this point. She was too much a part of his plan. Of course, there was nothing to say he couldn't stop sending business her way after this project. She'd survive, if that happened. And so would HomeWork. Maybe it wouldn't grow as fast without his seal of approval, but it wouldn't die a slow death, either.

And, when it came down to it, she didn't really even want to think about it right now. Houston's ire paled in comparison to the anticipation of meeting Gib and the kids for the recital.

As Janet pulled up in front of the town hall, she saw Carly waving excitedly at her. Janet parked the car and hurried over to her. "Where's everyone else?"

"Heidi already went behind the curtain. Gib and Emma are saving our seats for us."

Janet hung up her coat and Carly's in the large cloakroom of the old town hall and followed Carly down a side aisle. She slid into a seat beside Gib, and he handed her a happy-so-far Emma, who snuggled into her lap with a sigh. Janet pulled her in close and nuzzled the baby's downy hair, taking a deep whiff of sweet baby-smell. She let the breath out on a sigh and looked at Gib.

He raised an eyebrow. "How did it go?"

"The presentation went great. Houston's irked—*really* irked—that I bowed out of dinner. But, surprise of surprises, the client's a working mom. She wasn't exactly the cavalry, riding to the rescue—she thought I should have planned things better—but she saved me, at least for now. We'll see how it goes later. Houston's a little behind the times on the whole issue of business versus family obligations, but he's not an ogre. And if I can just figure out how to get this client firmly on my side, I'll be in good shape."

Carly nudged her. "Aunt Jannie, look, there's Heidi!" She jumped up and waved frantically at her sister, who was peeking out from behind the heavy gold curtain. "Here we are!" Janet waved, too, and when Heidi spotted her, she beamed and popped her head back behind the curtain. Then the lights dimmed and Miss Rita stepped out on stage to introduce the program.

The first dancers were the youngest—the two- and three-year-olds, even younger and chubbier than Heidi's class. They all wore tiny leotards, stiff lace forming tutus around round little waists. They held their arms in the air, barely able to make their hands meet over their heads, and turned lopsided spirals in imitation of Miss Rita as she led them across the stage.

Two little girls fell down flat on their bottoms, arms still raised high, and there was a sprinkling of quickly muffled laughter.

Another circuit of the stage, this time holding arms out straight and pointing toes more or less to the front with each step, and the first act was over and the toddlers exited in a ragged line stage right. Loud applause brought them back on stage for a series of stiff, short-legged curtsies, and then Miss Rita led them off the stage.

Carly squirmed in her seat, barely able to stand the excitement. She leaned over to whisper, a little too loudly, in Janet's ear. "Heidi's next!"

Janet considered her, then leaned over to Gib. "Carly wasn't interested this year—the thought of a recital terrified her—but I wonder if after this, she might change her mind?"

He leaned out to look beyond Janet to Carly. She was on the edge of her seat, and her eyes were shining with excitement. "I think maybe you're right," he whispered back. "You know, you're really good with these kids."

His breath was warm on her neck, and a thrill ran up her spine at his nearness.

And at his approval, if she wanted to admit it to herself. "Shh, here comes Heidi's class." Gib pulled out the camera, and Janet was relieved his attention was focused somewhere besides on her for the moment. It was wearing on her, keeping up the appearance of casual disinterest.

Heidi, resplendent in lavender, led her classmates onto the stage, arms straight out at her sides, pointing her toe before each step. The little girls, only slightly less chubby than the class before, circled the stage once and then lined up, three little girls in pink on either side of Heidi. Heidi curtsied, holding herself in the curtsy as, two by two, the little girls on either side followed suit. From backstage, tinny music started up, and an older girl, maybe fourteen, all in flowing white, entered stage left *en pointe*.

Janet and Gib passed Emma back and forth a few times when she got squirmy, and they both took dozens of pictures, and Heidi remembered to curtsy to the Swan Queen but forgot she was supposed to exit left and exited stage right with everyone else instead.

They all clapped loudly when Heidi's class came out together, holding hands, for their final bow—except for Emma, who was fast asleep on Gib's shoulder by that point.

There were four more performances after Heidi's class, and then one final bow en masse, and then the recital was over. A few minutes later, Heidi came running out to meet them. "Aunt Jannie! I saw you come in! I forgot to go out that way, an' I went out *that* way instead! Miss Rita said it was okay, though. She said it's okay to forget, sometimes, even if it's important. Can we go get some ice cream at Mrs. Goody's?"

Janet looked at her watch, then at Gib. She shook her head. "Honey, I don't think so. I have to go do a little more work tonight, and Emma's already asleep."

Heidi stuck out her lip. "I want to go to Mrs. Goody's!"

Gib shook his head. "Heidi, it's already past eight o'clock. It's time to go home and get ready for bed."

"Ice cream! Ice cream! Ice cream!" Heidi shrieked each word more loudly than the last.

Janet leaned down to Heidi's level. "Heidi, I said no. That's the end of it. Now, no more screaming, understand?" Heidi's lip trembled, and she reached up to knuckle an eye hard.

Janet held out her arms, and Heidi stepped forward into Janet's embrace. Janet gathered her up and straightened, and the little girl put her head down on Janet's shoulder. Janet looked over the curly head at Gib. "Just tired," she mouthed. "And overexcited." He nodded.

Janet carried Heidi out to the car and buckled her into her car seat.

Janet turned to Gib and lowered her voice. "I don't know what to do. I feel like I should come home with you and help, but since I missed dinner, I really am expected to show up for at least a few minutes tonight."

Gib smiled. "Take a look behind you."

Janet turned. Heidi was sitting in her car seat, her eyes glassy, clutching the plastic rose Miss Rita had handed out to all the dancers. She blinked a couple of times, and then yawned.

"She's been wound up for days. She'll be asleep before we get home." Gib's whisper sounded in her ear, his lips brushing her hair, his breath warm on her cheek. "Besides, making the kids your top priority doesn't mean every minute of every day and in every situation. You're allowed to balance other needs against theirs.''

He was right. What a relief. She could have kissed him for understanding. Janet turned her head, and there he was, so close to her that she really could have kissed him.

He flicked a glance at her lips, and back up to her eyes. Well, maybe she shouldn't kiss him, but she could have hugged him for it.

She swallowed, thinking of a hard, smooth, chest, of naked broad shoulders, of a muscular back.

Nope, no hugging, either. Not a good idea.

On the other hand, she'd taken a pretty big risk already today. A risk she never thought she'd want to take. And look how well that had turned out so far.

On the other hand, that could backfire on her, too.

She turned, bringing her hand up, coughing into it, to cover her confusion. ''Well, then, thanks. I guess I'd better get going.''

She checked to make sure the other two girls were strapped securely into their seats, then hurried across to her own car. At the last minute, as she slid under the steering wheel, she couldn't resist sneaking one glance back at him. And found him watching her. She blushed and pulled her gaze from his, started the car, and pulled away.

Gib stood there, his hand on the open door of his van, watching as she drove away. She was an amazing woman. She was so many women, it seemed. A competent small-business owner, a harried but loving single parent, a power-suited saleswoman. A tigress in his bed.

He wanted them all.

WHEN GIB HEARD the key scrape in the lock late that night, long after the children were all asleep, his eyes were drawn up to the kitchen landing. He hadn't realized it until just this minute, but he'd been waiting for her.

She stepped into the pool of dim light, hesitating there for a moment, and their gazes met. And then, as if she couldn't help herself, she walked slowly toward him down the stairs.

His eyes followed her, down each step, and his mouth went dry as he studied her. She'd pulled the pins from her hair, and it curled loosely against her face. Gold disks still winked from her ears, but she'd unbuttoned the top two buttons of her high-necked blouse, and the collar hung in silky folds. As she came nearer, he could see the beat of her pulse at the base of her throat.

He opened his mouth to speak, and had to clear his throat first. "How did it go?"

She smiled, that smile that lit her face from within. "Really well. Amazingly well, considering how badly it could have gone. I ended up trading hair-raising child-care stories with Hildegarde Thomas, and Houston couldn't have been happier. He even seemed pensive at the end, after listening to us all night. As if he might be figuring something out about kids and families and priorities." She laughed self-deprecatingly. "Or maybe it was only the after-dinner brandy making him pensive, and I'm just indulging in a spot of wishful thinking. People don't really change their mind-sets that easily, do they?"

Gib swallowed. Maybe people did change their mind-sets, if they had a little help.

Especially if they had some help from Janet.

He watched her, feeling as if he hadn't looked closely enough before. His eyes took her in, drank in the sight of her, until she looked away, and he realized how intently he'd been staring at her.

He reached his hand, slowly, toward her cheek. Slowly, so she could pull back if she wanted to, if she thought about it. But she didn't, so he touched her, his fingers gentle, trailing over the skin of her cheek, her jaw, as if he'd never touched her before. Then he dipped his head to hers, and she took a small sudden breath just before he touched his lips to hers.

She kissed him, on a sigh, and he could feel it in her kiss, that this was what she wanted. But then she drew her head back, looked at him, blinked. "I'm not sure this is right."

He wanted to kiss her again, more than he'd ever wanted anything. He could feel her desire, too, and he knew it matched his. That much, he was sure of.

But she was right. He wasn't sure, either. Of anything, anymore, it seemed. He dropped his hand from caressing her, though it almost killed him to do so. "Then I guess this isn't a good idea."

She lowered her eyes. "I just don't know."

"Probably best that we stop, then."

"Yes. Probably best." She turned away, and it was all he could do to control his hand, to keep from closing his fingers around her arm, drawing her back, pulling her into his arms.

Where she belonged.

He almost gasped at the realization that she belonged in his arms. Because that meant something about him, and about where *he* belonged. Something, maybe, that he didn't want to face.

Something he needed to think about.

So when she walked away from him, he kept his arms by his sides. He only watched as she crossed to the stairs, climbed them in those silly heels, her hips swaying and setting her skirt swinging against her tanned legs. He watched her go, when everything within him screamed for him to stop her, to keep her there. He wanted her with him.

But was he sure? If he kept her with him, was he sure he wouldn't regret it later? He'd been waiting a very long time for…

What exactly *was* he waiting for? For freedom, right?

Did loving Janet mean the end of freedom?

He wasn't sure.

She disappeared up the stairs, and he turned away. One thing he was sure of—he wasn't getting to sleep any time soon.

At the very least, he needed a shower.

JANET TRUDGED upstairs and collapsed, face up, on the bed in her bedroom. She stared at the ceiling. She tried to control her lust and think rationally.

She wasn't sure, and neither was he. That much was obvious.

She stared at the ceiling some more. She tried to pretend he wasn't in the house, just one floor below, probably getting ready for bed right this very moment.

She pushed away thoughts of Gib undressing. *Think. Solve this problem.*

If she let herself fall in love with Gib, she'd be taking a big risk. She could get her heart broken.

On the other hand, sometimes risk-taking paid off, big time. She'd taken a risk today when she decided to tell Houston she wasn't coming to dinner. It could have blown up in her face. But it didn't.

And if she hadn't taken the risk, if she hadn't refused dinner, she would never have gotten into the conversation she had with Hildegarde Thomas. Oh, she might have connected with the woman over dinner anyway—they certainly had enough in common. But when Hildegarde had confided that she'd had to call poison control one day when one of her twins ate the heads off of sixteen marigolds, and Janet said, "I called *three* times one day, and they finally sent someone out to my house," and Hildegarde almost fell off her chair laughing—well, was there anything in trading stories about stalled faxes and just-missed connecting flights that could match that?

She'd risked it all—everything—and it had turned out fine. Better than fine. It turned out better than it would have if she hadn't taken the risk.

And even if it hadn't turned out so well, she still would have had the memory of Heidi's excitement and pride and joy in Janet's presence, which was more important than any dozen business deals.

She hadn't wanted to risk her heart. But sometimes risk-taking paid off.

A floor below, she heard the shower turn on.

All her carefully pushed-away-and-locked-into-a-corner lust came flooding back, almost taking her breath away.

She sat up.

She wanted him.

It would be taking a risk—he might leave her life forever, and break her heart. But he was leaving her house soon either way, and she might never get another chance. And if he did leave, at least she'd have the memory of the moment—surely that was better than sitting alone feeling virtuous because she hadn't taken the risk.

Would she regret it later? Maybe. Probably, even. But at least she'd know she'd gone for it.

Downstairs, the sound of the water continued.

Janet stood up and kicked off her shoes. No time like the present.

GIB STOOD under the shower, leaning against one of the glass-block walls of the open shower stall. Hot water streamed over his head, pounded down on his shoulders, ran along his back and legs.

He wasn't feeling much better yet. This could take a while—at this rate, he'd be emptying the water heater.

A sudden draft made him turn, and there stood Janet.

She stood there for a moment in the open bathroom doorway, gazing at him, quiet, still in her navy silk suit.

She pushed the door shut behind her and leaned against it. The steam swirled near her now that the door was closed, and she looked so beautiful through it, her hazel eyes and red hair an incredible combination, almost magical in the mist from the hot shower.

If this was a dream, it was a damn good one.

But he was definitely losing ground on the whole reason for the shower in the first place. Seeing her standing there, watching him, small droplets of water forming in her hair, her lips parted slightly to breathe in the heavy moistness of the air, was going to kill him if he didn't touch her.

Silent, not trusting his voice, he held out his hand to her.

And she stepped toward him.

Placed her small hand in his wet one.

He pulled her toward him, and she stepped into the shower, still fully clothed. He wrapped an arm about her waist, pulling her to him almost desperately, tipping her head back so he could taste her before he died of the wanting. He dipped his head and placed his lips on hers, trying to keep his kiss gentle, but when his lips touched hers, he just wanted more. He needed more.

He ran a hand along the fabric encasing her thigh, her hip, her waist, finally her breast. The damp material of her silky blouse rubbed against her skin, and she groaned, the first sound she'd made since she walked in, and the sound almost drove him over the edge.

But he had to ask. "Are you sure?"

She returned his look, her hazel eyes glorious, and she gave a small helpless shake of her head. "I'm not sure, but it's okay. It's okay not to be sure."

He didn't think any further, he didn't question anything else. He only wanted her.

The air was steamy, heavy in his lungs, and he pulled at her wet jacket, peeled it off her shoulders and dropped it sodden to the floor. He ran his hand up inside her blouse, up to close on her breast, the hot water running over everything, slick, stimulating new response with every pulse of the shower.

As his hand closed on her breast, she gasped at the feel of it, and her nipple hardened, provoking a similar response from him.

If that was possible—he was already as aroused as he'd ever been.

She tipped her mouth to his, running her tongue along his lips, and it almost drove him wild. He reached for her skirt, pulling it upward, and found nothing underneath, nothing but Janet.

That almost ended it all, right there.

With a groan, he kissed her, his tongue pressing into her mouth to explore, his hand running over her round, soft hip and thigh, and finally, down her belly to find her, touch her, and she gasped as he slipped a finger inside her, and she pressed forward with her hips against his hand.

She placed her hands on his chest, smoothing the silky, wet skin over his muscles, slicking over the ridges of his belly. He bent to her again, kissing her deeply this time, then pressing his lips down over her jaw, her neck, nuzzling aside the wet silk blouse and her flimsy bra to take one already-wet nipple into his mouth. She arched her back, moaning, pressing the length of her body to his, and the sound of her, the feel of her, sent his mind spiraling. He had to slip his hand from between the two of them, reaching blindly to the shower wall to keep his balance. She made a small sound of protest and pressed her hips against him, rocking against the hardness of him. He leaned with her up against the wall of the shower, and she separated from him long enough to reach for him, caressing the length of him.

He gritted his teeth, closing his eyes to shut out the sight of her, trying to control his reactions. "I can't stand to wait much longer."

"Then don't," she whispered, her voice a raw, breathless groan over the sound of the pounding water.

He lifted her slightly, pressing her between his body and the hot, wet wall of the shower, and when he let her slide down, bit by bit, upon him, she let out a moan of desire so deep, her face so transformed by raw pleasure, that he had to close his eyes once more against the power of it.

He gave a convulsive gasp and pulled her to him, dipping his head and kissing her lips, her throat, until the very feel of himself within her, even motionless, was almost too much.

Janet arched her back, her hair was brushed by the pulsing water as she tipped her head back in helpless pleasure, and Gib drank in the sight of her slender throat, her delicate shoulders, full breasts moving as she breathed, slick in the coursing water.

Gib rocked his hips forward, once, twice, then stopped. She shuddered and bucked, and he knew she was close. He pulled back for a moment, prolonging the pleasure for them both, and she cried out, deep, throaty, pleasure and frustrated desire warring in her cry.

She found his lips with hers and pressed her mouth to his, tasting of him, until his own breath came in ragged gasps. She rocked, sliding along the length of him, and soon he was controlling himself only with great effort. She kissed along his jaw, behind his ear, all the while moving against him, and again, until he clutched at her convulsively.

She pressed herself to him, taking him deep within her, as deep as she could take him, and she rocked forward again, once, and then stopped, and he pulled her hips to him to press himself yet deeper, and he held back a groan. Again she rocked, and stilled, and he couldn't hold back any longer. His face twisted with the effort of controlling his spiraling pleasure.

And her eyes opened, hooded with pleasure and rimmed with tiny droplets of moisture, and the desire he saw within them sent his feelings reeling out of control. When she moved against him again, and again, he could no longer stop himself, and he pressed himself deeper within her, rocking with her, and they both shouted as they found their release.

He stood there, gasping into her wet curls, clasping her tight to him for a long moment as deep moans tailed off into the final sighs of her pleasure. Then he kissed her again, tender, gentle, deep, lasting. He wanted to hold her, to kiss her, all night.

Holding her in his arms, he stepped from the shower, kissing her lips, her jaw, her throat as he peeled off the remainder of her clothing, her wet blouse, her bra, her skirt, dropping them one by one to the slick floor.

Undressing her like that, piece by piece, each piece wet and causing him difficulty, had some alarming results.

Janet glanced down at him. "Again?" She laughed, still gasping a little for breath.

"Again and again. I'll never get enough." He kissed her again.

Chapter Twelve

The next morning, Janet woke up feeling guilty. Happy, sated, unregretful, but still, guilty.

Okay, she hadn't planned to start a relationship with this man, but it looked like she'd done so. It was probably a bad idea, and she'd almost certainly regret it later when he left for parts unknown and she was in pain, and of course she had to keep it hidden from the kids at all costs.

Fine. She was every kind of idiot. It had been her day for jumping off cliffs and hoping she learned to fly on the way down. She could live with that.

But she was holding out on him. She knew something he didn't know, something he had a right to know. That, she couldn't live with.

So while Gib was making breakfast for the girls, Janet ran upstairs to her office and called Sheila.

"Janet! I was going to call you today! I quit school, I really did it, I have my tuition-refund check right here. There's no turning back now."

Janet felt a rush of alarm. No turning back, indeed. "Sheila, you have to tell Gib. When are you going to tell him?"

Silence.

"Sheila?"

"I know, I have to tell him. He's just going to be so mad. But you're right. Okay, I'll do it. Today. Now. I'll be right over." Click.

Be right over?

Oh, no, they weren't going to do this here. Janet didn't want to be anywhere nearby when this all came out. She dialed Sheila's number again, but this time the machine picked up. Sheila must have already left.

Damn. That meant she had maybe five minutes before Sheila got here.

Well, maybe she could take the kids and leave the house. She ran down the stairs and turned into the kitchen. "Who needs a ride to school?"

Gib, standing there with a plateful of pancakes, looked at her like she was nuts.

Carly said, "Aunt Jannie, it's Ms. Carmichael's turn this week."

Janet forced a weak smile. "Oh, yeah, but wouldn't you guys like to ride with me today? I might as well take you, since I have an early meeting."

Heidi pursed her lips at Janet's sweats. "You always wore your suit before, when you had a meeting!"

Janet reddened. "Uh, this is a client who likes things really casual."

Gib gave her a puzzled frown. "No one's going anywhere until they eat their breakfast."

Just as Janet was going to make one last attempt to get out of the house, the doorbell rang. Janet winced. Life as she knew it was about to end. "Uh, I'll get it." She hurried out to the front door.

Sheila stepped inside, speaking low as she took off her coat. "What kind of mood is he in?"

"Confused."

Sheila gave an evil smile. "I've always found that's a good start."

Janet led Sheila into the kitchen. "Gib, look who's here! Come on, girls, let's go finish getting dressed."

"I want another pancake!" Heidi grabbed the arms of her chair, as if she thought Janet might forcibly remove her from the table.

"Janet, what is wrong with you? Will you sit down and have some coffee?" Gib gave her a half-exasperated look, handed her a mug, then turned to his sister and smiled. "Not that I'm not happy to see you, but what's up?" He handed Sheila a cup of coffee, too, and she paced around the kitchen while Gib refilled his own cup.

"Nothing's wrong, exactly, Gib, but I have something to tell you." Sheila stopped pacing and looked straight at him. "I quit school yesterday."

Gib didn't say anything, he just slowly turned to face his sister.

She swallowed and plowed on. "I have your tuition money—three thousand dollars. It's only three-quarters of what you paid. I could have gotten all of it back if I'd dropped out last week, but they only refund seventy-five percent after the second week of classes." She pulled a check from her pocket and handed it to him.

He took it, looked at it, folded it, put it into his pocket. He still didn't say anything. Slowly, he sat down on a chair and rested his cup on one knee.

Heidi stopped chewing for a minute and looked from Sheila to Gib and then to Janet. "Are they havin' a fight?" she whispered.

Janet bit her lip and lowered her own voice. "No, honey, they're just discussing something. It's something that's important to both of them, but they aren't fighting. And swallow before you talk, honey.''

The silence stretched out, and Sheila hurried to fill the void.

''I know I said I'd try, and I did. I really did try, Gib. I even tried to find classes that would help me when I opened the studio. I took marketing, and management and accounting. I took teaching methods and a class in child psychology. I took an interior design class, in case I ever get the chance to plan my own studio rather than using an existing space. I took all the dance classes they offered, even the beginner stuff, figuring I could learn how to teach the basics to adults that way, because I want to offer a lot of mother/daughter classes. I even took basketball basics, and boxing, because I've been hearing a lot about how coaches in those sports are having their players take ballet classes to improve their movement skills, and I want to be able to do that. But I finally ran out of classes I could use. And my advisor started to pressure me to take the required courses—biology, and sociology and language. And I knew I'd just be wasting your money.''

Sheila had been pacing, but now she stopped and turned to glare at him. ''And if that doesn't bother you, I can tell you that it's also wasting my time, which bothers me a lot. Gib, the way I see it, you have a choice here. You can get mad and kick me out, or you can give me that check back and let me use it to take control of my own life for a change. I know you wanted a college degree for me—and maybe someday, I'll decide I want to get a business degree or a teaching degree to help me improve my business. But right now, I want to take this chance. There's an opportunity for me right now, and I want to take it.''

She stopped, a little breathless, and watched him, anxiety showing clear in her heart-shaped face.

Gib leaned back in the chair and gazed at her. "Well, I guess there isn't much I can do about this now, is there? But if you think I'm giving you this money, you've got another think coming." He glanced at the kids, who were still wide-eyed at this display of adult disagreement, and he very deliberately kept his voice level. No anger, just stating facts. "As of now, you are on your own. If you want to go back to school later, I doubt I'll be in a position to help you. You think you've been putting your life on hold for this silly idea of mine, this college education whim? Well, let me tell you, I've put my life on hold for the past twelve years. And I am not about to sit around waiting for you to come to your senses and realize that sooner or later, whether you're applying for a bank loan or putting together your résumé to give to potential students' parents, you're going to need that degree. You're going to wish you had it. And I am going to be long gone."

Sheila's lip trembled, but she held her ground. "That's fine with me, because I'll be long gone, too. As soon as I sign the contract, I'll pack my bags and move into Miss Rita's." Sheila flounced out of the room and banged the front door as she left.

Janet winced. Things had been going along fine, there, until Sheila mentioned Miss Rita. "Well, I better get to work." She hopped up, took one last sip of coffee, and crossed to the landing, being careful to fasten the gate before she hurried up the stairs.

But the mention of Miss Rita hadn't been lost on Gib. As she was settling herself into her desk chair, he stepped into her room. "She's going to be working for

Miss Rita? Isn't that Heidi's dance teacher? Janet, what do you know about all this?''

Janet sighed. "I've only known for a week. I wanted to tell you, Gib, but she begged me to let her tell you. And I thought that was her right.''

He got very still. "What about *my* rights? She's my sister, and it's my money she's wasting, and now there's nothing I can do about it. If you'd told me last week, before she quit school, I could have put a stop to this disaster. Now it's a done deal.''

"Gib, it was her decision. She's doing what she thinks is best.''

He snorted. "She's twenty years old! How could she possibly know what's best for her?''

Behind him, Emma's head appeared at the top of the stairs. Janet was on her feet, across the room, and through the door by the time Emma had peered around and smiled in delight when her eyes lit on Gib. As the little girl placed one shaky hand on the top step, Janet scooped her up. She turned to frown at Gib. "You left the gate off downstairs!''

He frowned at her in puzzlement. "I did?'' He sounded incredulous.

Janet carried Emma into the room and set her on the floor, where she made a beeline for Gib. "When you were twenty, did you know what was best for you?''

He rolled his eyes. "That's completely different. I was responsible for three other people when I was twenty. I had to think about what was best for them, too. I spent a lot of time thinking about what was best for Sheila.''

"Seems like you've made a habit of it, and that habit has worn out its welcome. Some of us would like to make our own decisions on what is right for us. Some

of us would like to make our own mistakes, even."
Boy, she was on a roll now. "You know, this is just
one more example of how you think you know what's
best for everyone. You do the exact same thing to me."
She put on a pompous face and mimicked his voice.
"'Janet, I'll know when you're ready to deal with these
kids on your own'—please! I think I'm perfectly capable of handling them right this very minute."

Gib sat down. "If I'm so overbearing, if I'm so
wrong, why am I still here? You know I'm right, that's
why. Deep down, you know you need me. You're only,
just now, with my help, starting to get your priorities
straight." He set Emma on the floor, and she crawled
across the room toward Janet's desk, where she reached
for the wastebasket.

Janet shook her head. "My priorities were always
straight. They just were overwhelmed. And maybe not
very well organized." She slid the wastebasket out of
Emma's reach and set it on top of her desk.

"Well, it's a good thing you had me here to keep
things together, because you show no signs of getting
them organized."

"Give me a break, will you. I've only been a parent
for three weeks." She handed the baby a crumpled-up
sheet of paper out of the wastebasket as a consolation
prize. Emma rolled onto her back and wrinkled and
unwrinkled the paper, happily making crinkling
sounds.

"My point exactly. Until you figure out you can't
have it all, you need me around to pick up the pieces.
You're trying to do too much. It's all a lie. You've
been told you can be both Supermom and Superca-
reerwoman, but you can't. You can't have it all.
There's no way. You have to let something go." He

leaned back in his chair, as if the argument was over. "So until you decide what it is you want to give up, I think I'd better stay. I think the kids deserve nothing less, don't you?"

Janet tried to hold her temper in. He wasn't fighting fair, using the kids and her fears about them against her. At her feet, Emma found something small and shiny on the floor. Janet scooped it out of her hand just as it was about to go into the baby's mouth. A bottle cap. She tossed it into the trash can on her desk and in the same movement pulled a teether out of her desk drawer and handed it to the child. "So you've got this all figured out, do you? Well, I don't think so. I don't think you've been paying attention. And I can, too, have it all—I just need a little help with all of it. I'd have been happy to have you stay and give me that help, too. But you don't think it's help I need—you think it's something much more profound. You think I need to give something up? I think I'll give *you* up. You can go any time. I'm perfectly capable of handling this myself."

And, she realized to her shock, that was actually the truth. She really was capable of it.

She scooped up Emma, hit the switch on her printer to print out her invoice file for mailing, and marched out the room and down the stairs, leaving him gaping at her, caught in his oh-so-in-control posture on the couch.

Janet carried Emma down the stairs to the kitchen, where both Carly and Heidi were still eating breakfast. "Come on, you two, let's get dressed." As she herded them up the stairs, Heidi said, "We heard yelling. Did you two discuss something?"

Janet smiled at her. "No, honey, that was a fight.

But it has nothing to do with you, just with how things are supposed to be done around here. And we shouldn't have yelled."

After the kids were off to school, Janet picked up Emma and a portable child gate and went back up to her office. She put Emma down on the floor and started stuffing invoices into window envelopes.

She felt wrenched. Wrenched by the argument with Gib, and by her own feelings at the prospect of losing him so soon. By her remaining uncertainties about her ability to handle the kids on her own, no matter what she'd said to Gib. Things could end up exactly as they were before Gib came—total chaos, all the time, with Janet running constantly to catch up and never getting anything done and being both a bad parent and a bad businesswoman.

She remembered sitting with Laura Jason in the park. "He was right. He's always right," Laura had told her. She hadn't wanted to agree. But there was a lot of truth in what Gib said. She couldn't do it, not alone. Not everything. No one could do it alone. Well, she was sure some women could, but she wasn't one of them.

Priorities. What did she really want?

Besides Gib, that is. She needed to keep her feelings for him out of the equation.

She snorted. As if she could do that!

But she pushed them aside for the moment. What she wanted was to have a business and still have time for the kids. Georgie's kids now, and her own later.

What she wanted was to have her cake and eat it, too.

And she could. But she was going to need some help. All she needed was someone organized, someone efficient, someone who could make the customers feel catered to and the temps feel cared about. Someone who could take a complicated process and make it seem simple. Someone who liked kids and had a rapport with them.

Someone like Gib. She pushed away the small mocking voice in her head.

Great! She'd figured out how to do it, now all she needed was this paragon of virtue to carry out the plan.

Oh, well, something would come to her. Something always did.

Janet sat up, startled. When did she start thinking like that? When did she start thinking life would take care of itself with no help from her? Well, not *no* help, exactly, but when did she start thinking she didn't have to plan everything down to the color of her toenail polish before things would go her way?

When Gib showed up. That was when. When Gib showed up, he'd brought with him spontaneity and controlled chaos and a sense of fun as irresistible as his smile.

She sighed. No way was she going to be able to leave him out of this equation. He was in it.

DOWNSTAIRS, Gib finished the breakfast dishes. He carefully folded the dish towel, arranging it so it would dry quickly on the handle of the oven. He wiped down the counters one more time, although they were spotless.

Finally, he stopped himself. The print of a cat curled up on a hearth rug, with the caption Contentment, was hanging slightly askew, and his fingers itched to straighten it, but he didn't. It would just go crooked again, the first time anyone slammed the door. And besides, Janet saw it every day; she knew it was crooked. If she wanted to fix it, she was perfectly capable of doing so.

He looked around, to see if there was anything else he was still responsible for. Then he shook his head—to look at him, anyone would think he didn't *want* to get out of here unencumbered. Anyone looking at him would think he actually wanted to get himself involved with these kids, with this woman. And he didn't.

Oh, for one crazy moment there last night, he had thought it might not be so bad, getting involved. But he'd forgotten that when you get involved with people, they get involved with you. They started adding complications to your life. As a result, he now had Sheila to deal with—again. He knew he'd never be able to cut her off. If she needed that tuition refund, well, it was her money, wasn't it? He'd marked it with her name when he earned it. It was still hers.

But then, that was it. He'd had enough of entanglements to last him a lifetime. He'd be ready for a family and kids in about ten years. Maybe. He sure as heck wasn't ready for them now. He had things to do, places to go. People to meet.

Unfortunately, right at this moment, none of those people seemed half so fascinating as Janet Resnick and these three little girls.

He shook that off. That was how he felt now. When he got some space between himself and this little family, he'd feel differently. He'd realize he'd made the right decision. Besides, if he found he'd made a mistake, there was no reason he couldn't come back—Janet wasn't going anywhere.

Kids were different, though, a little voice intruded. If you looked away for ten minutes, when you turned back around you were looking at a different kid. What would Emma be like in six months? She might be talking by then. She'd definitely be walking. She'd probably be climbing everything.

He made a mental note to check the house for climbing dangers.

In fact, he'd better leave a list of things Janet should watch for in the next few months as Emma became more and more mobile.

He also should remind Janet that it was still important to keep reading to Carly, even though she could read now herself. Kids needed to be read to until they were in sixth grade, at least. The longer you read to them, the better, really. And he should also talk to Janet about not putting too much responsibility on Carly—it was easy to do with the oldest, especially in a single-parent household. Janet would want to make sure Carly got every bit of childhood she could get.

And Heidi. There was so much to know about middle children, especially middle children who were of the same sex as their older and younger siblings. They could grow up feeling there was nothing special about them. People tended to treat them as if they were in the middle—just sort of average little people. They tended to be grouped in with the other kids instead of treated as if they were just as much individuals as their siblings. There was too much to simply tell Janet about that—he'd better leave her a reading list.

He knew that, even though Janet's mom would be home soon, Janet would never be able to go back to being just an aunt. She was part of these kids' lives now, inextricably. It was just one more reason he had to get out—even if he thought he could have Janet, he couldn't have another ready-made family to be responsible for and still have his dream. It was time to go, now. Time to take that last step toward his freedom.

Time to start his new life. And the last thing he had to do was sever the last of his responsibilities. He took a deep breath and started up the stairs.

As he reached the top of the stairs, he could see Janet off to the left in her office, playing with Emma while she tried to get some work done. She'd given Emma her wastebasket to empty. A little pile of bent paper clips and an empty pen sat on a shelf above Janet's head—she must have gone through the wastebasket and taken out anything dangerous before she handed it to the baby. Emma sat of the floor gurgling with delight as she pulled a piece of folded paper out of the wastebasket. "Ah! Ah!" she shrieked, and crumpled it. It crinkled, and she laughed in delight and shot a sunny smile up at Janet, who smiled back at her while she carried on a phone conversation.

"What I need is someone who has two very different sets of skills. I want someone who can manage the day-to-day details of the business—scheduling assignments, handling the books, answering the phone, sending out requests for information. And I also need this person to be able to deal with my kids when I'm out of the house for occasional meetings."

Gib stopped, stunned. Janet was hiring someone to baby-sit for her?

"Great! Why don't we schedule an interview, and you can come over and meet the kids." Janet pulled her desk calendar toward her. "Tuesday it is, 10:00 a.m." As she made the note, Emma picked up the wastebasket and put it on her head, and Janet stuck her leg out just in time to provide enough support to keep the toddler from tumbling over backward as she suddenly lost all visual orientation cues. "I'll see you then."

Janet hung up the phone and grabbed Emma up, pulling the wastebasket up to peek at the baby, who shrieked in delight and tried to throw herself backward out of Janet's arms. "Oh, no you don't, silly girl. Whew, are you fragrant. Come on, let's go get that stinky diaper." She stood and turned, giving a small start at the sight of Gib on the top step, just outside the door to the bedroom. She gave him a brittle smile. "I'm going to change a diaper. Want to give me my final exam?" She stepped over the gate that she'd set up in the door of the bedroom office.

He didn't move out of her way. "What were you just doing on the phone?"

"What do you mean, what was I doing? I was hiring some temporary help for my business. For as long as I'm going to stay a single mom, I'd better get some help, don't you think? I went through my HomeWork files, looking for likely candidates, and I've already got four people lined up for interviews tomorrow." She laid Emma on the changing table and rested one wrist on her tummy while she pulled open the wipes box and removed several baby wipes. She handed Emma a stuffed clown to play with, then pulled out a diaper, unfolded it, and set it out of Emma's immediate reach.

Gib frowned. "But you were discussing mostly helping with the business end of things. Who's going to take care of the kids?"

"I am, silly." Janet pulled the tape tabs back and pulled the diaper carefully out from under Emma. She wiped the baby clean, applied a dab of ointment to a reddish spot, slid the fresh diaper under, and taped it securely in place before Emma finished examining the stuffed clown.

"What do you mean, you are? As if you're anywhere near being ready to take care of these kids on your own. You don't even know what it is you don't know.''

Janet's jaw tightened. She pulled up Emma's tights, fastened her onesie back over them, and picked the baby up. ''I'm going to assume you aren't really listening to yourself, because you've just said you haven't done your job very well. I feel like I'm well able to handle these kids.''

He snorted. ''And what about middle-child syndrome, huh? Have you thought about that?''

She gave him an exasperated frown, as if she thought he was manufacturing concerns. ''I've never even heard of it!''

Aha! ''Proving my point. You not only aren't qualified to take care of these kids yourself, you aren't even qualified to hire someone to take care of them for you.''

''Gee, and I thought I'd done such a good job the first time around. You know, you've been telling everyone who will listen that you've been waiting years to have no more responsibilities. Well, buster, you just got your wish. Your sister is on her own, and you're out of a job. Why are you still hanging around here, anyway?''

''If you think I'm leaving before I see what brand of incompetent you've got lined up to help with these kids—''

''Then I've got another thing coming? Fine, stick around until tomorrow. Frankly, I can use the help until then.'' She shook her head in exasperation and left him standing there, working his jaw as he watched her go.

THE DOORBELL RANG, and Janet ran to get it. A young woman dressed in black with long purple hair and very pale skin stood on the doorstep. She had a small gold post through the septum of her nose, and a ring through her eyebrow, just above the outside corner of her eye. Janet winced, wondering what else might be pierced.

"Yes?" What could she possibly be selling? Home body-piercing equipment?

"I'm here about the job."

"You're Violet?" Janet wondered which had come first, the hair color or the name. "Uh, okay. Come on in."

Violet followed Janet to the couch and plopped herself down. She pulled out a small black compact and looked at herself in the mirror. She licked one finger and smoothed down the eyebrow that had the ring in it. Janet could imagine that a large piece of jewelry would have a tendency to get caught in the short hairs. She shuddered as Violet's spit-slicked finger rubbed over the gold ring.

Janet was just about to ask Violet about her child-care experience when Carly, carrying Emma and trailed by Heidi, walked into the room. Heidi took one look at Violet and screamed and ran out of the room. Emma gave her a startled glance and buried her head in Carly's shoulder. Carly looked her up and down, and her eyes got very wide. "Are you a vampire?"

THE DOORBELL RANG, and Janet got up to get it. An elderly woman, exactly the picture she'd had in mind when she first called The Mommy School, stood on the doorstep. Janet smiled in relief. "Mrs. Martinson?"

"Yes, I'm Mrs. Martinson."

"Oh, please, come right in."

Janet led the way into the living room and seated

Mrs. Martinson on the couch. "Can I get you any-thing—a cup of coffee, maybe?"

"No, thank you, dear. I never take it."

"I have decaf, if that makes any difference." Mrs. Martinson seemed perfect.

"Oh, no, it's not the caffeine. It's my aura. Any brewed beverage will muddy your aura. At my age, I have to worry about such things." She smiled at Janet.

THE DOORBELL RANG and Janet stood up and walked over to get it. A young woman stood there, dressed in a blue corduroy jumper with a yellow turtleneck under it. She looked a little blank, but very clean-scrubbed.

"Hi, I'm Emily."

"Please, come in." Janet led Emily into the living room and they both sat down. "Why don't you tell me what kind of experience you've had?"

Emily, it turned out, had worked as a receptionist in a day-care center. Janet felt the first pricklings of hope—this girl sounded like she might work out! She was no ball of fire, maybe, but she could probably han-dle answering the phone and dealing with the kids for short periods of time. Janet would just have to find a way to keep up with the rest. After all, it was only temporary.

Only temporary. Why did she keep telling herself that? Because it was getting harder and harder to ac-cept?

As they finished the interview, Janet walked her to the door. "Well, I have to do a few quick checks, of course, but things look good. Can you start right away?"

"Checking? What do you check?"

"Oh, you know. Your references. Since you'll be

taking care of the kids part of the time, I'll do a police check.''

"A police check? Like, for a record?" Emily frowned.

"Yes, a criminal record."

Emily paused. "So, like, say you found a record, does that mean you wouldn't hire the person?"

Janet looked at her closely. "Well, it would depend on what that record was for. Possession of pot ten years ago might not kill the deal, but assault and battery definitely would."

Emily looked pained. "How about armed robbery?"

THE DOORBELL RANG. Janet sighed, and got up to answer it. A clean-cut young man stood there, but Janet knew looks were deceiving. Before he could introduce himself, Janet motioned him in. "And I suppose you're a firm believer in the power of angels, right?"

"I beg your pardon?"

"Or maybe you're the president of the local marijuana growers' association?"

"Miss Resnick, you don't recognize me, do you?"

Janet took another look at him. And reddened. "Mr. Dooley?"

"I'm required to make one unannounced visit within the first six weeks of opening a case. This is your unannounced visit."

Chapter Thirteen

Gib sat in the kitchen and handed Emma bite-size pieces of peanut-butter-and-jelly sandwich, one at a time. She tended to stuff too many into her mouth at once, if he gave her more than one.

Besides, this way took longer, and his spot in the kitchen was out of sight but definitely within hearing distance of the living room. He was enjoying Janet's day immensely. So far, Janet's possible helpers represented the worlds of alternative rock, alternative healing, and alternative values.

And now Mr. Dooley. Gib schooled his features into an innocent expression as Janet brought the social worker around the corner into the kitchen.

"Mr. Dooley, this is Gib Coulter, from The Mommy School."

"Ah, yes, I've been wanting to meet you. We've heard such wonderful things about your service." He glanced at Janet. "Mr. Coulter has even done some pro bono work on some of our cases. I'm so glad things are working out for you here." He tsk-tsked. "Such a need. But things look under control now."

Janet looked as if she had a metal rod up her spine.

"Actually, I'm just in the middle of interviewing for a new nanny. Mr. Coulter is leaving us."

"Oh, is that so?" Mr. Dooley frowned and made a note on his pad. "Well, I'm sure you wouldn't be leaving unless you thought things were working out, hmm?"

Gib looked at Janet. "Absolutely not."

Janet narrowed her eyes at him and led Mr. Dooley down the stairs to the family room, where Carly and Heidi were playing.

"Aunt Jannie?" Heidi's voice carried up to Gib clearly. "Carly says the new baby-sitter is a vampire. Is she going to drink my blood?"

After Mr. Dooley was satisfied—"Things look much more in control around here"—and took his leave— "We'll be in touch"—Janet stalked back through the kitchen and up the stairs. Gib smiled to himself. Janet would see that it wasn't so easy to hire someone to deal with something so important.

That afternoon, while Gib ran Heidi and Carly from one place to another, Janet split her attention between Emma and HomeWork. It was frustrating. Every time she sat down to play with or feed or read to Emma, the phone rang. And every time she got started on a project, Emma needed a diaper change or a bottle or just a cuddle. She managed to get a little work done, and by gating off the kitchen and working at the kitchen table, she kept Emma safe and in sight, but by the time she needed to start dinner—Tuesdays were Mrs. Murphy's afternoon off—she was feeling a little frazzled and as if she didn't have much to show for the amount of effort and energy she'd expended. She hadn't completed even one major project, and she hadn't had a single uninterrupted half hour with Emma.

But then, she hadn't made any calls to Poison Control, either, or received any calls from irate clients.

And maybe that was life. Maybe her expectations for herself were too high. Maybe she needed to be willing to accomplish a little on both fronts, instead of trying to be perfect in everything.

All things considered, she'd done okay.

But she was realistic about it. She'd handled one child for one afternoon, during which she'd had no business emergencies, and she'd really only managed to tread water. With all three kids, and even a normally hectic business day, she'd be back to pulling her hair out. She really did need some help.

She laid aside an estimate for a new project—thank goodness she'd been smart enough not to promise it until next week—stuck Emma into her high chair and put a handful of pretzels in front of her, then pulled out a can of refried beans and a packet of tortillas. Chop a few onions, grate some cheese, and dinner would be quick-and-easy tonight: bean and cheese enchiladas, something even she could make successfully.

The phone rang, and Janet picked it up, shrugging it between her shoulder and ear while she spread refries on another tortilla.

"Janet?" Sheila's voice sounded like she was in tears.

"What's wrong?"

A sob. "What if I'm making a mistake? What if Gib's right?"

"Excuse my saying so, but your brother is acting like a first-class jerk, on pretty much all fronts. I don't know what's come over him." Janet sighed. "Come on over, we'll talk about it."

Sheila seemed a little more in control when she

showed up, so Janet asked her if she'd deal with Emma for a few minutes while Janet ran out for a gallon of milk.

"Gib's not here?"

"He took the older girls to the park so I could work this afternoon. He's being ever-so-helpful. *Grrr.*"

When Janet got back, she found Sheila and Emma sitting on the kitchen floor feeding each other bites of banana, to their mutual hilarity. Sheila told Janet all the brilliant things Emma had done during the twenty minutes Janet was gone.

Janet smiled in delight at Emma, who had crawled into Sheila's arms. "Did she really say 'kitty'?"

"Plain as day! Actually, she screamed it while the cat was sleeping. Then she screamed again in delight when Clementine jumped two feet in the air and raced off down the hall."

Janet laughed, held out her hands, and Sheila deposited the gurgling Emma into her arms.

She sniffed. "Oh-oh, someone's fragrant." The three of them climbed the stairs to the bedroom, and while Janet was snapping the tape-tabs open and folding them back on themselves, the phone rang. "Can you grab that for me?"

Sheila trotted into the next room to pick up the phone, and her voice dropped into the warm tones Janet recognized from phone conversations they'd had. "HomeWork, this is Sheila." She listened for a minute.

"Well, Mr. Barton, you've come to the right place. If you'll just hold on for a moment, I'll need to get some information from you." She covered the mouthpiece of the phone and looked back across the hall at Janet. "A Mr. John Barton, he needs someone who can put together his company's newsletter each month. It's gotten to be too big a job for his secretary."

"Would you mind asking him to fax over a copy of the latest newsletter? Then tell him we'll call him back as soon as we get it."

Sheila's face lit up, and she uncovered the mouthpiece. "Mr. Barton? We'd like to see a copy of your most recent newsletter, so we can get an idea of what kind of work we're talking about." A pause. "That's right, certain jobs require certain skills, and we wouldn't want to choose the wrong person for your particular job." She raised questioning eyebrows at Janet, who gave her a thumbs-up.

Janet paid enough attention to realize Sheila had gotten the right idea, but not so much that she couldn't give Emma belly-busters before buttoning her into a fresh romper.

She carried Emma back into the office, listening while Sheila got the potential client's address, phone and fax numbers and hung up. "You're a natural! Do you want a job?"

Sheila gave a humorless laugh. "When can I start?" At Janet's quizzical glance, she shrugged. "I'm serious. I need a part-time job if I'm going to make a go of this."

Janet got the first glimmer of a brilliant idea. "Come on, I need to check those enchiladas." She carried the baby downstairs, while Sheila followed.

Janet slid Emma into her high chair and set a handful of raisins on her tray. Emma picked one up between her thumb and forefinger and placed it into her mouth. She chewed it diligently between her four front teeth.

Janet smiled, then bit her lip.

She was going to miss this.

She looked over at Sheila. "If you really want a job, it's yours. You would not believe the..." She winced, remembering Gib's prediction of incompetents. Right again. "The unusual and totally inappropriate potential employees I've had in here today. And, of course, Gib was here to witness the whole thing. At any rate, I need someone who can handle the phone and the kids, and you seem perfect. It's only temporary, three or four weeks, tops, until my mom gets back, but it'll give you some breathing room until you find a permanent job. Do you need a place to stay?"

"No, I've got the key to Miss Rita's already. I haven't moved anything yet—actually, I don't own anything except my clothes—but I'd rather sleep on the floor than stay one more night at Gib's. I can't wait to tell him I've found a job."

Janet could wait. If he was upset before, he'd be furious now.

As if on cue, they heard the van pull up out back.

WHEN GIB FOLLOWED Heidi and Carly into the house, he found Janet and Sheila making dinner. His sister was hanging around an awful lot. Sheila's eyes looked a little puffy.

"Late night last night?" He stepped past her and into the kitchen. She ignored him. Oh, what now? He heaved a sigh. Why couldn't women just come out and say it when they were mad at you? "Sheila, are you still upset that I'm not planning to support you any longer? Because you keep telling me how you're perfectly able to make your own decisions. How you want to be on your own. How you're tired of me interfering with your life."

No answer. He watched as she pulled a pitcher of

juice out of the refrigerator and filled four glasses. Finally she looked up at him.

"Are you staying for dinner?" She held the pitcher ready over a fifth glass.

"I live here, remember?"

Janet looked up. She was standing beside Sheila, and they were looking suspiciously like a united front. "You said you were only staying until you assured yourself I was hiring competent help, someone who would be able to deal with the kids. I've done that."

A really nasty suspicion reared its head. But Janet wouldn't do that. She wouldn't go that far. She wouldn't undermine him that much, not after they'd already talked about it. "What do you mean?"

"She means we've solved both our problems. I'm going to be working here, for Janet." Sheila sounded shrill, and Janet looked down for a minute. But then she looked back up at him, and her face was set. A united front it was.

"Sheila, could you leave me and Janet alone for a moment?"

Sheila glanced at Janet, who nodded. With a glance at her brother, she picked up Emma and carried her down to the family room, where Heidi and Carly were watching *Cinderella.*

Janet blurted out, "Before you start in on me, you were the one who told me I couldn't do it without help."

"So you stole *my* help? That's your solution to the problem? Maybe it solves your problem, but it sure doesn't solve Sheila's."

Janet gave a little gasp of incredulity. "You told her she was on her own, that you weren't in business any more, Mr. World Traveler with no commitments. You told her to go support herself.''

A tightening of the jaw. "I didn't mean it. I was just trying to make a point."

"I'd say you did a pretty swell job of it, then. Gib, she needed a job, something she could be happy doing. She wasn't happy working for you—you never let her do anything. You only let her answer the phone because you couldn't be there twenty-four hours a day."

"I wanted her to concentrate on her studies."

Janet tried to keep from raising her voice. "She didn't want to concentrate on her studies. She wanted to concentrate on her dream. You're getting in the way of it. It was your dream that Sheila complete college, not hers. Don't you see? You're making your dream more important than hers."

He wasn't convinced. "College is important."

"Why, Gib? Why is it important?"

Was she nuts? "Education is important. Learning is important."

"Why?"

Oh, please. She was being deliberately obtuse. "Well, for one thing, because you need it to earn a good living."

"And a good living is important because..." She stood there, arms crossed, mocking him like the worst of all possible teachers.

He matched her sarcastic tone. "Because you need to support yourself, to be independent, so you won't have to depend on..." He trailed off.

She stepped forward, moving in for the kill. "So she won't have to depend on others for a living? So she won't have to depend on you? Is that what you mean?" Her eyes snapped at him. "You're causing her all this trauma so you can save yourself from feeling responsible for her?''

"No! I just want her to be happy."

"And you figure she needs a good living to make her happy? Look again, Gib. What she wants to make her happy is a ballet studio. And you are doing your darnedest to keep her from it. This is how you think you'll make sure she's happy?" Janet shook her head in disgust. "You've got another think coming." She turned back to the stove.

He didn't know what to say. Was that what he'd really been doing?

Maybe it was—and maybe he'd have been aware of it, if he'd cared to look closely enough. He just hadn't looked at it in that way.

He looked back at Janet. Janet, who was wiping Emma's high chair and sliding it into place, who was pulling a pan from the oven and making a note on the grocery list as she poured the last of the juice, who was competently handling exactly what he'd spent the last two days telling her she couldn't handle.

She didn't need him.

"Janet, I'm—"

She cut him off with a wave of her arm, her back to him.

She was right. An apology now was too little, too late. He felt a wrenching sense of loss. He didn't know what to say. He could think of absolutely nothing, and it made him feel about as inadequate as he ever had. He struggled to come up with something, anything. "Well, then." Nothing. "I guess I'll go say my goodbyes."

It was rough. More than rough, it almost broke his heart. Heidi cried, even though he promised her he'd come back and visit. Carly told him in a very quiet voice that it was okay, she understood he had to leave. Emma waved bye-bye brightly, but then started to wail when he pulled his coat on. He kissed her, and he hugged Carly and Heidi tight. And then he left.

Janet, nowhere in evidence, obviously didn't want to talk to him. Sheila kept her back to him as he passed through the kitchen. As he walked toward the van, the red letters on its side mocked him, and as he drove away, the bright lights of the house depressed him.

JANET LISTENED to him pull away. She'd been crying in the kitchen, hadn't wanted to turn around so he could see her tears. She'd stood hidden around the corner while he said his goodbyes to the girls—it almost broke her heart—and as soon as he left, she'd run downstairs to comfort them.

Heidi had sobbed, "Is Gib going to die?"

"No, honey, he just isn't going to live here. He only came for a few weeks, and now he has to leave." Janet's heart had broken for her again, and for Carly, quiet as a mouse, pretending to read a book in the chair Gib had always sat in. She'd wanted to tell them that he'd come back and visit, of course, when he was in town. But how could she promise that?

THE NEXT DAY, things went amazingly smoothly for Janet. Sheila showed up at seven, and Janet worked all morning with just a few cuddle breaks with Emma. Sheila played with Emma, and answered a few phone calls whenever Janet was unavailable, and picked up Heidi from school, and fixed lunch for everyone.

At one o'clock, Sheila left for Miss Rita's, and Janet recorded a new message for her answering machine, saying she'd be in all-afternoon meetings every day for the next few weeks, and spent the rest of the day with the kids.

By the time she got everyone fed and bathed and into bed, Janet was exhausted, but she spent a couple more hours on paperwork and then fell into bed herself. She supposed she'd get used to the schedule, but even with help, things wouldn't be easy for the next few weeks.

And she missed Gib. She tried to tell herself that she was missing mostly his easy ability to handle the kids and the meals and the errands and everything else associated with running a household, but it was more than that. Then she tried to tell herself that she missed having another adult around full-time to share the emotional burden of raising three kids, but it was more than that, too.

She missed his touch, and his glance, and his laughter, and even his irritating habit of being right. She just missed him, period.

GIB SAT STARING at the check. Final Payment, it said on the memo line. Janet's big loopy signature at the bottom. It hadn't taken her long to write him out of her life—the check had been in the mail the day after he left.

He had no reason to contact Janet any more.

And with Sheila out of school and out of his apartment, he had no reason not to start his new life. The life he'd waited for so long.

The life he no longer wanted.

Or, it wasn't really that he didn't want it—he wanted to travel, wanted to write, wanted to start this new adventure. But he wanted Janet, too, and he wanted something to come home to. Surely he could have both.

Surely he could have it all? *You can't have it all. There's no way. You have to let something go.* His words to Janet mocked him. Of course he wanted to have it all—didn't everyone? As long as he was wishing for the moon and the stars, he might just as well throw in the three kids, because he wanted them, too.

He was miserable. He knew he was miserable. He just didn't know how to go about fixing things so he wasn't miserable.

Number one on his reasons-to-be-miserable list was Janet. Who would have thought he'd feel this bereft at losing her? He'd never minded changing partners before—why did he mind now? If this was love, it was damned uncomfortable. He'd remind himself not to ever do this again.

After he figured out how to get Janet back.

Get her back?

Gib smiled. Suddenly he knew how to go about fixing things. That is, he knew what he needed to do to stop being miserable—he needed to get Janet back.

But how?

He couldn't just race over there with a bunch of day-old roses in his hand. She'd just throw him out again. No, a woman like Janet required a plan. A careful plan. A well-planned plan.

Okay, so he needed a plan. How did he go about making a plan?

He'd seen Janet do it enough times. How did she make a damn plan?

He closed his eyes and heard her voice. "The key issue in formulating any plan is articulating the problem. If you don't correctly identify the problem, you can never hope to solve it.''

He must have been listening all that time, and not even known it.

Okay, the problem. He sat down at Sheila's desk and flipped on her computer.

Problem: Janet is unavailable, because I've made her mad at me.
Solution: Get her unmad.

Not good enough. Sounded pretty stupid, as a matter of fact. Okay, try again.

Problem: Janet is rightfully upset because I treated her condescendingly and as if she couldn't conduct her own affairs.

Ouch. But true, if he was willing to admit it.

Solution: Show her I've changed.

He sat back for a moment. How could he show her he'd changed?

Solution: Do something to show her I think she's perfectly capable of running her life. Show her I trust her judgment. Show her I think she's right when she says she can do it all. Support her decisions.

He frowned and leaned back in his chair. That was the solution, all right.

Unfortunately, he had no idea what might do the trick.

ALL THAT WEEK, Janet worked like a demon every morning, and actually, she got a lot accomplished.

Yep, she could do this. It was the hardest thing she'd ever done, but she could do it.

But it really was a lot easier with Gib around. What a difference he'd made with the kids.

With everything. Nothing was the same without him. Nothing.

But while she was lecturing him on not standing in the way of Sheila's dreams, she'd realized something. Something about Gib's dreams. She hadn't meant to, but by starting this relationship, she'd threatened his dreams. It wasn't her fault—it was nobody's fault—but the fact that Janet wanted something more than just a warm body in her bed meant the warm body couldn't be Gib's.

She stood, agitated, and started to pace. Why couldn't it be Gib's? She wanted him, but she didn't want every second of him, from now until the end of time. Why couldn't they work this out? Why couldn't he go off to Mali or wherever, then come back home to her? She could stand that—if that's what it took. Would she rather have him around all the time? Of course. But if the choices were having him around some of the time and not having him at all, she'd pick part-time, every time.

Plus, once the kids were back with her mom, Janet could use the time Gib was gone to bury herself in her work.

Well, that part didn't sound so good. Not as good as it once would have. Especially the part about the kids being back with her mom. And even the part about burying herself in her work didn't sound as appealing as it would have two months ago.

She shook that off, impatient. It couldn't be helped; that was life. The kids would still be in the same town, and Janet could see them as often as she wanted.

It wouldn't be the same, though. Nothing would ever be the same.

She had a brainstorm. Maybe she could move in with her mom! This single parenting couldn't be any easier for Mom than it was for Janet, even without the added pressures of a business to run.

Of course, it would make those times when Gib was around a little awkward.

No showers, that was for sure.

Okay, so it wasn't perfect. It was better than what she was looking at right now—a future with no Gib and no kids, with just work, never ending, stretching out into the distance.

She was going to do it. Or, at least, try.

Besides, she just had this funny feeling she should really call her mom.

She picked up the phone and dialed Aunt Mary's number in Florida. On the second ring, her mother answered.

"Mom, it's Janet."

"Janet! Merciful heavens, what a coincidence! We were...we were just talking about you."

Janet heard the crack in her mother's voice. There was something wrong! She'd known it, last time they talked. "What's wrong, Mom?"

"Nothing's wrong, honey. Things are good, really. Very, very good."

And now she was denying that anything was wrong! "Oh, God, Mom, what is it?"

"Honey, I'm getting married."

Janet sat down. Luckily, there was a chair just there; otherwise, she would have landed on the floor. "Married? To a man?"

Her mother laughed, a joyful sound Janet hadn't heard from her mother in...how long?

Maybe never, she thought, tears stinging her eyes.

"Of course to a man, Janet. Did you think maybe I was going to marry Mickey Mouse?"

"Who...what's his name?"

"His name is Morris Bronstein, and he's standing right here next to me. He'd like to speak to you."

Janet heard her mother hand the phone to someone, and then a deep, calm voice boomed into the phone. "Janet? This is Morris. Your mother has told me so much about you. I'm looking forward to meeting you."

"I'm so...so pleased to meet you, Mr....Bronstein, is it?"

"No, no, please call me Morris. After all, we're going to be related soon. And I want to meet you as soon as possible. Your mother and I will be flying up to Ohio to see you, as soon as we get a few things taken care of on this end." He spoke away from the phone for a moment. "Hmm, what's that? Oh, yes, okay. Janet, here's your mother again." Janet heard the sound of a kiss being exchanged as the phone passed hands this time.

"Honey? It's me again." Her mother sounded so happy. So this was why she hadn't sounded like herself. There wasn't anything wrong at all—just something different. Something very, very good.

"Mom, I'm so happy for you. You sound wonderful."

"Oh, honey, I feel wonderful. But, Janet, there is a problem." Now her mother's voice sounded strained. "Morris lives in a community. It's a wonderful community, there's golf and bridge and a garden club, but there aren't any children here. For visits, there are, but they aren't allowed to live here. I don't think it would be a good place for the kids, even if they were allowed." Her mother started to cry, and Janet felt tears sting her own eyes. But her heart was pounding with excitement.

Her mother continued. "Morris says if we have to, we'll live in Ohio until the children are older, and then come back down here. Or we can move to a suburb somewhere down here in Florida. But, Janet, he's seventy. He'll be eighty-seven by the time Emma graduates from high school. I just don't think it's fair to make him raise a second family."

Janet's heart jumped in her chest, and started to beat fast and hard. "I'll keep the kids."

Her mother heaved a sigh, as if she'd been waiting for just that. "Oh, honey, of course that's what I was hoping for, but are you sure?"

"I'm sure. I've pretty much learned how to deal with them, and I think I've got things under control. I've found someone to help me with my business, and I'm running it out of the house now." A thought struck her, and she stiffened. "Oh, Mom, what about the house?"

"Janet, I think you and the kids should stay in it. That's the least I can do for the kids. I love them so much, and I feel like I'm abandoning them, like they're losing one more person." Her mother's voice broke.

"The least I can do is let them stay in their home, at least until Emma's through school. Then you keep it."

Until Emma was through school. Seventeen years. Janet would be forty-four then. And Gib, who wanted nothing of commitment or family, would be long gone, off to the Amazonian jungle or wherever he ended up. Well, at least she'd have the house. She'd be a dried-up old spinster, but at least she'd have a roof over her head.

And she'd have the kids. Even if she never had children of her own, she'd have these three, for the rest of her life.

"Janet, are you sure, honey? Are you really sure?" Her mother's voice took on a hint of its old worried, fretful, doubtful tone.

"Mom, I've never been more sure of anything in my entire life."

After her mom hung up, Janet sat there holding the phone. She felt a strange mixture of elation and grief. She was going to keep the kids! She wouldn't have to give up Emma's sticky grins and snuggles. She'd see her take her first steps, and she'd watch as the next tooth came in.

She'd be around to hear Heidi's funny, horrifying remarks. She'd watch while she learned to read and write, while she had all the fun that came with starting first grade.

She wouldn't have to give up Carly's shy hugs. She'd give her the security she craved, and watch her come out of her shell.

She'd be able to promise that she'd never leave them. No one was going to desert these three, never again.

Except Gib. He was gone for good. If he hadn't been

anxious for a commitment to Janet, this new develop-
ment certainly wouldn't change his mind. Oh, well, it
had been a nice idea while it lasted. Besides, he was
probably already packing his laptop for Timbuktu or
Nepal.

To hell with it. If she could do the single-parent
thing on her own, she could certainly do it with him,
even if he wasn't quite ready yet to be there every
minute of every day. She didn't need him there every
minute of every day—she just needed him there.

She was going to talk this out with him right now.

She jerked to her feet and grabbed her car keys. As
she slung her purse over her shoulder, she called upstairs to Sheila, "I'm going out for a while. Can you
keep an eye on the kids for me?"

"Sure thing, I don't have to be at Miss Rita's until
three today."

Janet pulled the door shut behind her. She jumped
into her car and backed it down the driveway.

As she slowed to a stop at the main intersection
through town, she spotted a street vendor selling flowers. She rolled down her window and waved at him.
"A bunch of roses, please." He trotted over, and she
shoved a five into his hand. "Roses for an apology—
might as well look like I have some sort of a plan."
He laughed and turned to get her change, but just then
the light changed, so she waved him off. "Keep the
change." The roses lay across her lap, wet and heavy,
filling the car with their heady scent, as she stepped on
the gas.

GIB SAT BACK, exhausted. This planning stuff could
wear you out. Much more difficult than just jumping
up and doing what needed to be done.

But it was worth it. He now had a foolproof plan, a plan that would solve everybody's problems and send Janet's head and heart spinning as she leaped into his arms to forgive him.

He hoped. He was still a little new at this.

He'd go over to Janet's house. He'd get her alone, somewhere quiet where they could talk. He'd tell her he needed her, and that he loved her, and that he couldn't stand not to be with her. He'd help her come up with ways they could make it work—like maybe she could travel with him. Maybe she could hire a manager, and telecommute. She did most of her work by phone and fax, anyway.

Well, that was the plan. It was definitely more than a little weak. But it was all he had.

And it might work. Something *had* to work—he was going to keep Janet in his life, and he'd do it any way he could. Even if he had to give up the whole stupid travel-writing thing. That was all pie in the sky, anyway. Janet was here and now, and real, and he wanted her more than he'd ever wanted anything else in his life.

Okay, he had a plan. Now for implementation. He pushed to his feet and grabbed his jacket, feeling in the pocket for his keys.

On the way over to Janet's house, he passed Jimbo on the corner, hawking his roses. Gib knew from past experience they'd last about two days before they started to droop, but considering the weakness of his plan, they couldn't hurt. He rolled down his window. "Jimbo! Better give me two dozen—I don't have much of a plan."

Jimbo jogged over with the roses. "Funny, you're

the second person to mention a plan in the last two minutes. Seven bucks.''

Gib paid him and set the roses on the seat beside him. Maybe they'd only last two days, but they sure smelled good now. And what woman could resist roses?

He pulled up at Janet's. Her car was gone. Damn.

And Sheila's car was there.

He took a breath. But he needed to have it out with his sister, once and for all. He'd talk to Sheila, and then he'd wait for Janet, and he'd talk to her, and then they'd all live happily ever after.

Leaving the roses in the car, he walked up the walk. Inside, he could see Sheila moving around. He reached for the knob, then remembered. He didn't live here anymore. He knocked, and Sheila opened the door.

She raised an eyebrow at him, and she didn't say anything, but she opened the door wide to invite him in.

He walked past her, sat down at the kitchen table, frowning a little in thought. ''Sheila, I've been thinking about what you said. I've decided you deserve the tuition money. It was always your money, and you ought to be able to spend it any way you want. I want you to have it.''

She just looked at him, and he could tell from the set of her jaw that she wasn't nearly as happy about this as he'd expected her to be. ''Oh, you've decided that, have you? So now, you've made the decision for me.''

Oops. Now he saw his error. Man, this was tricky.

Sheila wasn't ready to stop. ''You didn't listen to me when I came to you, begging and pleading. You didn't listen to my reasoned arguments. You took no notice of how upset I was over the whole thing. But now you've decided maybe I was right, after all. You know, you haven't changed a bit. I don't know why Janet bothers putting up with you.''

Boy, that pop-psych theory was true—women were from Venus, men from Mars. Gib felt as though he were dealing with an alien species. His every remark provoked unforeseen reactions, and he wasn't thinking nearly fast enough to keep up. He was going to need some practice.

He was just thinking that maybe he'd be better off winging it, after all, when Janet walked through the door. He hadn't seen her in almost a week, and he'd never seen anything so beautiful in his life as Janet, standing there with a dozen of Jimbo's roses in her hand. Her hazel eyes widened as she looked at him, and he felt as if he could step into them and get lost forever. In fact, he'd happily do just that, if he had half a chance.

But first, the plan. What was his plan again? Fighting with Sheila—he hated it when she was right—and seeing Janet again had him all flustered. He couldn't remember what he was supposed to say first.

She opened her mouth, and for a moment he just watched, fascinated, as she licked her upper lip, a quick nervous swipe of her tongue. "I was just looking for you." Her voice was a little husky, more than usual, and he watched the little ripple of muscle at the base of her throat as she coughed to clear it.

Boy, she looked good. He'd almost forgotten how good she could look, even in her ratty leggings and a big old sweatshirt. He swallowed. "I was here. Looking for you."

She opened her mouth, but he rushed on in. He wanted to get this out, tell her his plan, before he chickened out. "Janet, I think you deserve a full-time relationship." Her face froze, and he knew that hadn't come out the way he'd wanted it to. "What I mean is, I know you need that—any woman would. So I think you should hire a manager for your business and come with me, travel with me."

"Gib, I—" She started to voice an objection, but he plunged on. If he could just get it all out, maybe he could straighten it out afterwards.

"You can run your business by fax. You practically do that anyway."

"Gib, I don't need a manager, I—"

"I just want to do this right, give you what you deserve. And you deserve a full-time relationship."

"I don't need that!" Her eyes snapped at him.

"But everyone does." That surprised him. Not "every woman does," which was what he'd always thought. *Everyone does.* From the look of her, it surprised her, too, that he'd say it.

"I don't! I need full-time love, but that doesn't mean we're joined at the hip! And it doesn't mean you can make decisions for me, or that you know what's best for me. I deserve you, full-time? Let me tell you what I deserve—I deserve what *I* know I need."

"I'm just trying to make things easier for you." He couldn't seem to stop talking. Why couldn't he just shut up?

"If that's how you think you can make things easy on me, you're out in left field." From the stairs, a faint crying started, then grew to a full wail. Janet gave an exasperated huff and slapped the roses down on the counter. "Oh, now you've really made things easier for me." She turned and pounded up the stairs.

Sheila, who'd stood there avidly watching the entire exchange, crossed her arms in front of her and stared at him, shaking her head. "Unbelievable. You do realize, don't you, that you've just totally reverted to type?"

He looked at her. "I didn't mean to. I was trying to be supportive. I just meant to help her solve a problem. It just didn't come out right."

"What, are you dense? Haven't you figured out yet that she's perfectly capable of solving her own problems?"

"I know she is. She's more capable of that than anyone I've ever met."

"Well, you sure aren't acting like it."

He thought about that. "You're right. I am dense."

"And besides, you don't even know all her problems. She just told her mother she was going to keep these kids. She couldn't go with you if she wanted to. Like it or not, she's stuck right here, for the next fifteen or twenty years."

He stared at her, stunned into speechlessness. Janet was keeping the kids?

"Look, Gib, why don't you just go home. You really aren't helping the situation much here, and you aren't helping yourself any, either. Go home. And if you can't come up with anything better than this, then you ought to just stay there. I don't know why she even bothers with you, at this point—you've pretty much proven you won't change." She turned and followed Janet up the stairs.

Gib stood there for a moment, staring after her.

Janet was keeping the kids. He couldn't believe it. It was like some fond dream had come true and then exploded in his face. Absently, he turned and walked back out to his car.

And there were those damn roses, still sitting on the seat. Still smelling good. He picked them up. They'd been Plan B. Well, Plan A sure hadn't worked worth a damn.

He thought about sitting in his apartment, miserable. He was headed back to that same misery, if he left now. Only he'd be even more miserable than before. Three little girls' worth more miserable.

Janet wanted this as much as he did, he could see it in her. He could feel it.

He grabbed the damn roses, marched back up the walk. Through the window in the door, he could see Janet, sitting on a stool, staring down at the roses she'd bought for him.

No, she wasn't staring at them. She was crying into them.

He hated to see a woman cry. He hated it even more when he was the cause of the tears.

He swung open the door without knocking.

Janet turned to look at him, her eyes a little red, but she stopped crying and just looked at him. Just looked at him.

He had to have her. Any way he could. Whatever he had to do, he had to have Janet. "What can we do to make this work? What do you think we should do?"

She stared at him, and he didn't know what else to say, and besides he thought he'd better just shut up already this time, so he handed her his roses. Now her arms were full of the damn things.

She just kept staring. "What did you say?"

"I said, what do you think we should do to make this work? I just want it to work. I just want to be with you. I'll do it any way you want." He took a deep breath. "Sheila told me about the kids. I'll stay here, take care of the kids while you work, if that's what you need. I can be Mr. Mom, if that's what I have to do."

Her face softened. He loved it when she looked like

that. Especially when she looked at *him* like that. "Oh, Gib. I don't want you to be Mr. Mom."

"What do you need? Just tell me, and I'll do it."

"I just need you to love me. I don't need you to give up your dreams for us. We'll be fine here while you're gone. We'll be even better while you're here, but we couldn't be happy if you weren't doing what makes you happy."

He touched her hand, and a little spark flew from her to him, and she jumped, and looked into his eyes. He reached out to brush her cheek with his hand, and she gazed steadily at him, her eyes darkening as she watched him. He couldn't help himself. He just had to kiss her, right now.

He pulled her slowly to him, cupped his hand behind her head, and her lips parted just before he touched his mouth to them. He kissed her once, gently, and then again, as he lost himself in the feeling of kissing Janet, holding her, and he crushed her to him, crushing the roses in their paper wrapper against her. The scent of the roses mixed with the scent of Janet, and he gasped as he breathed the heady mixture deep into his lungs.

"I love you, Janet." He'd thought it would be more difficult than that to say, but it wasn't, so he said it again, amazed at the lightness of his heart as he spoke the words. "You'll be hard to leave behind."

She smiled, a wicked little grin that made him immediately horny. "I intend to make it the hardest thing you'll ever do, every time you go. I want you thinking about coming back, the whole time you're gone. *That's* what I want. *That's* what I need."

"It's a promise." And he kissed her again, pulling her into his arms.

Epilogue

Janet stood in the Florida sunshine with an exceedingly silly dress on. It had been chosen to suit the other bridesmaids, and it was far too young for Janet.

But it sure looked cute on Carly and Heidi. She smiled down at them, all frothy lace and ivory ribbons, and tried not to think about what a woman of twenty-seven looked like in the same fussy confection.

The organist started the bridal march, and Janet and everyone else turned to face the trellis through which her mother would enter the rose garden.

Her mother appeared in the trellis, framed in the twining yellow roses and escorted by Gib. His skin was tanned dark from a recent week in Egypt. Janet's heart raced at the sight of him—who would have thought a formal jacket would make him so blindingly hand-some?

She forgot to look away when he flashed her a grin, and she almost keeled over from the adrenaline surge. This was ridiculous—she was a married woman now, she needed to get used to it.

Her mother looked beautiful. Mom had spent months planning this wedding—she hadn't had one her first time around, and she said she was going to do this one up right. Janet had never seen her look so happy, so relaxed. So alive.

As Gib and her mother approached the gazebo, Morris, looking pretty good himself in his formal jacket, stepped forward to meet his bride. Gib kissed her mother's cheek and stepped over to join Janet and the girls. He stood with them during the ceremony, his hands on Heidi's and Carly's shoulders, until Emma got away from Aunt Mary and careened up to him, arms raised, demanding, "Up! Up!" He picked her up and settled her on his hip, and the amused congregation returned their attention to the ceremony.

Janet felt her heart would burst. If only Georgie could see the changes her children had wrought in all their lives. The night before, Heidi had drawn a picture of her new family, with Morris now included. In the left top corner, two figures sat on what was apparently a cloud. When Janet had asked her about them, Heidi had said, "That's Mommy and Daddy, waving from up in Heaven."

Janet raised her eyes to the puffy, white clouds high over the garden. "I love you, Georgie," she whispered. "Thank you. We'll take good care of them."

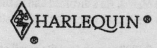

It's hot…and it's out of control!

BLAZE

Beginning this spring, Temptation turns up the *heat*. Look for these bold, provocative, *ultra*sexy books!

#629 OUTRAGEOUS
by Lori Foster (April 1997)

#639 RESTLESS NIGHTS
by Tiffany White (June 1997)

#649 NIGHT RHYTHMS
by Elda Minger (Sept. 1997)

BLAZE: Red-hot reads—only from

HARLEQUIN® *Temptation*

LOVE *or* MONEY?
Why not Love *and* Money!
After all, millionaires
need love, too!

How to Marry a
MILLIONAIRE

Suzanne Forster,
Muriel Jensen
and
Judith Arnold

bring you three original stories
about finding that one-in-a million man!

Harlequin also brings you
a million-dollar sweepstakes—enter
for your chance to win a fortune!

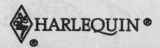

HARLEQUIN ®

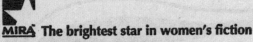

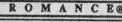